starting from scratch

Georgia Beers

starting from scratch

© 2010 BY GEORGIA BEERS

ISBN (10) 0-979-92546-0
ISBN (13) 978-0-979-92546-7

THIS TRADE PAPERBACK ORIGINAL IS PUBLISHED BY BRISK PRESS, NEW YORK, NY 10023
EDITED BY KATHERINE V. FORREST
COVER DESIGN AND LAYOUT BY TAMI BOX (www.tamarabox.com)

FIRST PRINTING: JANUARY 2010

Books By Georgia Beers

Novels
Starting From Scratch
Finding Home
Mine
Fresh Tracks
Too Close to Touch
Thy Neighbor's Wife
Turning the Page

Anthologies
Outsiders
Stolen Moments
The Milk of Human Kindness

Georgia Beers
website: www.georgiabeers.com

acknowledgments

This book has been a long time coming, and I have many, many people to thank for helping me get it into your hands, so bear with me…

First and foremost, my undying thanks and affection to the lesbian reading community, to each and every one of you who checked in on me, visited my site and my Facebook page, sent me an e-mail, kept asking when the next book was coming, plugged my appearances, spread the word, and generally stayed in touch with me. Your letters, encouragement, and enthusiasm kept me going when I was wavering badly. I offer my sincerest and most heartfelt gratitude, and I know it isn't nearly enough. I hope this book rewards your patience. Thank you from the bottom of my heart.

Thank you to my wife, Bonnie, the one who loves me unconditionally, despite my flaws (and there are many, I know). What a long, strange trip the last three years have been. Who'd have thought we'd end up right back where we started and be ecstatic about it? Thank you for helping me keep my chin up, and for not letting me languish, rocking in a corner and wailing about the injustices of the world. You pulled me up, sat me at my desk, and got me back to work with all the love, support, and understanding a person could ask for. Peter was right: we *are* powerful together. Heart. Always.

To my fellow authors and friends in the lesbian publishing world: Ruth, Katherine, Jamie, KG, Joanne, Karin, Rachel, Lori, Cheryl, Ann, Smitty, Jane, Catherine, Toni, Tarsha, Andi, Sheri, Susan, Lynn, Cathy, Kat, Cate, Linda, Gill, Cheri…the list goes on and on. You are the people who grabbed my arms and pulled me from the quicksand on those days when I thought maybe it was better to just stop struggling and let myself sink. I owe each of you a debt of gratitude for never allowing me to give up, for helping me to stay strong, and for making me understand that the best solution was to simply keep writing. And to that tiny handful who would have liked to see me fall apart and disappear completely, to those few who would prefer to splinter this amazing community in the name of power and greed rather than help it stay cohesive and strong by working with others to make it so: shame on you.

My eternal love, admiration, and gratitude to my editor and friend, Katherine V. Forrest, an icon to me in every sense of the word. When I asked her for guidance, and admitted that I was slightly embarrassed to do so, she said to me, "Hey, this is a sisterhood. We're here to help each other." After months of wondering if I was stupidly naïve in expecting my fellow lesbians to just be...*better*, Katherine echoed my internal thoughts and renewed my faith in my community. This *is* a sisterhood and we *are* here to help each other, and I know that one day, I'll be ready, willing and able to pay it forward to a younger writer who asks for *my* help. The lesbian literary community couldn't ask for a kinder, wiser, more genuine role model than Katherine V. Forrest. Thank you, Katherine, for being you.

To Tami Box, my WebDiva/cover designer extraordinaire, I bow to your creative brilliance. You make me look good, but more importantly, you make me look professional. My website rocks and you surpassed my wildest expectations by a long way for the cover of this book (with which I am crazy in love!). You are a true artist.

To JD Glass…what can I say? Life is so strange and the separate paths we started out on that ultimately met and united have been—for each of us—long, difficult, often lonely, and hard to navigate. But I have to believe we ended up on the same road for a reason and your friendship has grown to mean so much to me. Words are not enough to thank you for your love, support, willingness to listen, and clarity of advice.

To Susan X Meagher, I cannot begin to express my thanks for putting your time, money, and faith into my work. You gave me an opportunity with Brisk Press that any other writer would *beg* for, and I will do whatever I can to make all the effort worth your while. Mucho, mucho gratitude to both you and Carrie for your hard work and easy attitude.

To my Awesome Proofing Trio, Stacy Harp, Steff Obkirchner, and Jackie Ciresi, this one took a long damn time, but that doesn't mean your efforts were any less important. Thank you guys so much for spending your days off reading my stuff. Your dedication and honesty keep me grounded and your friendship means everything to me.

And Steff: the trailer for this book rocks harder than I can begin to put into words. You amaze me over and over with your creativity, your generosity, and your love. I'm lucky to have you. Thank you.

To Dr. Holly Raschiatore Garber, my friend of (gulp!) thirty-six years, for helping me look like I know what I'm talking about when it comes to medical details.

To my friend, Denise Ash, for the crash course in bank management.

To my sister, Lauri Whitney, and my friend, Tanja Atkins, for letting me pick both your brains (sometimes endlessly) about what it's like to be pregnant and then be a mom. You were both very patient with me, and I so appreciated your help and direction.

Finally, to Jaclyn, Frankie, Allyson, Anthony, Alexis, Joseph, Isak, and Emerson, for showing me that whether I'm being a godmother, an aunt, or a babysitter, this non-mother actually *does* have a little bit of maternal instinct (who knew?). I love you all.

dedication

To my maternal grandmother, Madeline DeRosa Pacilio, the strongest woman I know.

In memory of my beloved aunt, Joyce Meredith Beers, a woman before her time. I miss her every single day.

chapter one

"I want to speak to your manager. Now."

Uh-oh. I glanced toward the counter at the panic-stricken expression on the face of the young bank teller. Those were never happy words. The poor kid couldn't have been more than twenty-one and his forehead was already shining with sweat.

"Certainly, sir," he said, and his voice cracked like Shaggy's in the Scooby-Doo cartoons. "I'll be right back."

The man who'd uttered the fateful phrase was older—maybe sixty-five—and judging by the way he tossed his checkbook to the counter and sighed loudly, he was not pleased by having to resort to going over the kid's head. Or he was just a jerk. I wasn't sure which, so I took an exorbitant amount of time filling out my deposit slip at the little rectangular desk in the middle of the lobby in order to find out. My stalling tactics paid off, because a minute later, *she* walked by. Elena Walker, branch manager, stunningly attractive specimen of the human female, and woman of my dreams...or at least my fantasies. I only knew her name from the nameplate mounted next to the door of her office, which I passed during each visit.

I was always surprised that she didn't move in slow motion with a mysterious breeze blowing her hair in some sexy-chic fashion, she was that beautiful. Tall—a good three or four inches taller than me—with dark, silky hair cut just above her shoulders and styled in that sort of hip, flippy look that I believe only professional hairdressers know how to create. Olive-toned skin that looked tan all year round and caused me to speculate on her ethnicity (Latina? Italian? Greek?). Today's business suit was navy. Simple. Elegant. Sexy. The raspberry blouse beneath the jacket gave the outfit a fun splash of color, making up for any stuffiness the simple style of the skirt might conjure. Of course, stuffiness was the last thing that came to mind when you got a look at her legs. Long, shapely, strong. I wondered absently if I was drooling on myself, though I didn't care enough to stop staring.

Rather than go around the counter, she walked right up next to Mr. Irate Customer, introduced herself, and shook his hand with a smile. All I had to do was see a teeny, tiny glimpse of his face to know he was immediately smitten with her.

"Hey, get in line, buddy," I muttered softly and with a grin.

Elena kept her voice low, probably figuring the entire bank didn't need to know Mr. Irate Customer's business. Or that he was angry. I didn't hear what was said, just the murmuring of voices, but the conversation didn't last long. Within two minutes flat, she had him smiling and thanking her. Sweating Bank Teller Guy looked relieved at his stay of execution.

I jerked my eyes back down to my own stuff as I realized she was headed back to her office and would be passing me. I didn't want her to think I'd been staring.

"Morning, Ms. King," she said with a smile as she passed me. I looked up in surprise and caught the wink she threw at me. The color of her eyes made me think of melted chocolate. "Have a great day."

"You, too," I replied lamely, wanting to slap myself in the head for missing an opportunity to open some kind of dialogue with her. *She knows my name. How cool is that?*

I finished my business and floated on a cloud back to work, wishing I had more reasons to be out and about in the bright and sunny spring weather, and at the same time, wishing I had more banking to do. But it was a very small branch and I figured it would be noticed (and possibly thought of as creepy) if I ended up in there four or five times a week. Plus, I preferred to be somewhat stealthy in my ogling. Elena Walker didn't need to know I was seriously crushing on her and had been since I'd opened my accounts there six months earlier. I did have a *tiny* bit of pride.

Back in my office, I was very happy to see that the muffins I brought in earlier were almost gone. It's not really an office, more of a really large cubicle that I share with Josh Bacon, one of my best buds and the creative writer to my graphic design at T. Harrison Jones & Associates.

"Hey, Avery," Josh greeted me, not looking up from his keyboard as he chewed. "Your muffins suck, by the way."

Feigning prim-and-proper shock, I asked, "And just what would you know about my muffins, mister?"

"You'd be surprised."

I snorted. "What's that, your third one?"

"Fourth." He stuffed the last bite into his mouth and reached for a huge volume of *Roget's International Thesaurus* on the shelf above his head. The damn thing was so heavy,

I was continually amazed each time he pulled it down that he didn't knock himself senseless with it. Josh is a gadget man, up on every new piece of electronics on the market today, every camera, every computer, every video game, but he refuses to use the thesaurus on his Word program. He told me once he didn't trust it, that he was sure there were way more options for each word than the ones programmed into the computer and that Microsoft was exercising its worldwide control by making people use only the handful they designated. I told him he was a freak, which he didn't argue.

T. Harrison Jones & Associates is a small advertising firm. The staff amounts to just a dozen or so people, but we work very well together and we've come up with some pretty brilliant campaigns for some of the most successful companies in upstate New York. Small and mighty, that's what Tyrell likes to call us. He's the T. in T. Harrison Jones, as well as the owner, CEO, president, all that good stuff. He hired me a little over a year ago and I have done everything possible to give him the best I have to offer. He treats his staff with respect, something I hadn't seen much of in my past jobs, and I want to stay here as long as I can. Josh was here before me, and Anita Christopher was hired just after me as a senior account executive. The three of us make a formidable team and we helped THJ garner a reputation locally. An impressive one.

"How was the view at the bank?" Josh asked as he squinted at his monitor.

"As stunning as always," I said, tossing in a dreamy sigh for good measure. Since our computers are placed in the corners of our desks, we actually sit almost with our backs to each other. We'd carried on many a conversation without ever looking at one another. "And she had to talk an irritated customer off the ledge."

"I bet she did it in six seconds flat." Josh was also well-aware of Elena Walker, since he did his banking at the same branch I did.

"Easily." I opened up the file on the design for the microbrewery on which I'd been putting the finishing touches. "I think he fell in love with her."

"Well, he'll have to stand in line behind us."

"I tried to tell him that. Telepathically, of course."

"Did he get the message?"

"I can't be sure."

"Did you drool all over yourself?"

"I think I did."

"Pig."

I hung my head. "It's true. I'm such a guy."

Josh laughed, a loud bark of a sound that shocks most people the first time they hear it. "Well, we're happy to have you counted amongst us."

Our witty banter was interrupted by the ringing of my phone, which I snapped up mid-chuckle. "Avery King."

"Hey, you. Sounds like you're having fun over there. Shouldn't you be working and miserable like the rest of us?"

I grimaced at the voice on the other end of the phone. Lauren and I had been together for almost three years and broken up for nearly two. Our split had initially been ugly (what breakup isn't?), but I thought we'd gotten to a place where we were almost friends. Lauren seemed to think so too, and called me every couple of weeks or so just to say hi...and to check up on me, I was sure. I didn't call her at all.

"Hey yourself," I said, trying to twist the grimace into something more pleasant. Josh mouthed "the ex?" at me. When I nodded, he pantomimed hanging himself. I whipped my head in the opposite direction and looked away from him so I wouldn't bust out laughing in Lauren's ear. "What's up?"

"Not much," she said, releasing a sing-song sigh, a trademark of hers that told me she was bored and just wanted to chat. "I had a free minute and thought I'd call to say hello."

Lauren's one of those people with whom all you have to do is get the conversation started and then you barely have to participate outside of tossing in an occasional, "uh-huh" or "I see." I knew if I gave her a push, I could get some work done while she talked, and she wouldn't lay the guilt on me about not having the time for her. "So tell me what's new," I prompted.

Across the cubicle, Josh picked up his own handset and rapped it against his skull.

For the next fifteen or twenty minutes, Lauren rambled on about her job, her mother, the date she went on last weekend (I think she was hoping for a tinge of jealousy from me…which she didn't get), while I made some final adjustments to the color and outlines of the logo design I needed to hand off to Anita later in the day. She started her wrap-up with, "Well, I should let you get back to work."

I jumped all over that. "Oh, yeah. We're working on a big project today and I really need to get back to it."

"We should get together for dinner some time, you know?"

"You're right. We should," I lied, panic nearly seizing me. Dinner with my ex was not something high on my list of things I'd love to do with my evening. "Let me check my schedule at home and get back to you, okay?"

Josh snorted. I flipped him the bird.

"Okay," Lauren said, and I couldn't tell if she was on to me or not. "It was nice talking to you, Avery."

"Same here."

I barely let go of the handset in its cradle when Josh said, "You are *not* getting together with your ex, are you? What is wrong with you people?"

"What do you mean, 'you people?'" I teased, knowing exactly what he meant.

"You lesbians and the whole staying friends with your exes thing. What *is* that? Besides freakishly weird."

"It is freakishly weird, isn't it?" I shook my head. "I have no idea. It just happens."

"It's crazy, is what it is," he muttered. "You don't see straight men doing that."

"That's because the exes of straight men usually hate them with every fiber of their being."

Josh pursed his lips and exhaled through his nose as he nodded. "Yeah, there is that."

The rest of the day went by quickly, just the way I liked it. On the way home, I stopped at The Grape Stomper, my favorite little wine store, and bought myself a bottle of cheap zinfandel. Not because it was cheap, but because it was surprisingly good. I also bought a bottle of something a little more expensive to take to dinner with me.

7

When I unlocked the door to my townhouse, I was greeted by Stephen King, the love of my life. Well, not so much greeted by as looked at. He was stretched across the back of the couch and could barely be bothered to lift his head and acknowledge my presence. I set my briefcase on the floor by the coat tree, put the wine on the kitchen counter, then crossed to the living room and pressed a kiss to the wiry hair on his head. In response, he gave a huge yawn, his long tongue curling out, then in on itself like one of those New Year's Eve noisemakers.

"Hey, buddy," I said to him. "Have a good day?"

His thick black tail began to wag slowly as he came alive from his afternoon nap. He seemed to pour himself onto the floor, sliding down from the back of the couch to the seat, then from the seat, like a sooty black puddle of ooze. He stretched again, first his front legs, then his back ones. I shook my head with affection for the performance. Steve is not a dog to be rushed.

We'd met not quite a year before when I decided I wanted a dog to keep me company. I'd thought about a purebred and I'd even gone so far as to research some different breeds, look up some breeders on the internet, and talk to a friend of mine who's a vet. My timing couldn't have been better, though, because the local branch of the Humane Society in Rochester was in the middle of its annual fundraiser. During that time, they snagged a couple hours on a Saturday afternoon to have a telethon that was broadcast on a local television station. I'd been channel surfing and ended up watching the whole thing (not to mention calling in to donate fifty bucks). The shots of all those dogs dropped off or picked up and just waiting to be adopted really pulled at my heartstrings and I decided then and there that that was the kind of dog I wanted. I'm sure there are deeper reasons for why I chose this route, but the bottom line is, I went there the next Sunday and met Steve and the rest is history.

My vet friend and I had a rough idea of his background. She thought he was definitely some kind of terrier, either Cairn or Scottie, judging from his short, stubby legs and coarse, wiry hair. His stubbornness and inability to walk without his nose to the ground seemed to back her up pretty well. I suspected he also had a little Border Collie in him. His ears were pricked up, but then the ends flopped over. He tended to follow me around the house by walking right at my heel, herding me in a sense. And his hair was all black except for the white band that ran right around his chest and a touch at the very tip of his tail. He was easily the oddest-looking dog I'd ever seen and that was one of the reasons I was so drawn to him.

Another was his personality. He is like a little person trapped in a furry suit, and there are times when he looks at me and for a split second I get a flash of a person. I swear he's often thinking human thoughts. That's why I gave him a human name, which he grew used to in a shockingly short period of time. Plus, I thought having a dog named Stephen King was pretty funny. What can I say? The guy is a brilliant writer, and I am easily amused.

Steve went outside to do his business and then I fed him before packing him and the better bottle of wine into my car so we could head to dinner.

Maddie Carlisle and Joan "J.T." Thompson were my best friends in the whole wide world. I'd met them as a couple nearly ten years ago at the universal meeting place for lesbians: a softball tournament. I'd been called by a friend as a sub for somebody who flaked out at the last minute and I spent the entire weekend playing some decent third base. I didn't suck, but I wasn't an exceptional player. Many of these women were, though, and I enjoyed simply watching them almost as much as actually playing.

J.T. was particularly amazing. No matter what the sport, she's one of those women you pick for your team even before you choose your own girlfriend. She is the best first baseman I've ever seen in softball. She spikes a mean volleyball that leaves a reverse imprint of the word "Wilson" on the forearms of anybody brave or stupid enough to attempt to receive it. She was the star of her high school and college basketball teams. The woman has God-given athletic talent.

Maddie is pretty damn athletic herself, but knows enough not to get into any kind of competition with J.T. She just does her thing and smiles proudly while other people stand in awe of her girlfriend.

It's hard to explain exactly why the three of us became such close friends. They've been together since the dawn of time; they're the only lesbians I know who were one another's first girlfriends and are still together. They've seen me through more than one disastrous breakup and they've continued to love me even after I did some really, *really* boneheaded things. They are my lifeline and my conscience.

Their modest-looking house is in Penfield, about twenty minutes from my townhouse development in Brighton. Modest-looking from the outside, that is. The inside looks like it could have served as the photo model for one of those *House Beautiful* or *Home and Garden* magazines. What J.T. has in athletic ability, Maddie more than equals in her decorating skills.

I'd barely opened the car door and Maddie was coming out the side door, arms thrown open.

"Stevie-boy! Come here and give Aunt Maddie a kiss."

I shook my head in wonder as Steve scrambled across my lap and out the driver's side door, right up into "Aunt Maddie's" embrace and set to work bathing her with his gentle kisses. I never get that kind of greeting from him.

"What do you do, rub bacon all over your face before we come over?" I asked her as I followed the love fest into the house, my nose lifting just like Steve's as I caught the delicious scent of whatever Maddie was making us for dinner.

J.T. stood in the kitchen sifting through a pile of mail and still wearing her police officer's uniform. My mouth went dry, as it always does when I see her imposing figure in full regalia. She is nearly six feet tall, with skin the color of the unsweetened cocoa powder my grandmother used to make brownies from scratch, deep and smooth and even. The uniform was cut surprisingly well for her; it didn't look like she was a woman trying to wear a man's clothes. Her waist tapered in, her hips flared slightly with her gun holster on one side and her nightstick on the other, and her broad shoulders told you how alarmingly strong she is. Any lesbian who doesn't immediately entertain fantasies of J.T. pushing her up against the wall and slowly, thoroughly, frisking her from behind (my fantasies include use of her handcuffs) needs to have her libido checked.

11

"Hey, Red," she said as she saw me come in, using the familiar nickname she'd given me when I was twenty-five. "You look as sexy as always."

"What did I tell you about making me blush," I scolded her, feeling my face warm as I playfully slapped at her arm.

She bent down to kiss me on the cheek. "That it clashes with your hair."

"That's right."

"Not my fault. You're too damn good-looking." She gave me a lazy wink. Nope. No hot-blooded woman would stand a chance resisting J.T.'s charms. Not a one.

"I'd give your wife a hug," I told her, "but she's too busy loving up my dog."

Maddie laughed. "Oh, all right. I can't help it if he's the man of my dreams." She set Steve on the floor and he gave J.T. a quick sniff as she bent down to ruffle his fur, then set off on his usual tour of the house, the first thing he always did when we came to visit. Well, second thing after lavishing attention on Maddie.

She wrapped her arms around me and squeezed. Maddie gives the best hugs of anybody I know; you feel like you really mean something to her and she's happy to have the opportunity to show you.

"How's the knee?" I gestured down with my chin as she limped to the stove.

"Open that wine and I'll tell you all about it," she ordered.

We sat and chatted and ate dinner and drank wine, catching up on the weeks since we'd seen each other. Maddie was scheduled for knee surgery the following week. Torn ACL. I don't handle medical, surgical, or any kind of 'cal' very well. As soon as Maddie got into any sort of sentence that began with, "then they cut this," or "after they slice through that," I slapped my hands over my ears and began to sing "She'll Be Comin' Around the Mountain" at the top of my lungs. I'm ridiculously squeamish. Pathetically so. I can't even have *Grey's Anatomy* on my television during a surgical scene. The second I see anything bloody, I run squealing from the room in horror. So, Maddie knew better than to go into detail about what they were going to do to her in that operating room. As far as I knew, she was going into the hospital, they were going to fix her knee, and then she'd come home and recover. And that's all the information I needed to have.

"Are you nervous?" I asked her as J.T. set a cup of after-dinner coffee in front of me. My stomach was full to bursting with the pot roast Maddie had cooking in her crock pot all day long, and the sips I took from my cup were miniscule. Steve was crashed out under the table, his chin resting on my foot.

The sigh Maddie blew out told me she didn't really want to admit what she was about to tell me. "Yeah. Yeah, I am." She took a sip of her coffee. J.T. reached over and covered Maddie's hand with her larger one. "I know everything will be fine. I'm not really all that worried about the surgery itself. I just want my recovery and rehab to go quickly. And they've already told me it may not. I ain't as young as I used to be," she added, trying for a cocky grin but it ended up looking more like she smelled something foul.

At thirty-eight, Maddie was four years older than I, and I couldn't imagine trying to get around on one leg for longer than a couple hours without wanting to pull my own hair out, so I understood her worry.

"You just have to remember to take your time, not to push harder than your body tells you to, and let J.T. wait on you." I gave that last comment with a wink.

"I've already told her that," J.T. said. "But you know how stubborn my wife can be."

"It's not stubbornness that's going to be the problem," Maddie told us. "It's going to be the frustration. I'm going to get frustrated and that's going to piss me off."

J.T. and I nodded in unison, knowing Maddie spoke the absolute truth.

"So," she added, eyes on me, "I'm going to ask you to call before you pop in. Okay?" I knew her well enough to read her face. She was trying not to hurt my feelings, but was also trying to make a point. "I don't want you showing up unannounced on a day when I'm crying my eyes out or throwing dishes."

I smiled, not the least bit offended. "Understood. I promise to call."

"Good. Thank you." She sipped again. "Which brings me to something I need to talk to you about."

"Well, that's kind of ominous," I said, because it was. "Are you breaking up with me?"

She laughed. "Never, baby."

"Okay, good. What's up then?"

"Remember when you left Christine?" She gazed into her cup.

"Of course." Christine was an ex from many years ago with a taste for alcohol and a volatile temper. We were together for about six months. I made her angry once. She slapped me once. That was the end of that.

"And we helped you go get your stuff from her place without a moment's notice, just dropped everything we were doing and got you the hell out of there?"

I squinted at her, wondering exactly where she was going with this, thinking I wasn't going to like it judging by the fact that she hadn't looked up from her coffee yet. "Uh-huh."

"And you thanked us so much and said that you owed us, big time, and whenever we had a favor to call in just to name it?"

"Uh-huh..." I drawled it out, feeling the sudden need to squirm. J.T. seemed to find her fingernails very interesting and my eyes zipped back and forth between her and Maddie. They obviously needed something from me, and I was okay with that. They'd taken great care of me more than once and I loved them both like family. "All right. What's going on? What is it?"

Maddie took a deep breath. "When I scheduled my surgery, I forgot about one teeny, tiny thing. I have something that starts two days later and I won't be able to do it because I'll be laid up. Plus, with rehab and physical therapy, it's probably going to be at least three or four weeks before I can even think of participating."

"Participating in what?" I asked, a sinking feeling settling over me. I set my cup down, the coffee suddenly sitting like lead pellets in my stomach.

"And I apologize for the short notice. I've been sort of preoccupied." She indicated her knee with her eyes.

"Participating in what?" I asked again.

"Tee-ball."

And there it was.

I groaned.

15

Starting three years before, each spring and summer Maddie coached a tee-ball team of five- and six-year-old boys and girls. She enjoyed it immensely, despite the fact that it was sometimes stressful. She had done it as a favor initially. The computer consulting company she worked for sponsored a team each year, a dozen little kids running around in bright green T-shirts with the company logo splashed across the front, trying hard to learn the rules of the game and have fun at the same time. Maddie's boss asked her if she'd be interested in coaching a team. Maddie said yes, more out of a desire to please the boss than a desire to actually lead a bunch of kids. To her surprise, she found it to be fulfilling.

Which, by no means, meant I would. I groaned again and dropped my forehead to the table in front of me.

"You'll be great at it," Maddie said, as the buttering-up began. "It's just practice. The first few weeks. I'll be able to take over after that."

"Me and kids, Maddie?"

"Kids *love* you."

"I never know what to say to them," I whined, knowing the chances of me getting out of this were slim to none, but vowing to protest as much as possible anyway.

"That's why they love you. You talk to them like they're grown up."

"I talk to them like they're grown up because I don't know what to say to kids." Maybe repeating myself would help me get through to her. "Can't somebody from your office do it?"

"I don't trust anybody there with my kids," she said, surprising me.

"God, I don't know…"

"It's only for a few weeks, Avery," Maddie said. Her voice had changed, from "hey, this'll be fun" to "all right, I know you don't want to, but you owe me."

And she was right. I did owe her. Them. Maddie and J.T. had gotten me out of a really bad situation. I was truly afraid of Christine, but there were a few things I'd really needed. If I went to get them alone and she caught me, she might snap. Paranoid? Probably. I didn't care. Having J.T. there in uniform was a huge comfort. Surprisingly, I'd never heard from Christine again...not that I didn't change my phone number and jump every time my doorbell rang for the next month.

I sighed the sigh of defeat, knowing there was no way out. I owed Maddie big, she needed me, and that was all there was to it. "Fine."

"Oh, thank you," she squealed, popping up from her chair and hobbling around the table to throw her arms around my neck. Her blonde hair smelled like lilacs and I couldn't help but smile at her exuberant gratitude. "You're the best."

"Yeah, yeah. I hope you'll be a character witness at my trial after I kill all the children for driving me up the wall."

"Not going to happen. They're going to love you and you're going to love them."

I shook my head. "I haven't the foggiest idea how to coach a tee-ball team."

"No worries. I'll give you my notes."

"Notes? You have notes?" I got up and helped myself to the last of the wine from dinner, exchanging my coffee for something a bit stronger. And more numbing. J.T. chuckled from her seat. I turned on her and pointed a finger in her direction. "And you. Don't you sit there and laugh. You haven't helped at all."

She shrugged, still grinning. "Hey, I know who's boss. It ain't you."

"Yeah, no shit." I sat back down and took a slug of my wine.

chapter two

My grandmother's assisted living apartment complex didn't have some fancy name that made it sound like a nursing home. It wasn't Shady Acres or Whispering Winds or Lofty Pine Manor. It was just 217 Jefferson Road and I think that's why she liked it.

As far as I'm concerned, Colleen Avery King was truly a woman ahead of her time. She was a career woman when it was uncommon—and frowned upon. She was the right hand of the County Commissioner and pretty much ran his office for the better part of thirty-five years. She retired at seventy with a notable pension, as well as income from the smart investments she'd made. Her financial prowess was the reason I was able to go to a good college without more than a couple of small loans.

It was true that she didn't need my financial help (she'd been insulted when I offered to help her with her rent, and she'd told me so in no uncertain terms), but she was still my grandmother and she'd raised me, so I liked to help out any way I could. Thus, the grocery bags I unloaded from my car on Sunday afternoon. Eggs (you can never have enough eggs), half-n-half (Grandma hates plain milk in her tea), boneless chicken breasts, bread, and a sour cream coffee cake I'd baked that morning. I figured she could serve it to her coffee klatch—three friends in the complex that came over every Monday for lunch. I knew she'd scold me for bringing her these things, but I also knew she was eighty-five years old and just couldn't get out and about to the grocery store as often as she liked. Not that she'd ever admit it. So, it made me feel like I was helping her out, which would be worth the reprimand.

"Hey there, Ms. King." The front security desk was manned by Jamal, as usual, and his teeth gleamed like new-fallen snow in a face as black as pitch when he smiled at me. He was probably around the same age as me, but he always treated me with the respect he showed his elderly tenants.

"Jamal," I said as I signed in on the visitors log. "How many times do I have to tell you to call me Avery?"

"A few more, I guess," he replied with a wink.

Tossing down the pen, I sighed with feigned exaggerated irritation. "Kids today. They just don't listen."

"Have a good one, Ms. King."

I exited the elevator on the third floor and headed down the hallway with my two grocery bags, nodding to Mr. Schwartz and saying hello to Mrs. Rossi along the way. Grandma had been living here for five years now, so I knew the residents pretty well, at least well enough to say hi and offer a friendly smile. Grandma told me there were a lot of elderly people there who never got visitors, whose families moved them in and then pretty much forgot about them. The thought made me sad. No way I wanted my grandmother to be lonely and forgotten like a pair of old shoes. So I made sure I said hello to each and every person I came across, whether I knew them or not.

At apartment number thirty-seven, I set down one bag so I could knock, but Grandma pulled the door open before I had a chance. Knowing she'd been waiting for me made me all warm and mushy inside.

"Hi, Grandma," I said as she pulled me into a hug.

"You're too skinny," she said, tightening her arms around me. It was the exact same line she opened with every time she saw me. "Don't you eat?"

"I eat plenty, Grandma, trust me."

I was one of the only women I knew whose grandmother was actually taller than she was. Needless to say, height was not something that showed up in my genes, and I obviously didn't inherit that from Grandma. At about five-six, she had me by two inches. Apparently, my mother was also a shrimp, not that I'd have any way of knowing that, since she'd been gone since I was four. My coloring, on the other hand, definitely came to me through my grandmother. Her hair was now a steel gray and rich-looking but when she was younger, it was the same auburn shade as mine. We weren't really traditional redheads, as we both had fair skin but no freckles. Our hair was more like a burnished copper, kind of rust-colored with lighter natural highlights. My hair was definitely one of my better features and I tended a little bit toward freakishness with it, spending way too much on designer shampoos, conditioners, and styling products. Grandma said the same thing about hers, that she too used to fret a bit more than necessary over her locks. I'd seen old pictures when her hair was the exact shade as mine, and it was beautiful. I also got her eyes. My mother's were apparently hazel, but Grandma's were a clear green the color of a shimmering summer lake and she'd passed them on to me.

The scent of warm chocolate drifted through the air and caught me by the nose. "Hey," I scolded. "Did you bake something without me?"

"It's just brownies," she said, waving her hand dismissively as if her brownies weren't the most awesome confections ever. "Mr. Davidson down the hall hung a picture for me last week, so I told him I'd make him some in return."

"Yeah, you watch out for Mr. Davidson. He's got his eye on you." I put the grocery bags on the counter in the small galley kitchen and took a quick peek in the oven.

"Nonsense," Grandma said, though the slight pinkening of her cheeks gave her away. "What did you bring?" she asked, changing the subject as she emptied the grocery bags. "Avery, I told you that you didn't have to bring me food all the time."

"I know, but I like to." Her nearly empty carton of half-n-half I found in the small refrigerator made me happy I had. I knew she felt better, felt more independent, if she could protest a little, so I let her, knowing I'd done the right thing.

We sat at the round table in her little dining area and chatted, just like always. Her apartment was small but just what she needed. She even had a little balcony off the living room where she could sit and read on nice days. I bought her a wicker rocker for a housewarming present when she moved in and it sat proudly in the spring sunshine. Parting with some of her big, heavy pieces of furniture was probably the hardest part about moving her from the house she'd lived in for almost fifty years. What she'd been able to keep lent it a feel that was very similar to her old house, homey and comfortable and neat as a pin.

I told her about Maddie's bombshell as we sipped our tea. I drank mine just like she did, with a little sugar and a lot of cream, and we took mirror-image sips. She dabbed at her mouth with a linen napkin and reached for the plate of lemon cookies she'd baked the day before.

"Well, you're very good with kids."

I looked at her in disbelief. "Since when am I good with kids?"

"Avery, just because somebody doesn't want to have their own children, it doesn't make that person unable to handle them. You handle them very well."

Who were these people? I wondered. First Maddie and J.T., then my own grandmother, telling me how well I deal with children and determined to turn me into some kind of babysitter. "Well, I'm certainly not looking forward to it."

"But you'll do it because you owe Maddie."

The tone of her voice was firm enough that it made me flash back to being twelve years old. "Yes, Grandma, I'll do it. I told her I would."

"Good. Maybe it'll be fun."

"Maybe money will fall from the sky, too."

The corner of her mouth quirked up and she brought her cup to her lips in an attempt to hide it. Yeah, my grandma was finding my situation amusing. I narrowed my eyes at her. "I'm going to drag you to one of the games, you know," I threatened. "That'll teach you to mock me."

"Hey, if it gets these old bones out of the house and into the sunshine, I'm all for it." She winked at me and bit into a lemon cookie.

I couldn't help but laugh. "You're evil."

"And don't you forget it."

That night, I spent hours online researching tee-ball, how to play it, and how to coach it. Shockingly, I found a handful of websites on the subject, as well as a couple books, which I put in orders for. I wasn't sure exactly how they would help, but I held out hope anyway. If I was going to do this, I wanted to do it right. Or at least make the attempt.

I sifted through Maddie's notes. What I found most interesting was that she made some observations along the margins that had to do with not worrying about winning or losing. The line that made me laugh said, "The kids don't really care if they win or lose, they just want to learn to play and have a little fun. Let the score roll off." I made myself a mental note to ask her if she'd gotten a little too wrapped up in the number of runs during her first season as a coach, because I knew first hand how competitive Maddie could be. At the same time, it gave me pause. I liked to win just as much as the next girl. I took my red pen and wrote in big letters at the top of one page: TEACH THEM HOW TO PLAY. From the blurbs on the various websites I'd checked out as well as Maddie's notes, that was going to be the thing to remember. And as the coach of these oh-so-young children, that was my job.

Maddie was scheduled for surgery the next morning, so I called to wish her luck and get the details of where she'd be so I could visit later. She confirmed the time and place for practice on Wednesday and said she'd have J.T. zip to the room they used as an office and e-mail me the list of names for the kids on the team.

I took a deep breath as the e-mail arrived, and I scanned the list of twelve names. Five girls and seven boys. Eight five-year-olds and four six-year-olds. And they were counting on me to teach them how to play ball.

I dropped my head into my hands and groaned loudly. Steve lifted his head from my reading chair and regarded me with curious brown eyes. Then I got up and headed downstairs to do what I always did when I was stressed out and nervous.

I made cookies.

chapter three

They're five-year-olds. They're kids, for Christ's sake. Relax.
I said it over and over again in my head, but the nerves were still there and I felt like somebody was shooting billiards in the pit of my stomach. I'd gotten to the field a little early—Tyrell was far too amused by the fact that I was actually doing this and kicked me out of the office a full half hour earlier than usual. J.T. had dropped by the office parking lot the day before and transferred all Maddie's supplies to the trunk of my car, so I had everything I needed.

I'd decided that one large benefit to tee-ball was that I didn't really have to pitch, and therefore the chances of me getting nailed in the face with a line drive by some kid who was on track to be the next Barry Bonds were pretty slim. I hauled out the bases and Maddie's pre-cut twine and set them up, making the infield a little smaller than actual size for the time being. Five-year-olds had short legs.

The tee was made of heavy duty plastic, as were the bats, and we would use plastic balls as well. The idea was to get the kids used to the rules and the feel of the game, not to overwhelm them with heavy equipment. It was sort of glorified whiffle ball, not that any of these little tykes would have any idea what that was.

I was swigging from my water bottle and running through the list of names again when the first car pulled up and two kids got out. A minivan pulled up a few seconds later, followed by another. I glanced at my watch. Five forty-five on the dot. Nice. These would be the kids that were punctual, I suspected.

Once the seventh member of my team appeared, I decided I wasn't going to bother trying to learn their last names. First names were hard enough, especially considering I had two Brittanys, a Samuel not Sam, a Mikey, and a Mikki. By six o'clock, the last kid showed up, a little boy named Max. His mom followed him from their Lexus and was chatting on her cell phone as she took a seat in the bleachers with the one other mom and one other dad who'd also decided to stick around for practice. (Maddie hadn't mentioned the possibility of spectators on my first day and I was not happy about them...I felt I didn't really need anybody over the age of six to see that I had no idea what I was doing.)

"Okay, guys. Okay." I raised my voice to get the attention of all of them. "Let's have a seat right here." I waited until they all grabbed some grass between home and the pitcher's mound and then I took roll call. "All right, first things first. It's going to take me a while to remember your names. I'm old, like your parents, so my memory stinks." That got a little chuckle out of them, which was kind of cool. "So, you're going to have to help me out until I get used to you, all right?"

There were nods all around and one little blond girl (Isabella?) raised her hand. When I pointed to her, she asked, "What do we call you?"

"That's a good question. Coach is just fine."

"Coach what?"

Hmm. Another good question. Avery seemed kind of a weird name to expect them to remember. "How about Coach King? Does that work for you guys?"

"A king is a boy." Okay, so the little blond girl was a smarty-pants.

"That's true," I said to her. "But it's also my last name, so it makes sense."

"Oh." She shrugged and that was the end of that, apparently. Deceptively easy, I suspected.

Keeping their attention turned out to be the hardest part. I was pleasantly surprised to find that the majority of them knew some of the basic rules of the game—which bases were which, for example—so I decided to get right into hitting, thinking that if I spent a short amount of time on the boring details and most of the time on actual participation, it would all work out. I also crossed my fingers and toes, figuring it couldn't hurt.

I set them up in the field using the imaginary line in tee-ball that I'd read about in Maddie's notes as well as online. It meant that the fielders all stood back beyond an invisible forty-foot arc from home plate that ran from first base to third. This was a safety measure so nobody got blasted by a ball right off the tee. Plus, it helped the kids learn to move to the ball and gave them time to do so. Nobody played any particular position at that point; I just wanted them to get used to being in the field, to going after the ball. I also didn't want to have them run the bases yet. Just to have fun batting. We'd run the next day.

A petite African-American boy named Gabriel was up to bat first. He knew very well how to hold the bat and he sent the ball sailing on his very first try. *Hey, maybe this'll be easier than I thought,* went zipping through my head as he proceeded to connect with the next eight balls I set on the tee for him. Of course, I jinxed myself right then because Gabriel was the only kid who hit it on the first attempt.

When one of the Brittanys was up, I heard a woman's voice from the bleachers. "Come on, Britty! You know how to do this!" I took a quick glance; she was on the edge of her seat, hands fisted, looking way too invested in whether or not her five-year-old could hit a plastic ball off a tee with a plastic bat. The phrase Helicopter Parent flashed into my mind. Terrific.

Brittany proceeded to whack the crap out of the tee itself, but had trouble actually connecting with the ball.

"Eye on the ball, Brittany! Just like at home! Come on!"

I was reasonably sure her mother's continual shouts weren't helping. When I saw her big brown eyes start to well up, I felt a little ache for her and spoke softly. "Hey, let's try again tomorrow, okay? Give yourself a break for now. You'll get it. Don't worry."

She nodded and sniffled, quite obviously trying not to cry as she picked up her glove and went back out into the field. I noted no encouraging comments from the bleachers, only silence, and it forced an irritated breath from my lungs.

Max the latecomer was next. He was a really cute kid with enormous brown eyes and hair that was almost black. His eyelashes were the impossibly long variety that most women would kill for and when he gripped the bat, his tongue poked out at the corner of his mouth in concentration. I couldn't help but smile at him. It took him three tries, but the third one, he hit over the heads of the first line of fieldsman.

"Nice!" I cried.

The first thing Max did was whip his head around toward the bleachers, his face a glowing smile of pride. His mother was still on her cell and wasn't even looking in his direction. His smile dropped right off his face and he turned back to the tee. I wondered what the opposite of a Helicopter Parent was.

"Okay, gang, bring it in," I called as the last kid, David, finished his round at bat. Various vehicles were starting to pull into the parking lot and I was happily surprised to see that an hour had already passed. "Come here and sit down for a minute." It had only been one practice, but I felt like I'd learned a few things and I wanted to talk to the kids about them. "You did great. You did really, really great. I'm proud of all of you."

Gabriel snorted a laugh. "Brittany and Jordan couldn't even hit. At all."

"Shut up," Jordan snapped, his manhood obviously bruised. Brittany just flushed a light pink.

I bit my lip to keep from snapping out a retort that Gabriel's parents probably wouldn't appreciate. "You know what Gabriel? First of all, this is a team. We're all supposed to work together and do you know what that means? It means that the people who are good at certain things need to help out the ones who might not be and that way the whole team will get stronger together. So just because you can hit the ball, it doesn't mean you get to laugh at those who might not have the hang of it yet. Making fun of your teammates is not something I want to hear happening. Understood?"

31

Nods and murmurs rippled through the group, at least from those who were paying attention. Katie was pulling grass out by the roots and Mikey was sprawled out on his stomach looking so comfortable that I wondered if he might actually be napping.

"So, the fact remains that you all did well. You tried your best and you'll do it again tomorrow. That's why we have practice, so we can get better. Right?" At their nods, I waved my hands as if shooing them away. "Good. Go. Go home. I'll see you tomorrow."

They scattered like leaves in the wind.

I was picking up balls and putting them into Maddie's nylon bag when the lone male from the bleachers came to say hi.

"Jake Weber," he said, shaking my hand in a grip that was both solid and friendly. "I'm Samuel's dad."

I fumbled in my brain to try to pick out which of the boys was Samuel and finally settled on the quiet redhead with the freckles and shy smile. "Of course," I said, noting Jake's darker version of Samuel's hair. "Samuel not Sam," I teased, using the phrase the boy had used to tell me his name. "I'm Avery King."

"Pleased to meet you." His smile was kind and I liked him right away.

"Samuel seems like a really nice kid."

"He is. A little shy," he added with a chuckle, "but a good boy. He's been looking forward to this since winter." He scratched at his neck. "Anyway, I just wanted to say hello and meet the coach."

"I'm glad you did," I replied and meant it.

As Jake headed back to his son, Brittany's mom approached from the bleachers. Maddie hadn't warned me

32

about all this parent interaction and I made a mental note to slap her the next time I saw her.

"Hi there," she said, holding out her hand. "Marjorie Sullivan." Her clothes were designer, her makeup was flawless, and her short hair was the color of spun gold and perfectly highlighted. Everything about her said this was a woman who was used to being listened to, used to getting what she wanted.

"Avery King," I responded, shaking her hand and using effort not to wince as she overdid the firmness on her end. "Nice to meet you. You've got a really nice kid there." I nodded in Brittany's direction.

"Thank you. I was just wondering if there was anything my daughter should be doing at home to help her with her batting skills."

It was difficult, but I managed to keep my face neutral. At least I hoped I did. "I think she'll get the hang of it during practice. This was only the first day and sometimes it takes a little while. No need to worry, there's plenty of time. She'll be fine." What I wanted to say was, *Are you serious? She's five, for Christ's sake. Give the kid a break.*

Marjorie Sullivan didn't look all that impressed with my answer and I suspected I'd just dropped a couple notches on her list of esteemed teachers and coaches. "Well, maybe I'll have my husband work with her anyway."

I nodded, not that it mattered because she was walking away. I followed her with my eyes, still just this side of a little freaked by the amount of pressure she put on her kindergartner. Before I pulled my gaze back to my own world, I noticed Max and his mom. She was finally off the phone and as she handed him a water bottle, she looked at me. And totally sized me up. She was a good twenty feet from me, but her eyes crawled up my body so intentionally I could almost feel them. I didn't normally mind when somebody checked me out. Hell, it was flattering most of the time. But this just felt...a little dirty. She wasn't unattractive, but the way she leered at me made her less good-looking than I might have originally thought.

Okay, so Max's mommy might be family. I wonder if Max's daddy knows that.

I filed it away, along with the fact that though she couldn't be bothered to come and introduce herself, she apparently had no qualms about undressing me with her eyes right there on the baseball field with her son standing next to her. Shaking my head, I forced myself to look away and continue cleaning up. When I finally ventured another peek, the Lexus was pulling away.

―――

"So? How'd it go?" Maddie's voice wasn't quite as exuberant as usual, which I blamed on pain medication. Much as I wanted to give her a hard time, I suspected she was feeling crappy enough on her own without me adding to her misery.

"Not bad at all. It was interesting, that's for sure. And different." I mixed some tuna in with Steve's dry food as I spoke into the phone. He did a little tap dance on the kitchen floor at my feet, giddy with anticipation. "You didn't tell me some parents might stay and watch."

"Ooo, did I leave that part out?"

"Conveniently, yes."

"Sorry about that. It doesn't happen often. Usually they just want to dump their kids and come back later. Anybody give you any problems?"

The way she said it made me think she'd had some in the past and a feeling of dread sat in my belly like a peach pit. "Not today. Though there was one mom who was a bit overzealous in her cheering. I mean, it was practice, for God's sake."

"Yeah, you'll get that." Maddie sighed and I could hear her grunt as she shifted positions. "Some aren't involved enough and some are so over-involved you're afraid you might bump into them, they're so close." She seemed to hesitate a little bit and then said, "Um, did anybody ask about your marital status?"

"My what?"

"It's just…I tend to keep my sexual orientation under my hat." I groaned and she went on. "I know, I know. I don't like it either, and I know how you hate feeling closeted, but it's just better that way. Trust me, there will always be somebody who thinks a homosexual teaching their kid is a gigantic no-no, and they'll be sure to make a big stink out of it."

I hoped my silence told her how much I hated this little wrench in the gears.

"I know," she said again. "I know."

I let her off the hook after a couple more seconds of icy quiet. "How are you feeling?" I asked as I set Steve's bowl down before his little head exploded from the waiting.

"Owie."

"I'll bet. Pain meds helping at all?"

"If I take extras, they do."

35

"Yeah, well, be careful of that," I warned sternly. "The last thing we need is for you to become a Vicodin addict or something. That stuff can mess you up."

"Hey, you know what would make me feel a lot better?" she asked, her voice softening. "Some of those triple chocolate cookies you made around Christmas time. Remember those?"

A few minutes later I poured myself a glass of Cabernet and donned my favorite apron, a simple black one with brightly colored spatulas all over it that Grandma bought me at least ten years earlier. Pulling mixing bowls and ingredients out of cupboards, I set to work making cookies for Maddie.

My love of baking comes from my grandmother. I know it. She was a practical woman stuck raising her daughter's child, not something she ever expected to be doing, I'm sure. She was fifty-five when my mother took off and left four-year-old me with her, an age where she'd been thinking about retirement, not how to entertain a small child. She wasn't the kind to play catch with me or teach me to ride a bike (though she managed to do the latter), but she made a mean chocolate chip cookie, among other sweet confections. I still remembered shards of the very first time I helped her. I must have been five or six and she was working at the counter. I slid my little chair over and stood on it so I could see what she was doing. Once I was quiet enough, she simply began giving me instructions "I need an egg. Be careful with it." "This is a sifter; just pull on this handle until all the flour goes through." "There's a bag of chocolate chips in that cupboard. Grab it for me." And that's how it began. It was sort of unspoken, but that ended up being the quality time

I spent with Grandma and it didn't take long for me to grow to love it. Cookies and cakes were her way of showing me love, because I think she was so frustrated and disappointed in her own child, she didn't know what to say to me.

So we baked.

I sometimes thought how weird it might have seemed to somebody looking in from the outside. Somebody who didn't know, who wasn't there during my childhood. But Grandma took care of me; she clothed me and fed me and put off her own retirement so I could go to a decent college. She wasn't terribly verbal in the emotions department, but I knew in my heart that she adored me, and if the best way she could show me so was to bake me an angel food cake with marshmallow icing, that was good enough for me. I loved her right back. And as will happen with things that are handed down within a family, baked goods became a tool for me to show my love as well, at least in some cases. In other cases, I just like to bake. It is my cure-all. I bake when I am stressed out. I bake when I am sad. I bake when I am ecstatically happy. I bake when I'm nervous. I don't know why. Something about the focus, the way I can concentrate on measuring and sifting and stirring just helps to relax and calm my frayed nerves. Very few problems in life can't be made at least a teensy bit better by a mouthful of cookie dough.

I finished up the last batch and left them to cool on a wire rack while I did up the dishes. It was late, but Grandma always hated to wake up to a sink full of dirty dishes, so I always clean up my mess even if I've been baking at three in the morning which is not unheard of. After wrapping up a package for Maddie, I took a cookie for myself, along with the essential glass of milk, and Steve and I headed to bed.

chapter four

My townhouse development was a bit classier than most, in my opinion. Instead of being a bunch of giant buildings with doors all in a row, each building only housed two units. So, it was almost like living in a sort of duplex, rather than a structure with four or six or even eight units. And each building was slightly different, whether it was the pitch of the roof or the path of the front walk, or the color of the siding, so we didn't look like we lived in a bunch of cookie-cutter homes. There were three pods set up in semi-circles and inside each semi-circle was a happy little courtyard with benches and a swing set, so our back yards all looked over one another, but we were far enough apart to feel like we had at least a little bit of privacy.

As I opened my car door, I waved across the street to Mr. Watson. He was a nice man, old enough to be my father and widowed for about two years. He always snow-blew my driveway right after he did his in the winter. I, in return, kept him supplied with rum balls throughout the holiday season. It was an agreement that worked well for both of us.

"Morning, Avery," he greeted as he crossed toward me. He pointed down the street a ways with his square chin and asked, "You see the Sold sign?"

I nodded. "I noticed on my way home last night. How long has it been there?"

"'Bout a week."

I made a face that said I obviously hadn't been paying enough attention. "I wonder who bought it. Any clues?" Getting into our development was tough and we liked to keep it a closely guarded secret.

"Not yet, but according to Mrs. Greeley, it's been sold for a while and the sign should have been up weeks ago. The closing's next week some time."

"Wow." I tossed my briefcase into the car, wondering, not for the first time, how Mrs. Greeley always managed to get a hold of such detailed knowledge. Some would call her a busybody. I thought she was a wealth of information. If it wasn't for her, I'd never know anything going on around my home. "Then I guess we'll know soon enough, huh?"

"Looks that way."

Fridays are always a lot of fun at the office, with the dress code moved to casual and the atmosphere a bit lighter than at the beginning of the week, but that particular Friday was more festive than usual. The campaign we'd been working on—for a new local microbrewery—had been received with great fervor and excitement. Josh sent the praise my way for my colorful yet simple design. I tossed it back into his lap because of his catchy wording, and we both heaped the majority of the success onto Anita, who did the actual pitching, which we all knew she did with stylish presentation and expert coaxing. Tyrell was absolutely psyched, as we'd beat out several larger competitors. The microbrewery was owned by a much larger company, so the money they had to spend on additional ad campaigns was quite a bit more than what a small company would be able to fork over. This could turn out to be a really big client for THJ and we all knew it. Tyrell told us in no uncertain terms that we were all going out for Happy Hour after work, and drinks were on him.

Even though Tyrell said he was buying, I didn't like going out to a bar without any cash at all; it made me feel dependent upon others. This happened to me—finding myself with no cash—more and more often since the invention of the debit card. I wondered if other people had the same problem. I could rarely buy myself a pack of gum without using plastic because I just never thought to carry cash any more.

Of course, in order to get cash, I'd have to visit the bank. Elena Walker's bank. You could call me a lot of things, but "dummy" isn't one of them.

Rather than use the ATM, which would keep me from having to actually go *inside* the bank, and thereby preclude me from catching a glimpse of my fantasy woman, I entered the lobby and proceeded to fill out a withdrawal slip at one of the little desks. I could see right into Elena's office, see her sitting at her desk, talking to somebody on the little earpiece she wore so she didn't have to hold the handset of the telephone, and typing on her computer keyboard. The day's suit was black with very subtle white pinstripes and big silver buttons on the jacket. I couldn't see if it was a pantsuit or a traditional jacket and skirt, but the creamy blouse was unbuttoned enough to show off a tan expanse of collarbone and the tiniest tease of cleavage. I bit my lip when the conversation she was having sent her into amused laughter, and forced my eyes back down to my pen. Did anybody have a right to be that damn good-looking? That sexy? Wasn't it dangerous? Shouldn't there be a law of some kind?

When I glanced up again, she was looking right at me, those deep melted-chocolate eyes sparkling even as she continued to talk to whoever was on the other end of the phone line. She tossed a little wave in my direction. And then she winked.

She winked at me.

My knees almost dropped me on the floor right then and there like a pile of dirty laundry.

I left the bank whistling a joyful little tune that I made up on the spot.

By five-thirty that evening, we were having a blast. Tyrell was a different kind of boss, more like a big brother or cousin, always looking out for those he cared about. He was one of the nicest men I'd ever met and as I watched him joking with Josh over a beer, I remembered the first time I'd come out for drinks with the team, only a couple weeks after I'd started working there. He'd introduced himself to me as Tyrell Jones, so I asked if he named his company T. Harrison Jones because it sounded more professional, more sophisticated. He said, matter-of-factly, that he named it what he did because it sounded less black. I wasn't really sure how to respond, but I felt uncontrollable sadness over the fact that it was the 21st century and we still had to deal with ridiculous crap like racism and homophobia and misogyny. Tyrell was not only one of the sweetest guys I knew, he was also one of the smartest and one of the most talented businessmen in the city. But he had to be careful not to make his company name sound too African-American because he might lose clients. Sometimes the world just made me want to weep.

Josh bellied up to the bar next to me, his dark hair looking like he'd just rolled out of bed. I reached up to fix it, trying to brush it with my fingers like he was five years old.

"What is going on with your bangs?" I teased as he tried to swat my hand away. "Does your wife really let you out of the house like this?"

"She leaves before I do in the morning."

"That explains it. I'm calling her and telling her that her husband needs a haircut."

He laughed. "You will do no such thing." He caught the bartender's eye and made a gesture with his finger that encompassed both our empty glasses before asking me how tee-ball was going.

"So far, so good," I said to him, and meant it. "I've only had a couple practices, but I haven't murdered any of the kids yet, so I'd say it's a success so far." I held up my glass and he touched his to it.

Josh swallowed a mouthful of beer and then chuckled. "I remember going to watch my niece Jasmine play in her first soccer game. She was, like, five or six, I think. And the ball is coming her way, all the players are running in her direction, and what is she doing? Picking a dandelion she found on the field. They all went running right by her. I'm not even sure she noticed."

I thought of little Katie's fascination with yanking handfuls of grass out by the roots and shook my head. "I'm just hoping I have the patience for this. We'll have our first game before Maddie's ready to come back."

"You'll be fine. Got any ringers?"

My mind flashed to Gabriel, who proceeded to whack the crap out of the ball any time I put him near the tee. I told Josh about him. "He's a little condescending to the other kids, but he's got some real athletic potential. There's Brittany, who I suspect is only playing because her mom wants her to. She's not bad, though. She tries hard. And Max. He's adorable and he wants so badly for his mom to pay half the attention Brittany's mom does, but she's always absorbed in her Blackberry or her cell phone or whatever and can hardly be bothered to look up."

Josh just grinned at me.

"What?" I asked him, wanting in on the secret.

"I just find it interesting that I asked you about the kids and you told me all about the parents."

I groaned. "See? I'm just not good with kids."

"What are you talking about? Paying attention to the parents means you're more in tune than most people."

I shrugged off the remark and tossed him a change of subject. "So. How goes the baby-making?"

"Well," he said, and then arranged his expression into something resembling "thinking really hard." He took a gulp of his beer before continuing. "You'd think it would be awesome for a guy to have his dick at a woman's beck and call, wouldn't you?"

Beer went up my nose as I snorted over his choice of words. He'd always treated me as one of the guys, so using the word "dick" in conversation with me didn't faze him in the least. Once in a while, it caught me off-guard, though. I wiped my dripping chin as I laughed and then mimicked dialing a phone and putting an invisible handset to my ear. "Hey, Joshua," I said in my best come-hither voice. "I need you. Now, big fella. Come and have your way with me."

He pointed at me and nodded with enthusiasm.

"Like that?" I asked.

"Exactly."

"Yes, I would think most guys would love that."

"Yeah, well you would be wrong."

"I would?" I had to admit, I was surprised.

"It's a lot of pressure," he whined.

I rolled my lips in and bit them to keep from busting out laughing at his little-boy tone. "What, you can't just..." I cleared my throat. "Stand up on cue?"

"No!" He must have realized my mirth because he narrowed his eyes at me. "Most guys can't."

"Porn stars can."

"That's because they have—what do they call them?— fluffers to help them along."

"Maybe you need one of those."

He arched an eyebrow at me. "You offering?"

"Hell, no." I scoffed. "I don't want to be anywhere near that thing. No offense."

"Gee, thanks."

I noticed that he wasn't quite his happy-go-lucky self all of a sudden. We'd always taken each other's ribbing well, knowing that's all it was: ribbing. The flinch of pain that zipped across his features bothered me.

"What's going on, Joshie?" I asked, quietly and with more seriousness. "Are you having trouble?"

He studied what was left in his glass and pursed his lips. When he spoke, his voice was as quiet as mine and it struck me how we'd gone from playfully poking to softly serious in the space of about five seconds.

"It's just…like I said. It's a lot of pressure." He finished off his beer and gestured for a refill. "I think Nina's getting frustrated and maybe a little depressed that it hasn't happened yet. And every time she's *not* pregnant, I feel like a failure."

My eyes actually misted, I loved him so much. Laying a hand on his shoulder, I tried to think of the right thing to say, realizing with unobstructed certainty that revealing such feelings to a woman rather than one of his male buddies was a true sign of how much our friendship meant to him. That he trusted me with such a personal thing…I was truly touched and I didn't want to ruin the moment. Nor did I want to stretch it out too long.

"It's gonna happen, sweetie," I said with a confidence I definitely felt. "It just takes time and that has nothing— *nothing*—to do with anything resembling failure on your part. Nina would slap you for even thinking such a thing and you know it." That made the corner of his mouth twitch up. Nina was a little spitfire and she'd have his ass in a sling if she knew he was taking on full responsibility for conception. "When it's ready to happen, when it's supposed to happen, it will. You have to believe that."

"You really think so?"

"Absolutely. And in the meantime, stop bitching about the pressure and just relax and enjoy the multitude of opportunities to fuck your wife silly."

That time, *he* sputtered, sending beer spittle across the bar and making me grin. Just as he could mess me up by using raunchy guy talk with me, I could do the same to him. I handed him a couple napkins.

"Slob."

chapter five

I sucked so furiously on the straw in my water bottle that I was surprised my entire skull didn't cave in. It was the following Thursday, the day before the long Memorial Day weekend and the air was chilly. I didn't know if the kids were tired from their week, too cold to play, anxious about maybe taking a family trip for the holiday weekend, or just trying to make me pull my hair out. Whatever it was, they were driving me mad with their lack of attention and focus and I was trying hard not to blow a gasket in front of the four parents who occupied the bleachers that day. I couldn't for the life of me figure out how moms and dads did this every single day of their lives.

I had them set up in fielding positions, but Jordan was sitting on his butt just behind second base, and Katie kept wandering away from third to get a sip from her bottle of juice that sat next to the bleachers. After her fourth abandonment of her post, I gave up.

"All right. Bring it in," I called, waving them toward me at the pitcher's mound. "Grab a seat." When they were all parked on their little rear ends in a horseshoe around me, I studied them. I was hoping my hands on my hips, coupled with my expression of quiet disapproval would resonate and make it clear to them that I wasn't happy with this practice session, but a couple of their gazes began to wander and I sighed. *They're five and six,* I had to remind myself. *They probably don't get body language yet.* I'd have to spell it out while reminding myself to stay positive.

"Our first official game is next Saturday," I told them.

They murmured and actually sounded excited about it, which brought a little grin to my lips.

"But we've still got some work to do before we're as ready as we can be." A couple grimaces told me how they felt about that. "You didn't concentrate today as much as I would have liked. I know there's a long weekend coming up and you're probably excited, but we have one more practice, on Tuesday, and I want you to come ready to play, okay? No fooling around." I noticed Mikey smiling and waving at a car that had pulled up. "Mikey? What did I just say?"

He looked at me blankly, and pursed his lips. "Um." Then he studied the grass.

"That's what I thought. Max, would you tell Mikey what I just said?"

Max sat up a little straighter, as if he'd just been given a big responsibility. "Coach King said we have to come here on Tuesday and contrate. No fooling around." He smiled at me and I couldn't help but smile back in return, he was so cute.

"Exactly. Got it?"

"Yeah," Mikey said quietly, looking sheepish.

"Everybody? Got it?" I looked around at the rest of the team as they nodded. "Good. Okay, grab me the bases and then go. Have a great weekend." I shooed them away like flies.

They scattered as various cars pulled up, some parents getting out, some not. I bagged the equipment as bases

50

were dropped at my feet, muttered "Bye, Coach"'s floating by me. I was completely exhausted and looking forward to the long weekend without having to deal with the kids. I was hoping to plant some flowers, take Steve to the park, and try a new cookie recipe with Grandma. So lost in my upcoming plans was I that I didn't hear the approach of one of the parents.

"Hi there."

It was Max's mom, the one who'd leered at me so openly that first day of practice. She hadn't stayed for every practice; in fact, I'd only seen her once or twice since that first time. Max carpooled with another kid the other days. I hadn't paid her much attention, and she'd apparently returned the favor, disregarding not only me, but Max and his tee-ball play as well. He still turned to her when he did something well, his adorable face lit up with pride. Each time, I watched it fall with disappointment when he saw her absorbed in whatever electronic device she happened to have brought with her that day.

Forcing myself to remain professional, I replied, "Hi. You're Max's mom, right?"

With a nod and a smile, she stuck out her hand. "Cindy Johnson."

I returned the handshake. "Avery King."

Max saved me from more small talk when he ran up to us. "Did you see my hit, Cece?" he asked Cindy, all dignified and proud.

I stayed focused on him, well aware from my peripheral vision that Cindy's focus was not on him, but on me. "I must have missed it, buddy," she said with little interest.

I met her gaze. "It was a very solid hit," I told her.
"He's doing very well."

"I've got a knot," Max said, looking down at his shoe.

"Are you new around here?" Cindy asked me. "I don't
recall seeing you before."

"No, I'm not new, but it's a good-sized city," I replied,
trying to take her in without giving her the wrong idea—
which was exactly the idea she wanted, I suspected. Her
gaze was intense, her eyes a light brown with gentle crow's
feet at the corners. She wasn't a small woman—not heavy,
just rather big-boned—but her expensive clothes hid it
pretty well. Her brown hair was cut in a stylish bob, the
slightest hint of gray showing at the part, telling me she
was due for a coloring soon. I saw no ring on her left hand,
which made me feel only minutely better about her
obvious flirtation.

"It is. It's just…I've been here my whole life and I'm
kind of surprised we haven't run into each other, you know,
at Blink or the Pink Rhino or something."

Two of the gayest places in town. She was fishing for
my sexuality and much as it made me a little
uncomfortable, I had to admire her smoothness.

"Yeah, well, I don't go out much," I offered, caught
between embarrassment and amusement.

"I've got a knot," Max said again, louder this time,
bouncing up and down impatiently. I squatted to help him.
Anything to get out of the spotlight of Cindy's stare.

"We could fix that," she continued, apparently not at
all fazed that her son was right there and I was working on
his shoelace. "Maybe we could have a drink some time."

"Oh, I don't know," I hedged, wishing I had the balls
to simply say that I thought her approach was

inappropriate, given the close proximity of her son and me being his coach. But before I could figure out the right wording, her cell phone rang and I knew she'd answer it. It was impossible for her not to answer it. She was one of *those* people, the ones who lost part of their identity if they didn't have the damn thing within their grasp at all times, who didn't find it at all rude or annoying to be chattering away in a restaurant or a library or a grocery store, who had no grasp of the fact that the rest of the world was really not all that interested in listening in on their side of the conversation.

"We'll continue this next week," she informed me with a wink as she put the contraption to her ear, grabbed Max's hand, and backed away from me. The certainty in her tone unnerved me.

—

"You know, if you soak those in a mix of water and a little dish washing liquid while you're watching television tonight, they'll clean right up." Grandma gestured to my hands as I dropped spoonfuls of cookie batter onto her cookie sheets.

"Really?" It sounded like a great solution for my stained fingernails. The topsoil I'd been digging in the day before left a bit of a shadow under the white of each one.

"You always did like to dig." She shook her head, as if in dismay, but her wry grin told me she'd found it amusing.

"Did I?"

"You were such a quiet kid," she went on, as if once she'd started talking about the past, she just had to keep going. "I worried."

This was the first I'd heard of that. "Why?"

"It just seemed so unusual."

I slid the cookie sheet into the oven, picked up my tea and followed her to her small table.

"Children were supposed to be loud, screechy, running around shouting at the top of their lungs with all the other children." She sipped her tea. "You didn't do any of that."

These facts actually didn't surprise me. I was a quiet, fairly solitary adult; it wasn't shocking that I would have started out my life that way, too.

"So I did a little research," she went on. "Your friendly, local librarian pointed me in the right direction."

"And what did you come up with?"

"You were an introverted child."

I grinned, happy with the diagnosis. "And I am an introverted adult."

Grandma nodded. "I wasn't the only person back then who worried. Lots of parents who had quiet children did."

"Was my mom like that, too? Quiet, I mean?"

The subject of my mother, Grandma's only child, wasn't something we touched on frequently. In fact, we rarely touched on it at all. Grandma almost never brought her up and I was always too shy or embarrassed or worried about causing anger to ask, so we went on with our lives together as my mother took the shape of the elephant in the room that we both knew was there, but that neither of us was brave enough to talk about. I didn't know much. Samantha King had been a kind of wild child of the sixties who (I suspected) rebelled against her rigid mother by sneaking out, partying, and hanging with the wrong crowd of people. She got pregnant at sixteen, had me, made a half-hearted attempt to be a mother before leaving me with her own mother and running away just before her twentieth birthday. Not long after that, Grandpa King left too, not having signed on to raise another child when he was in his fifties. Or maybe he'd been simply waiting for an excuse to leave his wife of more than twenty years, I don't know. I hadn't seen either my mother or my grandfather since then, and I carried a lot of guilt into my adulthood, feeling responsible for Grandma losing half her family.

"No. No, your mother was not a quiet child," Grandma said and I was sure I caught the ghost of a wistful smile play at her lips. "Quite the opposite. Just like her father. Rambunctious. Full of piss and vinegar, as we used to say. I had a hard time keeping up with her."

"Oh." I sipped from my own mug, unable to put a finger on the reason I felt disappointed.

"No, you were more like me, I think."

That lightened the mood for me and I felt myself sit up a little straighter. "Really?"

"If I recall correctly, my mother used to tell me how much of a loner I was, that if given the choice between a party and a book, I'd choose the book every time."

"We're two peas in a pod, Grandma."

The timer chimed and I jumped up, anxious to see how our cherry chocolate drop cookies had turned out.

"Sinful," I pronounced, helping myself to a second cookie. "Mr. Davidson will be scratching at the door the second the scent makes it into the hallway."

"Oh, hush," Grandma said, pushing playfully at my arm. But again, her blush gave her away.

Steve was his usual laidback self when I got home that afternoon, lounging in a square of sunlight cast onto the carpet from the sliding glass door, like always.

I let him outside into the yard where he did his usual "perimeter sniffdown." My backyard was small but I had a white, four-foot picket fence on either side, just like everybody else. When I first adopted Steve from the pound, I bought a roll of two-foot high chicken wire-type stuff to run across the back of the yard, connecting the pickets on either side. Steve wasn't a jumper but he was part terrier and I worried that he might take off on me. The chicken wire fencing was more for my peace of mind than anything else, and of course, Steve could plow right through it if he was so determined. Instead, he tended to wander along the fence with his nose to the ground, check out every inch of his very own twelve by twelve square of the world, then plop down on the cement of the patio and bake himself in the sun. It was still cool and the breeze offset the heat of the sun nicely, so I suspected he'd be out there for a while.

An hour later, I was parked in my favorite reading chair, a glass of zinfandel on the end table next to me, the latest Mary Higgins Clark novel open in my hands.

I glanced out the window to see if Steve had burnt himself to a crisp.

And I froze.

"Oh, crap."

Steve was sitting at the end of the yard, along the chicken wire part of the fencing. On the other side, also sitting, but with his arm dangling over the chicken wire and moving gently along Steve's dark, wiry fur, was little Max from my tee-ball team.

Wondering if I were seeing things, I squeezed my eyes shut, then opened them again. What was he doing there? Was he visiting a friend? There were two kids on the swing set in the center of the courtyard, but they paid him no mind whatsoever and I had to conclude that they didn't know him.

Steve stretched out and rolled over so Max could scratch his belly, a move that seemed to delight the boy as I could hear him giggle through the glass of my door. I groaned out loud, suddenly realizing the most logical explanation for Max's presence. Had he and Cindy moved into the newly sold townhouse down the block? I muttered, "No, no, no," under my breath; I didn't want Max to know I lived here. I mean, I liked the boy and all, but my house was my sanctuary and I didn't want it invaded by some messy kid I barely knew leaving his fingerprints on my sliding glass door and leftover grape jelly in my dog's fur. Not to mention, the thought of Slick Cindy being so close gave me an instant, uneasy case of the jitters.

I watched him for a good fifteen minutes as he loved up my dog. Then, out of sight and earshot, somebody must have called for Max because I heard him shout, "Coming!" He gave Steve a final pat, then a quick kiss on the head, which made me smile; I couldn't help myself. I slipped out the door and watched him. Sure enough, he bee-lined directly for the seventh door down from mine, four buildings down, and went inside.

I spent most of the next day, my Monday off for the Memorial Day weekend, skulking around my own living room as Max showed up three different times throughout the day to visit with Steve. I supposed it made sense if Cindy was spending the holiday unpacking that he might be running around, exploring his new territory and trying to stay out of his mom's way.

Practice on Tuesday went surprisingly well. While I expected the kids to be restless and distracted having just come off a long weekend, they actually paid close attention and gave me a commendable amount of effort. Brittany with the helicopter mom had definitely practiced over the long weekend, because she made contact left and right with the ball. She didn't hit far, but she hit it every time. The way her face lit up at the *whack* of bat on ball made my heart warm and I thought, *This is why Maddie loves to coach.* I was finally understanding, finally getting it. And it did feel good, I had to admit. I felt…accomplished. Like I'd taught these young kids something totally and completely new and they were enjoying it. It must be how teachers felt when their lesson was finally grasped, when all the hard work paid off and the student got an A on an important exam. It must have been how a parent felt when she let go of the back of the bike seat for the first time and her child squealed with glee at the realization that he was pedaling a two-wheeler all by himself and not falling. Exhilarating was a good description.

Still not something I wanted to do on a regular basis, but it was all right.

I took my time packing up the equipment, glad beyond belief when Max got into the car with both Gabriel and Mikey. Not having to rebuff Cindy meant I could hold on to my good mood.

I decided to splurge for some take-out and swung by my favorite Thai place. I arrived home, fed Steve, and let

58

him out. I fixed my plate, poured a glass of Pinot Grigio, snagged two chocolate chip cookies from the stash I didn't take to work, and headed out to sit on my patio and enjoy the unseasonably warm almost-June evening.

And wanted to kick myself for letting my guard down.

Max was already sitting in his usual spot on the other side of the chicken wire, running his fingers through Steve's fur. My dog barely worked up the energy to glance in my direction. I stood like a deer caught in the headlights and when Max looked up, I knew escape was impossible.

"Coach King!" He stood up, his dark eyes bright with excitement. "What are you doing here?"

Swallowing back the defeated sigh, I replied, "I live here." I set my plate and glass down. "What are *you* doing here?"

"Me and my mom just moved into a new house." He pointed vaguely in the direction of the previously for sale townhouse, confirming my suspicions.

"I see."

"Is this your dog?" he asked.

Nope, never seen him before in my life, why don't you take him home with you? I almost said as my canine turned indifferent eyes on me. "Yep. That's Steve."

Max giggled, the easily amused, infectious giggle of a kid barely out of kindergarten. "Steve? That's a funny name."

"You think so? How come?" I took a sip of my wine. "Don't you know any Steves? I have a friend named Steve. And I went to school with a guy named Steve."

He laughed harder and when his eyes crinkled with mirth, he struck me as somehow familiar. "But he's..." He gestured at Steve, who hadn't budged an inch since Max stood. "He's a *dog*." The way he said it, there was an unspoken "duh" in his words.

"Well, what do you think his name should be?"

Max shrugged. "I don't know, something… something…doggie, you know? Like, like…Duke or Rover or…something like that."

Amusement enveloped me like a mist and suddenly my annoyance at the intrusion was pushed back into a corner. I wasn't sure what it was about Max, but I found him to be rather charming company. I used my chin to point to a ratty rope toy that had been left in the corner of the yard. "If you throw that, he might fetch it and bring it back to you."

"Really?" Only a small child could put such hope and anticipation into one word the way Max did.

"Yep." I crossed the yard and helped him hop over the chicken wire. He ran right to the rope toy, Steve hot on his heels. I returned to my seat to watch them. "Does your mom know where you are?" I asked.

"Yeah."

Of course I didn't believe him, but we were within shouting distance of his back door, so I let it go. I worked on my Thai and watched him play with Steve for a while. When I was just about finished eating, I said to him, "Hey, I make the best chocolate chip cookies around."

"I *love* chocolate chip cookies!"

"Do you?" I held one out to him. "Here you go."

Max turned to me, chewing. "Wow. This is really good."

Though I didn't think that six years on this earth warranted him to be any kind of cookie connoisseur, I was still inexplicably flattered. "Thanks. Glad you like them."

We heard somebody call his name. Twin grimaces crossed our faces. His because he didn't want to leave Steve and mine because I didn't want to deal with Cindy. She called again and Max looked at me. I gave him a shrug and a half-grin.

"I'm over here," he said loudly and—his inflection told me—grudgingly.

I could hear footsteps brushing through the late-spring grass a couple of yards down, and knew it was too late to do anything but be neighborly. Bolstering myself with a big breath and a bite of chocolate chip goodness, I was ready. But when the figure finally came into view, I nearly choked on my cookie, stunned into speechlessness.

Elena Walker—Smokin' Hot Bank Manager, as Josh liked to call her—stood on the other side of my chicken wire fencing. "There you are," she said to Max, hands parked on her hips.

"Hey, Mom," Max said.

chapter six

If I found Elena Walker incredibly sexy in the business suits she wore to the bank every day, it was an enormous treat seeing her in worn jeans and a plain white, long sleeve T-shirt with *Life Is Good* printed across the front in faded green ink. Good Lord, was it ever. Her hair was tousled and the color of blackstrap molasses. She had a smudge of what I assumed might be newsprint along her jawbone, and she looked absolutely exhausted.

She was the most invigorating sight I'd ever seen.

With her eyes on Max, she said to him, "Are you bothering our neighbors?" but when she looked up and saw me, her faced changed from gentle embarrassment to stark surprise. "Ms. King," spilled from her mouth.

"*Coach* King, Mom. *Coach*," Max corrected.

"Wait, wait, wait." Elena waved her hand in front of her face as if trying to erase what she thought she knew. "*You're* Coach King? You coach Max's tee-ball team?" The corners of her mouth lifted in an easy smile, telling me she liked that idea.

I'd managed to swallow my fortifying bite of cookie without finding myself in need of the Heimlich maneuver, and for that I was grateful. I stood up and crossed to where she stood on the other side of the chicken wire. "Guilty as charged," I said, hoping I came across as charming, rather than dorky as I suspected. "And...*you're* his mother?" I tried to phrase my question in the right tone so as to not be insulting, but to let her know I was slightly confused.

"One of them. I think you've probably met Cindy."

I nodded. Okay. Max had two mommies. Who knew? I tried not to dwell on the one question that was certainly going to torment me for the rest of the evening and beyond: where the hell was the justice in this world when a self-absorbed creep like Cindy Johnson could land a catch like Elena Walker? It was *so* not fair.

Pulling myself back into the wonderful arena of small talk, I rested my hand on Max's head and noticed his hair was exactly the same rich color as his mother's. When he glanced up, I realized his slightly almond-shaped eyes were just like hers. No wonder he'd looked familiar to me. "He's got some potential," I told her. "He tries really hard and he's a pretty good listener."

The glance she favored him with was filled with equal parts pride and love. "I'm glad to hear that. He's always been good about making an effort. The listening part? Not so much."

"Mom," he said, drawing the word out to make it sound like it had three syllables. He led Steve to a different part of the yard, obviously wanting to be away from the embarrassing adult talk.

Elena lifted her gaze back up to me and my heart did a weird, triple-thump kind of thing in my chest. "I know we see each other in the bank fairly often, but it's a pleasure to meet you officially, as neighbors." She stuck her hand out. "Elena Walker."

I almost snorted. Like I didn't know her name. "Avery King." Her skin was warm and soft and everything I thought it might be and I didn't want to let go of her hand. She held mine tightly and...for two or three seconds longer than necessary? Or was that just my wishful thinking? I wasn't sure. "Welcome to the neighborhood."

"Thanks."

"How goes the unpacking?"

She groaned and I laughed. "I think the boxes are multiplying in the night," she said.

"I've been here for two years or so and I still have boxes I haven't unpacked. They say if you haven't opened them after a year, you should just throw them away without looking inside. They're obviously filled with stuff you have no need for."

"I think I'm too much of a worry wart to do that."

"Understood."

"But at least I'm putting everything where I want it to go, so if I can't find something next week, I'll have nobody to blame but myself."

Together we watched Max toss the rope for Steve. "Cindy do the packing and you do the unpacking?" I asked. It was an honestly innocent question, just me making small talk with her, not wanting her to leave and not trying to wrest any personal information out of her, but she certainly gave me some.

"Oh, no. Cindy and I have been separated for quite a while. It's just me and Max in the new place."

How I managed to not whoop with joy and do a little dance right there on the grass, I'll never know. Instead, I glanced down at my shoes and gave her my sympathy. "I'm sorry. I had no idea."

She brushed away my apology. "Don't be. It was over a long, long time ago. It just took me a while to realize it."

"I hate when that happens."

She gave a little snort at my lame attempt at humor, and for that I was thankful. "Well, anyway, it was really a pleasure to meet you. Come on, Max."

I wanted her to stay and talk to me forever, but it might look a bit weird to be inviting her in so quickly. I decided right then to make more cookies and bring them over.

Max patted Steve on the head. "I'll come and play with you again really soon, Steve. Be a good boy."

I couldn't help but smile at his gentle words. Steve actually looked sad to see him go. My dog and I were going to have a little talk about loyalty in the very near future, that was for sure.

"Now, I don't want you bothering Coach King all the time," Elena said to her son calmly as she took his hand and helped him over the little fence.

I wanted to protest, to tell her he wasn't a bother at all, but I didn't want to step on her toes when she was being Mom. What Mom says, goes. Even I know that. I kept my mouth shut.

"Can I come back and play with Steve again, Coach King?" His big brown eyes were wide and his smooth face was so sweet I'd have given him the keys to my car if he'd asked.

"As long as your mom says it's okay."

"Cool!"

Elena caught my gaze and gave me a half-grin that was so damn sexy I felt a little pang low in my abdomen. I wondered if she had any idea at all how incredibly attractive she was. "It was nice chatting with you," she said.

"Same here. Welcome to the neighborhood."

"Thanks. I'm sure we'll see each other again."

"Well, you do have all my money," I joked.

"That's true." She winked at me (God, since when did my knees turn to Jell-O at a simple wink?). "Then I'll definitely see you again." With that, she tugged Max along as she headed home.

Steve waddled up to me and sat near my feet, both of us watching our new neighbors as they walked away, both of us with the same enamored looks on our faces, I was sure.

chapter seven

"Oh, my God, I'm bored out of my freakin' skull."

It was the answer I'd expected from Maddie when I asked how she was doing, but she said it with such frustration that she surprised me.

"That bad, huh?" I shoveled my last forkful of mashed potatoes into my mouth, savoring the final blast of the roasted garlic J.T. had stirred into them. Maddie was the cook, but she'd taught J.T. well.

"Do you have any idea just how bad daytime television is? Do you?"

"No, but I bet you're going to tell me," I teased.

"I don't even have the words," she replied, holding her hands out, palms up.

"How have you been able to survive without your brain turning to mush?"

"I'll tell you how." She sat up as straight as she could while J.T. cleared her place setting. "I've had to find other means of entertainment, that's how."

"Uh-oh." I asked, "Do I even want to know?"

"Probably not," J.T. answered grimly from over my shoulder as she topped off my wine. Then she took my plate and retreated to the kitchen.

Okay, now I was feeling a little uneasy and I posed my question to Maddie, point blank. "What did you do?"

Maddie wet her lips. "Now, keep in mind that I've been bored to the point of wanting to hang myself."

"Maddie..."

"And I didn't lie or post any kind of misrepresentation."

She was talking too fast and I was feeling more and more dread. I narrowed my eyes at her. "Madeline..."

"It was for your own good. I did it for you."

"What the hell did you do?"

"I posted your profile on Lesbian Link dot com." She blurted it out so fast that I had to replay it in my head to figure out exactly what she'd said. Then my eyes went wide.

"You did *what?*"

"Posted your profile on Lesbian Link dot com?" The tiny voice barely sounded like her, a telltale sign that she knew she'd overstepped her bounds in a big way.

I just sat there, blinking at her incredulously. I opened my mouth and shut it again two or three times as I tried to absorb the fact that my dearest friend in the world thought I needed a date so badly she'd posted my profile on the biggest lesbian dating site in the area *without my permission.*

"What...what..." I shook my head, unable to form a sentence. "Why?"

"Why?" Maddie flinched as if I'd asked her the single stupidest question ever. "What do you mean why? You haven't had a date in, what, six months? Eight? I've been telling you to put up your profile for the hell of it, just see what's out there."

"And I haven't done that, have I?"

"No, so I did it for you." She was so matter-of-fact, I wanted to kill her.

70

Through gritted teeth, I asked, "Did it ever occur to you that I haven't done it myself because I didn't want to?"

She had the good sense to look chagrined, but replied, "I just figured you were too chicken."

"Too—?" I couldn't even compute that one. I pinched the bridge of my nose for several seconds, harnessing my temper. "Take it down."

"No."

My eyes snapped back to her face. "No? What do you mean no? Take it down!"

"Not until you look at the interested parties."

When I re-focused on her, she was pressing her lips together and trying not to grin at me.

"Interested parties?" I wasn't sure I wanted to know.

"Eight of them."

"Jesus Christ, Maddie."

The fact that I didn't tell her to go to hell was all the encouragement she needed and she grabbed on with both hands. "Just look. That's all I'm asking. There are a couple you'll definitely cringe at, but there are also a couple that you might find…appealing."

It didn't make me happy to realize that she'd piqued my curiosity, so I sat quietly for several long moments, staring at the crimson-purple beauty of the wine in my glass as I turned it slowly, my fingers on the base. "And how long has my profile been up?"

Maddie threw me a grin of self-satisfaction. "Less than twenty-four hours."

Eight responses in less than twenty-four hours? That was good, wasn't it? I had no way of knowing. Maybe it was a spectacular failure. But eight interested parties seemed like a lot to me. Eight lesbians who wanted to get

71

to know more about me? To explore the idea of dating me? To say that didn't appeal to my ego would have been a lie, but at the same time I didn't want to let Maddie off the hook quite that easily.

I began my tirade. "You were so out of line."

"I know. I'm sorry."

"I don't even have the right adjectives to describe how out of line you were."

Maddie nodded soberly. "I know. J.T. told me. But in my defense—"

I cut her off with an upheld hand. "No. No, you don't get a defense here. Next time, listen to your wife. I don't care how bored you were. You had no right. You're not my pimp."

She winced at my choice of words, but didn't object. "You're right. I'm sorry."

"You should be."

We sat in silence for long moments, sipping our wine and not looking at one another. Maddie spoke first.

"So, when do you want to look at the responses?"

"How about after the game tomorrow?"

"Cool."

Behind me at the sink, I was certain I heard J.T. snort.

chapter eight

I thought it would be kind of weird to have Maddie at the game, since she's used to coaching and I was a little insecure about the job I'd been doing, but it was actually good. She gave me some pointers as she crutched around, suggested ways to help me get the kids to focus a bit more . on the ins and outs of the game, and was incredibly encouraging for the players. They warmed right up to her and I think Gabriel developed an immediate crush, carrying things for her and picking items up off the ground that she couldn't reach.

"J.T.'s going to be so jealous," I muttered to her at one point as he took his turn at bat, tossing a happy glance in Maddie's direction to make sure she was watching.

"Maybe. But I think he could take her," she responded with a grin.

Also hoping to show off his prowess at the plate for somebody was Max. I was disappointed that Elena was nowhere to be found and instead, Cindy was in the bleachers. As usual, she was engrossed in her electronic device, alternately punching buttons with her thumbs and then smiling as an apparent response showed up. I don't know how many times she actually looked up to watch her son, but judging by the disenchanted expression on his face and his inability to make much contact at all with the ball, I guessed the answer was not many.

He plopped down on the bench next to me with a frustrated sigh and I ruffled his dark hair.

"Don't worry, buddy. You'll get it."

He shrugged, telling me he didn't believe me.

"Hey, where's your other mom?" I tamped down the little voice that scolded me for pumping a six-year-old for information on my eye candy.

"She had to work."

"Well, maybe she'll come to the next game."

He shrugged again and added a pout.

We only played five innings; that was about all the kids' attention span would allow. Despite the fact that we didn't officially keep score, I knew we lost by about seven runs and I tried not to let the fact weigh on me. It was only the first game and my players were a step above toddlers, so getting upset by being beaten in tee-ball would have been silly and was certainly not a reflection on my coaching skills.

"It's not about the win or the loss," Maddie said quietly to me as I was packing up the equipment. "It's about the learning." She slapped me on the back and used her best phys ed teacher voice. "Shake it off."

The laugh slipped out before I could catch it. Maddie always did know how to make me feel better. I continued to pack things up as the crowd dispersed. Several parents came up to tell me how much their kid was enjoying tee-ball—or to offer me some pointers on improving things, over which both Maddie and I managed *not* to roll our eyes.

Cindy looked in my direction as she descended the bleachers, but tossed me a quick wave and left with Max as she chattered into her cell.

"Ready to check out the bevy of hotties who want to meet you?" Maddie asked with a flourish of her hand.

"Not with you hovering over my shoulder."

She looked totally crestfallen. "What?"

"I'm not looking at them with you. I want to look alone."

"Why?" She did a spot-on impression of a three-year-old. The only thing missing was a foot stomp.

There was no way I was going to look at potential dates with her breathing down my neck. I knew she'd mean well, but she'd have a comment, suggestion, or editorial to give me on every single one, along with judgments on my own opinions. No, I wanted to dive into this all by myself, find my own way around, figure out if I even wanted to be there. "I'm dropping you home," I told her, "and you'll just have to wait and see what I think of the big, giant misstep you took with my identity."

She must have thought better of arguing with me, decided the sooner she took her medicine for what she'd done, the sooner she'd be allowed back into the *Inner Sanctum of Avery King's Dating Hell*. She nodded.

After helping her into my car and stowing her crutches, I handed her a small notebook and a pen. "Write down everything I need to know to get into my profile."

Once I was home, I did a lot of different things to avoid getting down to it and seeing exactly what Maddie had done to me. Finally, I set my laptop up at my little kitchen table and called up the site.

Sucking in a big breath that was supposed to steady me, I signed in under the name Maddie gave me: BttyCrokr. Apparently, she thought that was fitting as well as humorous. I already wanted to kill her.

Scanning my profile with trepidation, I was pleased to see that she really didn't offer up that much information on me. Ultimately, there wasn't all that much that somebody couldn't find out about me by simply asking around or seeing me on the street.

Age: 34
Ethnicity: Caucasian
Religion: none
Height: 5'6"
Hair: auburn
Eyes: green
Body Type: feminine/athletic
Status: single
Sign: Virgo
Smoke/Drink: no/yes
Kids: maybe someday
Pets: dog
Occupation: graphic designer

Though she'd given me an extra two inches in the height department, and I questioned the "feminine/athletic" body type simply because I wasn't a fan of those kinds of labels (who got to decide if I looked feminine or masculine or somewhere in between?), the vital statistics were pretty straightforward. She'd warned me in the car about the "maybe someday" on the subject of kids, even though she knew I wasn't the mom type. She said it would make me seem more approachable. I just shook my head.

It was in the section featuring my hobbies that Maddie had really let her creativity come out to play. I winced as I read.

Hobbies: reading in front of a cozy fire; romantic strolls along a wooded path, a sandy beach, or even a tree-lined street; baking sinfully good, sweet and tasty concoctions...I make the most wonderful cookies and cakes around; it's my favorite way to show my love...

"'It's my favorite way to show my love?'" I read aloud. "Christ. These women aren't going to want to date me; they're going to want to laugh at me!"

I dropped my head into my hands and thanked my lucky stars that she hadn't included a photo of me. At least I could remain somewhat anonymous. As I groaned into the quiet of my kitchen, the laptop gave a tiny beep. When I looked up, the little mailbox in the upper right hand corner was flashing the number ten, telling me that I now had ten "interested parties," as Maddie had called them.

"Damn it."

I got up, pulled out of the refrigerator the fresh blackberries I'd gotten at the farmers' market that morning before the game and dumped them into a plastic bowl.

When I looked back at the computer screen, the little number ten was still flashing, looking all cheerful and tempting, daring me to look at what lay beneath. I glared at it, grabbed my Tupperware canister of sugar and sprinkled some over the berries. Tossing them in the tiny crystals seemed to calm me the slightest bit and I took a step toward the table. Without allowing myself time to chicken out, I clicked on the number ten.

Ten profiles of women popped up in list form on my screen.

My job was to look them over, decide if I found anybody appealing, and send them an e-mail telling them so.

Ugh.

I skittered back to my counter like Steve escaping the bathtub and snatched some butter out of the fridge. It was softened in the microwave and beaten in with more sugar until it was light and fluffy before I finally ventured another look at the screen.

HckyStix.

I could only assume that meant she was a hockey fan. I scanned her profile quickly as I toyed with a small bottle of vanilla. She was thirty-eight, 5'5", and had brown hair and blue eyes. She listed herself (or her best friend listed it for her without telling her, I reminded myself) as athletic/solid and her hobbies were playing hockey or pretty much any other sport, watching hockey—Go Bruins!—dancing at clubs, throwing impromptu parties, and hanging with her friends. I was sure she was probably very nice, but her hobbies seemed to include a lot of people most of the time and I immediately felt that inner panic that always seizes me with regard to impending over-stimulation.

I added the vanilla to my butter mixture and retrieved three eggs from the refrigerator.

One down, nine to go.

I added the eggs one at a time, mixing each in before cracking the next. When they were all beaten to within an inch of their lives, I looked at prospect number two.

Luv2Camp.

That was all I needed to see. Since I absolutely did *not* love to camp, it was pretty obvious that we wouldn't mesh. Maddie and J.T. had informed me more than once I could have my lesbo card taken away from me for that travesty, but up to that point the Lesbian Camping Police had yet to track me down.

In another bowl, I measured out flour and baking powder, then pulled out my handy-dandy, razor sharp zester to wreak havoc on the rind of the lone lemon in my fruit bowl. As I did so, I stared at the next profile on the list.

By the time I'd finished melding all my ingredients for my blackberry buckle, folded in the blackberries, and slid the pan into the oven, I'd gone through all ten profiles. I was alarmingly surprised to find that there were three of them who actually interested me. Really *interested* me, as in, "I think I might contact these women." Whether I'd be able to get up the nerve to actually do so was another story entirely, but for the moment, I was proud. I sat down and reviewed them again, the vague tick-tick-ticking of my egg timer the only background noise—when it wasn't being interrupted by Steve's occasional snerfs and snorts as he napped.

DrCutie was thirty-two, Hispanic, a dermatologist, and liked movies, racquetball, dogs, and spontaneous road trips.

Pinot72 was thirty-six, a mom, worked in finance, and liked hiking, foreign films, suspense novels, and a good red wine.

LilMinx was thirty-five, also a mom, was a teacher, enjoyed beach volleyball, picnics in the park, and volunteered at the Humane Society.

I marinated on the whole thing for the forty-five minutes it took the buckle to bake. If I contacted these women, I'd never hear the end of it from Maddie. See? She was right. How well does she know me? And yada, yada, yada. And because of the way she overstepped, I didn't want her to have that satisfaction. At least not yet; I was still mad at her.

On the other hand, she *was* right. I hadn't been on a date in so many months it was closing in on a year. It was true, I was perfectly fine being on my own, spending time alone or with Steve or with Grandma. It wasn't like I didn't have any friends or hadn't had other relationships, like I was some reclusive loner with no contacts. But there were times, every now and then, when I felt…well, lonely. Lonely for somebody to share life with. It would be nice to wake up again next to somebody that I was happy to see first thing in the morning.

I opened up a Word document on the laptop and began trying out different letters—no, *notes*. Different notes. I decided a letter would be way too long and possibly make me seem desperate (like the screen name for one of my ten prospects that sent me running for the hills: HelpMeLuvU. Sorry, just…no.). I wasn't really sure about the next step. Opening an e-mail dialogue, I assumed?

Thanks for sending your profile. Looks like we might have some things in common. Can you tell me more about yourself?

I grimaced. It sounded like I was conducting a job interview.

Got your profile. Let's chat!

My snort apparently disturbed Steve who lifted his head to glare at me.

Hey, got your profile. Looks good! Wanna have sex with me? Because that's ultimately what we're talking about here, right?

The thump my forehead made against the table must have been the last straw for Steve. He got up and headed for the living room, evidently to find a quieter place to nap.

chapter nine

"It's not funny, Josh."

My lips pressed together in a thin line, I glared at him as he rolled with hysterical laughter at his desk, taking a great deal of pleasure in my misery. I kicked at his chair to no avail. Finally, I folded my arms over my chest and waited him out with a sigh.

After wiping tears from his eyes, he reached for the plate on his desk that contained the moist, dense blackberry buckle I'd made over the weekend.

"You must have been freaking," he said. "What'd you do?"

"I made a buckle."

The furrowing of his forehead told me I'd lost him. "What the hell's a buckle?"

I gestured to his plate.

"Ah." He bit his lip as if deciding whether he should say what he was thinking. The answer obviously came through as yes, because he then said, "After all, it *is* your favorite way to show your love." And he crumpled into more laughter.

I, of course, promptly snatched his plate out of his hand. "Yeah, well, not feeling a lot of love for you right now," I snapped. That stopped the ridiculing of the graphic designer pretty quickly.

"So…is Maddie still alive? Or is her body now somewhere on the bottom of Lake Ontario?"

I returned the plate. "Not that death wasn't appropriate," I began, chewing my own cake as I clicked my mouse to open the project I'd started the previous week. "But I decided to spare her. Just this once."

"But you'll hold it over her head, I hope?"

"For years to come."

I hadn't seen Josh since the Friday before the long weekend. Included in my synopsis had been Max showing up in my back yard, our first tee-ball game, the revelation that Max's mom was actually Elena the drool-worthy bank manager, Maddie's admission that she'd posted my profile online, and my attempt at actually e-mailing three of the women from the dating site. He'd sat there for several long moments and I got the impression that if his head could literally spin, it would have. Then he'd burst into laughter.

"Well, let's see." He was studying his monitor, but I knew what the tone of those three words meant. He dealt with work the same way, mentally examining the overall idea of the project he was handed, viewing it from every possible angle, then presenting a detailed, most often brilliant, solution to marketing the product with words. To me, his method was what made him so incredible an ad writer. "I will definitely help you with a couple of e-mail replies. That'll be easy. And fun." The lascivious waggle of his eyebrows made me grin in spite of myself. "But I do have one really obvious question first."

"Which is?"

"Why don't you ask out Rockin' Bank Manager?"

The snort came unexpectedly and nearly had me choking on my coffee. "Excuse me? Elena? Are you kidding?"

"You said she was nice and funny and gorgeous even all dirty—which doesn't surprise me in the least, FYI. You know she plays for your team, so no worries there. And she offered up the fact that she's single without any prompting whatsoever. Right?"

I shook my head adamantly, not wanting to analyze why the prospect frightened me so much. "She never said she was single. She said she and Cindy were separated."

His expression said "duh" so clearly that no words were needed.

"Josh, you've seen her. She's so far out of my league, we're not even playing the same sport."

"Honey, when was the last time you looked in the mirror?" he asked, his voice dropping to a soft and gentle nudge. "You're a hottie, babe, and I bet she thinks so, too."

I squirmed under his stare, felt my face heat up, and shook my head again. "No, she's just for looking."

He somehow knew not to push, but his quick drop of the subject clued me in to the fact that we'd revisit it later. For the moment, though, I was happy to focus on something else. The idea of spending time with Elena Walker scared the hell out of me for reasons of which I had no understanding. Evidently, instead of a real, live, incredibly attractive woman that I could talk to face to face, I preferred an unknown entity whose only information available to me was through an e-mail profile that may or may not be telling me the truth.

There was something seriously wrong with my logic.

We worked in companionable silence for a few hours, Anita, Tyrell and a couple other employees dropping by to pay their compliments on my blackberry buckle. It was a big hit and I looked forward to telling Grandma during my visit on Wednesday.

During a lull in my design of a new restaurant logo, I remembered Josh had taken some time off the previous week.

"Hey, what'd you and Nina do on vacation?"

"Oh, you know, the usual," he replied, squinting at his monitor and continuing to type even as he answered me. "Caught a couple movies, saw her parents, went to a game, visited her OB/GYN."

I nodded as he spoke, listening but not carefully. A couple minutes went by before what he'd said actually registered in my brain. "Wait. What?"

"What what?" he said, still focused on his document.

"You said you visited Nina's doctor. Why?"

"Well, they say that's what a woman's supposed to do when she's pregnant. Not that I'd know for sure since I'm a big, macho guy and all, but that's what I've heard."

I blinked at him.

He lasted about fifteen seconds before he turned to me with the most joyous expression on his face I could ever remember seeing.

"Nina's pregnant?" I asked, whispering for some unknown reason.

He simply nodded.

I jumped up and threw myself at him with a squeal, falling into his lap and hugging him with all my strength. Tears sprang unexpectedly into my eyes as I held on to him. I knew how badly he wanted this and I was elated that he was going to have it.

"I'm so happy for you, Joshie," I said softly in his ear.

He responded by tightening his grip on me and though I couldn't see his face, I had the feeling he was as choked up as I was.

Finally pulling away, I returned to my ergonomically correct chair and took a seat, simply staring at him while we each collected ourselves.

"How do you feel?" I asked him.

He gave a sarcastic chuckle as he answered. "Ecstatic. Nervous. Elated. Relieved. And my personal favorite: scared shitless."

"I can't be certain, but I'm pretty sure those are all normal responses. How's Nina?"

"The same, but without the scared shitless part."

"Doubt it. Are you telling people?" I looked around and lowered my voice a hair. "I mean, everything's okay, right?"

"So far, everything's fine," he said, and I let out an unintentional sigh of relief. "We thought about keeping it hush-hush for a while, but…" He shrugged as if he had no choice. "We're too damn happy about it. But I haven't told anybody here yet. I wanted to tell you first."

"Aw." Love swept over me. "I'm honored."

We stared at each other, twin smiles on our faces, and then I shooed him away. "Go! Go tell the others. Anita will be so happy for you. And Tyrell will have tons of Daddy Advice. Go!"

He jumped up and scampered down the hall to spread his merry news. I could tell where in the office he was by the sounds. Shrieks of joy from the reception area. Slaps on the back from Tyrell's office. An idea came to me as I listened, and I quickly typed out a couple of words in a new document, then printed them in pink and blue. I cut them out of the paper until I had a small piece about two inches square. Then I taped it to a toothpick so I had a tiny little sign. Scurrying into the kitchen, I cut an enormous piece of the blackberry buckle, brought it back to Josh's desk, and stuck the toothpick in it. I sat back and surveyed my handiwork with a smile.

When Josh returned, he'd sit down and be faced with the dessert and its sign.

For Daddy.

chapter ten

"Seriously, they ate like starving refugees." I sipped my tea and smiled as I recalled the success of my blackberry dessert. I'd made it the first time with Grandma and the key had been gently folding the blackberries into the batter at the last minute, being careful not to mush them into a pretty purple sludge.

"And your berries stayed whole?" Grandma asked, adding some cream to her own cup. We'd just finished a wonderful lunch of cheese, crackers, hummus, and some veggies.

She'd been studying me; I could feel her gaze on me. Grandma didn't say a whole lot, but nothing got by her, not when I was a kid, and not when I was in my thirties. "What's bothering you today, Avery?"

"Nothing." I shook my head.

"You think after thirty-four years I don't know when you're lying to me?" It was a reproach, but its tone was gentle and made me smile.

"I'm not lying because nothing's bothering me. I've just been thinking about..." I trailed off as I searched for the right words. Grandma let me hunt without interruption, sipping her tea and waiting me out. "It's kind of weird," I told her. "I feel like I'm suddenly surrounded by kids."

Her silvery eyebrows knit together. "What do you mean?"

"Well, Josh is going to be a dad. I've got the tee-ball team. Max keeps showing up in my back yard. They're everywhere."

"That's hardly everywhere, dear."

I squinted at the telltale movement of her shoulders. "Are you laughing at me?"

"Yes."

"Thanks." I sipped my tea, annoyed at being found so entertaining.

"You have such an aversion to children, Avery. How come?"

I gave my shoulders a lazy lift, looking, I'm sure, every bit the sulking teenager. I was certain Grandma knew full well why I had "such an aversion." She wanted to hear me say it. "I just think too many people have kids without thinking about it, without thinking about the responsibility and effort that goes into raising them."

"I agree with you," she said simply.

"You do?"

"Of course. But just because your mother was a failure at being a parent doesn't mean you automatically will be as well. For the record, I think you'd make a wonderful mother. It's precisely those hardships you had to endure with your own parents that will make you a better one."

I was mulling that over, basking in the glow of the confidence my grandmother had in me (as well as her use of the word "hardships"), when there was a knock on her door. We blinked at each other for a second. "I'll get it," I said, hopping up before she could think about it.

Mr. Davidson was built like a lamp post, tall, thin, and sort of bent forward at the top. The snow white of his hair and the ice blue of his eyes were equally startling and I always found myself doing a double take whenever we were face to face.

"Well, hello there, Avery," he said with his usual friendly smile as he bent to kiss my cheek. He smelled like Old Spice.

"Mr. Davidson, always nice to see you," I said as I stepped aside. "Come on in. What brings you by?"

He stepped in from the hall so I could shut the door behind him. "I just came to make sure your grandmother was feeling better today."

"Feeling better?" I snapped my head around to meet my grandma's already guilty-looking gaze.

"She had a bit of a dizzy spell yesterday at lunch. I had to help her back to her apartment. Her heart was racing. Didn't she tell you?" The trailing off of his voice clued me in to the fact that, like most men, he realized far too late that he'd stepped in it and would probably have hell to pay later.

"Why, no," I said, lacing my voice with artificial sweetener as I narrowed my eyes at my grandmother. "No, she didn't tell me."

Apparently, Grandma found her tea suddenly very interesting. "It was nothing," she muttered into it. "I just had too much sugar or...got up too fast."

At eighty-five years old, there wasn't much my grandmother *could* do too fast any more. I went to her and squatted by her chair.

"How often does this happen?"

"Avery, sweetie, it was nothing. Really." She looked me right in the eye and I searched for any deception as she patted my hand.

"Maybe we should give Dr. Garber a shout," I suggested.

"No, we're not going to bother her with something as meaningless as a dizzy spell," she informed me. "I have an appointment scheduled for my regular check-up in a couple weeks. I'll go then."

I wanted to argue with her, but Grandma was always a tough nut to crack and if she said everything was fine and she wasn't going to call the doctor, then everything was fine and she wasn't going to call the doctor.

I sighed loudly when I stood up, just so she'd know I was annoyed at her lack of concern. Mr. Davidson was sort of shifting his weight from one foot to the other, obviously uncertain what to say after opening his can of worms. I gestured to my chair.

"Here, Mr. D. Sit. I've got to get back to work anyway. Can I get you some tea?"

"No, no. I can't stay." But he made himself comfortable and it was hard to miss the way Grandma's face softened when she looked at him. *Ah, young love,* I thought, and I was glad she had somebody who looked at her the way he did.

My windbreaker was on a hook behind the door and I grabbed it, then returned to the table. "If the dizziness happens again, I want you to promise you'll call me," I ordered her before kissing her on the cheek.

She patted mine in return. "Yes, dear."

"Don't yes, dear me. I mean it."

"Yes, dear." She winked at me and I shook my head.

92

"Don't let her give you too hard a time, Mr. D. She's a handful."

"Don't I know it," he said with a twinkle in those eyes.

I took my leave and left them to be alone. As I walked to my car, it occurred to me how mind-bogglingly strange it was to realize I was jealous of my own grandmother's budding romance with a man closing in on ninety.

chapter eleven

I smiled at the laptop as I sat at the kitchen table and clicked send. Once Josh had helped me get started with initial e-mails to the three women I'd chosen, it had moved rather comfortably as we tested the waters with each other for the rest of that week. I was now conversing with all three of them, still on a somewhat superficial basis. No real names yet, not many personal details, just small talk.

DrCutie and I had discussed movies for several days and we seemed to have similar tastes, including most Scorcese films and anything that featured Susan Sarandon. LilMinx was all about political causes, which I found admirable, but I was trying to find a way to steer things to other subjects so I could learn more about her. Pinot72 was witty as hell and had me laughing out loud on more than one occasion. It occurred to me that it might be approaching time to exchange photographs, but I wasn't sure how to bring it up. And I wasn't ready.

The situation—meaning online dating…or in this case, sort of *pre*-dating—was such an odd thing and I was sure Grandma would find it all very tedious (yet amusing). It was like dating foreplay. You could chat somebody up, but you couldn't really go too far without seeing a picture because, callous as it might have sounded, physical appearance *did* mean something for most people. It certainly did for me. I could find a woman to be devastatingly charming on paper, but if she didn't *look* attractive to me, that was it. We had to have physical chemistry or all the chatting in the world would be nothing but a waste of time.

The worst part of it, at least for me, was the matter of self-confidence. Yes, I wanted the women I was chatting with to be attractive to me. Of course I did. But worse, and more nerve-wracking, was the fact that I wanted to be attractive to them. Just as I would pass judgment on their looks, so would they do the same thing to me.

I hated to even think about it.

It was a cool Sunday afternoon and Steve and I were enjoying a quiet day at home...my favorite kind. We'd gone for a long walk in the morning, and Steve was now crashed out on the couch in the living room.

I closed the laptop and stared out the window at a sky the color of dull metal, wondering when it would rain.

Such weather seemed to cry out for warm chocolate chip cookies, so I began pulling out the ingredients for them. I'd only gotten as far as creaming the butter and sugar together when a knock on the sliding glass door scared the bejesus out of both me and Steve, who leapt off the couch as if he'd been ejected from it and started barking his head off.

There, with his nose pressed against the glass, probably hoping to be able to see inside, stood Max.

"Damn," I muttered. So much for my relaxing Sunday at home. Alone. Cruel as it sounded, I briefly entertained the thought of ignoring him. But when Steve jumped at the door and Max's face lit up, I had no choice. I had to let him in.

"What are you doing outside?" I asked him as he entered and immediately dropped to his knees to cuddle Steve. "It's going to pour."

"Cece brought me home and she was being loud, so I left."

My eyebrows met above my nose as I tried to process. "Cece?"

"My mom," he said with a slight hint of annoyance that said I should have known that.

"Oh." She was being loud? That didn't sound good. "Was she fighting with your other mom?"

He shrugged and kept his eyes on Steve. "They always fight."

"What were they fighting about?" I cringed, the realization that I was totally going to hell for siphoning information from him about his moms' dysfunctional relationship tapping me squarely on the shoulder.

He didn't look at me when he spoke and kept his eyes and hands on Steve. "Mom said Cece was early. She asked her if it would kill her to spend more time with me." Then he shrugged again, such a kid thing to do. "Whatever."

Even at thirty-four years old, the childhood pain of not being worth the time of your parents could sneak up on me and whack me over the head like a board and I suddenly felt great sympathy for this little boy who, just moments ago, I was wishing would disappear. I was ambushed by the unexpected need to make him feel better.

"Hey," I said, making my voice sound sort of conspiratorial. "Guess what I was just doing."

He blinked those deep dark eyes at me, so much like his mother's. "What?"

"Making chocolate chip cookies."

97

His eyebrows made a show of trying to climb up into his hairline and his big eyes grew even wider. "You were?"

"Yep. Want to help?"

"Can I?"

"Absolutely."

Sharing my kitchen and my baking duties with anybody but Grandma was not something I was good at and letting Max help was an exercise in self-control. It took all the energy I had to let him do stuff himself, like measuring and stirring, because my instinct was to take over and do it right. I bit my lip whenever he spilled something and made myself look away while he cracked eggs. I guess the fact that I was well aware of my control freakishness was a good thing, but by the time we had the batter ready to go, I had a splitting headache from clenching my jaw.

Instead of occupying his usual space in the living room while I cooked, Steve stayed in the kitchen with us—and by "us" I mean Max—the whole time we were working. I shot him a betrayed glare every now and then, but he pretended not to notice.

By the time we got the first batch of cookies into the oven, half an hour had gone by. Upon shutting the oven door, Max and I high-fived and I tried not to look as relieved as I felt.

"Nice work, Mr. Assistant Chef," I said to him.

His little giggle was so cute, I couldn't help but giggle a little myself and ruffle the top of his brown head. He dropped to his knees in front of the oven and watched the cookies bake through the window. When the timer dinged nine minutes later, he was still there.

As I backed him up and put an oven mitt on my hand, there came a banging on the front door. Apparently, I didn't move quickly enough getting the cookies out of the oven because there was more banging before I was in any shape to answer.

"All right, all right," I muttered as I nudged a barking Steve out of my way with my foot.

The knocker was a harried-looking Elena Walker, hair disheveled, eyes darting. Before either of us could speak, her gaze landed on Max and she flew at him, falling to her knees and crushing him in a bear hug.

"There you are," she said, a frantic note of desperation in her voice.

It was only then that I realized we probably should have let her know where her son was. I winced as the guilt seeped in. How stupid could I be?

"I'm so sorry," was all I could get out before she started jabbering to Max, as anxious mothers are wont to do.

"You *cannot* just leave the house without telling me," she said to him, gripping his shoulders tightly. I got the impression she wanted to shake him, but was holding herself back with great effort. "I was worried. I didn't know where you were. I called you from the backyard. I checked the playground. I knocked on doors. *I didn't know where you were.*" She seemed to run out of steam then, and simply pulled him into another hug.

"You were busy with Cece," Max said, his words muffled by his mother's shoulder. "I didn't want to bother you."

"You are *never* a bother." Elena was almost frighteningly firm when she said it, shoving him back to arm's length so she could look him in the eye. "Never. Do you understand me? You're my son and I love you and you are *never, ever* a bother to me. Okay?"

Her voice cracked and I had the sudden fear she was going to burst into tears right there in my foyer. Feeling intrusive, I looked around for an escape, but found none, so I stood there like an idiot.

"What's on your face?" she asked him once she pulled herself together, and swiped a finger across his cheek as she stood.

"We made cookies." His giant grin was contagious and I couldn't help but catch it.

Elena turned her gaze my way and I could tell she was annoyed with me, as she should have been. It also felt a little like maybe she didn't *want* to be, so I decided it was a good time to re-launch my apology.

"I'm so sorry, Elena," I said as I moved into the kitchen. "I assumed you knew where he was and I didn't ask him and I should have. It won't happen again." I hoped my accompanying grimace was pathetic enough because having her flash fire at me from those espresso-colored eyes was too much for me to bear for very long.

How I managed not to jump when she reached toward my face, I'll never know. She ran a fingertip along my chin and held it up, showing me the flour I was apparently wearing. "It got you, too," she said, her voice colored with amusement as she rubbed her finger and thumb together.

I swallowed hard and tried to fight the sudden surge of nearly overwhelming arousal she'd just caused by holding up a chocolate-chippy confection. "That's because we made cookies," I offered and tried to mirror Max's grin.

She pursed her lovely lips and cocked an eyebrow at me, very clearly telling me that she was still irritated, but my silly facial expressions were making her rethink things. Or maybe she just liked chocolate chip cookies. Regardless, she took it from my hand and when she bit into it, I felt forgiven.

"Oh, still warm," she said, nearly moaning. I had to look away.

"Coach King just took 'em out of the oven, Mom," Max informed her, in case burning the roof of her mouth wasn't enough of a clue.

"And you helped?" She swiped again at the splotch of flour on his cheek. Like me, she must have concluded it was just too damn cute to wipe off.

"He was a huge help," I told her as I spatula'd an entire tray of cookies onto a plate. "I hardly did a thing."

Max beamed at the praise. "I was sistant chef."

"Wow," said his mother, looking impressed. "You got a title and everything?"

"Yup."

"Hey, we don't mess around here," I said. "You do the work, you get a title."

Elena seemed to have let go of her initial anger and panic and was now smiling softly at her son. A good time to offer refreshments, I decided.

"Can I get you something? Coffee? Tea? A big glass of milk?"

The small crinkles at the corners of her eyes deepened. "That's very sweet of you, but I'll have to take a rain check." To Max, she said, "We have to go to dinner and Nana and Papa's."

"Oh!" Max exclaimed. "I forgot."

"No kidding."

I quickly put some plastic wrap over the plate of cookies. "Here you go, Mr. Assistant Chef. You get to share in the fruits of our labor."

"There's no fruit in them," he said with slight confusion.

"Figure of speech. Here, take these home and make sure you share."

"Thanks, Coach."

"Thank *you* for your help." At the door, I reached out and touched Elena's elbow, said her name, which felt as smooth as cream on my tongue. "I really am sorry."

"It's okay." The size of her smile and that usual twinkle in her eyes told me she was over it. "I didn't mean to come across as a madwoman. I had some residual junk carrying over from earlier and I should probably apologize to you."

Deciding not to ask her to elaborate, I simply shook my head, telling her that it wasn't necessary, that we were good, and held the door for them.

"Bye, Steve!" Max waved as he ran down the sidewalk toward his own home. Steve looked too much like he wanted to follow, so I held his collar.

I wanted to stand there and watch Elena walk all the way home in the low-slung jeans that were evidently made just for her, but I decided that might seem a bit lecherous and forced myself to shut the door.

I did watch her from the peephole for a couple extra seconds, though.

chapter twelve

We were slowly phasing Maddie in and phasing me out as coach of the tee-ball team and it seemed to be working well. She'd been sitting in on practices, which I continued to run since her mobility was still limited, but she'd begun taking the lead since our last game and I was perfectly okay with that.

She was somehow able to see that coaching was not something I wanted to do on a regular basis. I even managed not to say "I told you so." But we agreed that I'd stay on even after she was able to hobble around without crutches. Hell, there were only six games all together anyway. I figured I could tough it out.

Plus, letting Maddie take the lead left me more time to hover around the bench and happily notice that Elena had made it into the bleachers. I suspected that she often had to work Saturday mornings, since her branch office was open from nine until noon, but she must have shifted some things because she sat high up in the stands (or high-ish given there were only five rows), clapping and cheering for her son. And looking devastatingly beautiful while doing it.

June was turning out to be an incredibly pleasant month and that morning was sunny and warm. Elena had traded her worn and sexy jeans for a pair of worn and sexy khaki shorts and I felt warm and mushy inside just glancing at her knees.

God, what the hell was wrong with me? I'd never felt such a visceral reaction to any other woman before in my life.

I ripped my eyes from her legs and lifted them up to her face, only to have my heart start jackhammering inside my chest at the realization that she was looking right at me. Then she winked and my insides turned to goo.

I'd had no idea I was so easy.

It was embarrassing, really.

At Max's turn at bat, the difference between what I usually saw and what I saw now that Elena was there to watch him was shocking. He picked up the bat and turned to the bleachers. Elena smiled and waved at him, all her focus centered on him, and his face lit up like the Christmas tree in Rockefeller Center. I was so used to seeing his expression fall in disappointment when he understood that Cindy was paying no attention whatsoever to me that I actually did a double take when he beamed.

Elena's support was all he needed. He hit the crap out of the ball.

"Run!" I yelled to him when he turned to grin hugely at his mother. "Run to first!"

"Oh, yeah," he responded, running toward first base, taking the bat with him.

Maddie shook her head with a knowing grin, and I shrugged as I met her eyes. Who knew the hardest lesson to teach about baseball was which direction to run and when? Training the players to drop the bat after a hit was next to impossible.

Surprisingly, we ended up winning the game (not that I was keeping score or anything). As usual, by the end of things, the kids' attention spans had reached their limits and they were all over the place. Katie found a patch of dandelions that apparently needed her tending. Jordan was lying down in the dust near the equipment. Mikey bounced up and down on his toes, holding his crotch. With a jerk of my chin, I sent him scurrying to his dad, as I had no intention of cleaning up little boy pee.

Players and parents alike from both teams mingled and mixed as some of us gathered equipment, answered questions, congratulated kids, and gave pointers when asked. That time after the game was almost as exhausting as during it.

The crowd began to thin as I reached the bench and collected the remaining bits of our stuff.

"Did you see me, Mom? Did you? Did you see me?"

Max's excitement was palpable as he danced around next to me and watched Elena approach. I busied myself with tee balls and the canvas bag.

"I did," Elena answered. "I saw."

"I hit the ball. I hit it hard!"

"Yes, you did."

"I hit it hard, Coach." He looked up at me, his eyes big and wide, his pride swelling his little chest.

"Just like we've been working on," I said with a nod. "You did good, buddy."

His grin was enormous as he turned it on his mother. Six-year-olds were so easy, I thought, bringing my eyes up to Elena's. The white shirt she had on only accentuated the deep olive tone of her skin and I thought it odd that at that moment, the thing I noticed most was how smooth she looked. I wanted to touch her cheek, her forearm, her collarbone. It was an odd sensation. And oddly arousing.

"Avery…" Elena started, then stopped, pressing her lips together in what seemed to be uncertainty.

I absently wondered if it was wrong that I loved the way she said my name.

"Avery!" Maddie's voice came from behind me, snapping me into reality with a jerk as if she'd whipped me, and I hoped the gritting of my teeth wasn't too obvious, as it felt like I might crack a molar.

"Never mind," Elena said hurriedly, waving away whatever she'd been about to say.

"No, wait," I pleaded, barely keeping myself from grabbing at her as she backed away.

"It's okay," she assured me and I felt Maddie come up behind me. "It can wait."

"Hey," Maddie said as I watched Elena walk away and tried not to launch into a Lucille Ball whine.

"What?" I snapped, whipping my head around to glare at Maddie. The good thing about close friends was that you could bite their heads off for no apparent reason and they'd still love you the next day.

She held her hands up like a robbery victim. "Whoa. Sorry. I just wanted to make sure you didn't forget to grab the clipboard." She gestured with her eyes to said item that was sitting on the bench.

"The clipboard."

"Yeah."

I poked the inside of my cheek with my tongue as I worked hard to keep myself from throttling her then and there. I scanned the parking lot in time to see Elena pull the door of her Accord shut and drive away. Still poking, I picked up the clipboard and thrust it at Maddie.

"Here you go."

"Thanks," she said, squinting at me, but evidently aware that opening her mouth at that point might prove detrimental to her health.

She knew me well.

⸻

There was nothing quite like peace, quiet, and solitude for me. I lived for it. The ideal evening in my opinion, consisted of a good book, a good glass of wine, and a good chair. That night, George Winston joined me and I basked in the rich, smooth, emotional sound of his piano emanating softly from the stereo speakers. It was blissful and I sank into my reading chair as if it were made of marshmallow.

The phone rang. I picked it up without peeling my eyes from the page I was on.

"Hi there, sexy," Lauren asked. "Why are you home on a Saturday night?"

I managed to keep myself from replying truthfully and saying I had no better offers and I was trying desperately to stay off my e-mail account so I didn't get sucked into another Let's Bash the Republicans discussion with LilMinx. Plus, all three women were starting to talk about exchanging photographs (I got the impression they were as nervous about it as I was) and I was avoiding that subject as well. It was alarmingly hard to stay away, though, something that had me a little freaked.

Ignore it all; shove my nose in a book. That's how I dealt with many difficult issues in life. Hey, it seemed to work the majority of the time.

"My pumpkin-shaped coach is in the shop," I told Lauren instead, and she giggled.

"And your glass slippers are being polished?"

"Exactly. What's up?" As always, I only had to get Lauren started and she'd take off from there. Surprisingly, I actually found the sound of her voice to be comforting that night. I wasn't sure if I'd been feeling lonely and didn't realize it or what, but I actually put my book aside and paid attention to what she was saying, which I didn't always do. I even actively participated—when I could get a word in edgewise.

"I do have some news," she said after fifteen or twenty minutes of chatting.

"Because all the other stuff you just told me isn't news?" I teased.

"Not big news," she said, and I could sense the tentative excitement in her voice. It had me curious.

"Tell me."

She took a deep breath; I could hear it through the handset. "I'm going to be inseminated." She blurted it out so quickly that it took my brain several seconds to comprehend the words.

"Insem—you're going to have a baby?" I sat there blinking in shock.

Lauren laughed the sweet, joyful laugh of a truly happy person. "Well, not yet, silly. But my mom and I have been talking about it for a few months now. She knows how much I want to have a baby and we all know I'm not getting any younger. Tick tock and all that."

"Thirty-five is far from old, Lauren," I said, still absorbing.

"In terms of baby-making, it's up there. Anyway, my mom has agreed to help me so I don't feel like I have to wait for the right person to come along."

"Uh huh."

"Of course, I *would* wait for you, you know." Her voice got softer and my red flags started springing up all over the place. "We were pretty good together. You remember."

I was not going to take that bait, and I felt cornered, a feeling with which Lauren was a master at supplying me. I didn't want kids (more accurately, I didn't want kids with *her*, but I didn't stress that caveat, of course). I'd made it perfectly clear to her from the beginning, but she was sure she'd be able to change my mind. There were dozens of reasons why we didn't work out as a couple, but I clung to that one, knowing it was the best way to get her to let go. I wasn't proud of the deception, and I suspected she still had some residual anger about it, but I couldn't change that now. As I sat there, a shred of me wondered what it would feel like to be celebrating this decision with her.

"Avery?" Her voice poked me back to the present. "Did you hear what I said?"

"You sound very happy, Lauren. I'm glad." I waited with my lip held tightly between my teeth until she sighed loudly, a classic sign of her annoyance. Then she let it drop, though I suspected it would be revisited and I was already cataloging in my head ways of avoiding her calls in the future.

"So, Mom and I have narrowed it down to two donors and now it's just a matter of waiting for me to ovulate."

"Wow." I scratched absently at Steve's head as he lounged on the ottoman by my legs. "I just…that's…wow."

"I know. Pretty amazing, huh?"

"Well, I was going to ask you if you were sure, but you sound so great, I think the answer is pretty clear."

"I'm ecstatic. This is what I want. It's what I've always wanted. You know that. With my mom's help through the pregnancy and in the baby's first few months, I'll be fine."

"That's great, Lauren. I'm really, really happy for you." I was repeating myself, but I thought flattery was the best way to go, given the situation. "You're going to make a great mom."

"You really think so?"

I reminded myself to tread carefully. There were way too many pitfalls where Lauren was concerned. I didn't want to seem too aloof (and come across as a cold-hearted bitch), but I also didn't want to seem too into the whole baby thing (and risk her latching on to me again, which was apparently a more realistic danger than I'd thought). It was a fine line to walk, but somehow I managed. "I do."

"Thanks, Avery."

We chatted for a few more minutes before bidding each other goodnight. I sat alone in the quiet, George having finished up halfway through my phone conversation.

I felt weird; I had no other words.

Josh was going to be a daddy. Lauren was going to be a mommy. Max was at my house every other day and I was coaching a team of youngsters. I was suddenly surrounded by children or the idea of children and there was no other word to describe it.

I felt weird.

And on top of that—or because of that, I wasn't sure which—I felt lonely. Longingly, achingly lonely. It hit all at once and caught me off-guard. And I didn't like it.

I jumped out of my chair. Maybe chatting with one of my "interested parties" would help me deal with this unfamiliar territory I found myself navigating.

When I got signed in, I was happy to see that both Pinot72 and DrCutie had been online. They'd each sent a note a little earlier, checking whether I was around. I whipped two notes off quickly and clicked Send, wondering if I was too late for either of them. The gentle *ping* sounded a minute later.

Pinot72: I was wondering if you'd be around.

BttyCrokr: What else would I possibly have to do on a Saturday night besides sit in front of my computer? ;-)

Pinot72: I guess we're equally exciting, huh?

BttyCrokr: I can hardly stand myself, I'm so giddy. What are you doing?

Pinot72: I was reading, and now I'm just relaxing and enjoying the quiet. I don't get it very often, but I love the quiet.

BttyCrokr: Me, too. I can be easily over-stimulated and finding some quiet space helps me get back to feeling like myself.

Pinot72: Makes sense to me.

BttyCrokr: And are you having wine with your relaxation?

Pinot72: The wine IS my relaxation! LOL! You know me too well already.

BttyCrokr: It just didn't seem right that you'd be reading on a quiet evening and NOT have a glass of wine.

Pinot72: Glass? Who said anything about a glass? I just swig right from the bottle.

BttyCrokr: Certainly saves wear and tear on the dishwasher.

Pinot72: That it does. (You do know I'm kidding, right?)

BttyCrokr: You don't really have a dishwasher?

Pinot72: LOL! I'm not swigging from the bottle.

BttyCrokr: Too bad. ;-)

Pinot72: I do love my wine, but I draw the line at finishing a bottle all on my own. There has to be at least half a glass left in the bottom when I'm done.

BttyCrokr: LOL! Sounds reasonable.

Pinot72: What were you reading?

BttyCrokr: Ummm...<grimace>...Nora Roberts' latest.

Pinot72: Why are you grimacing? Isn't it any good?

BttyCrokr: No, it's actually great. I'm really enjoying it. I just...I don't know...it seems like the proper thing to do when you tell somebody you're reading a romance novel is look embarrassed.

Pinot72: I totally disagree. I think romance gets a bad rap. What's not to love about happily ever after? And Nora is wonderful. Now, if you'd said Danielle Steel...

BttyCrokr: LOL! Good point. This is my first novel of Nora's, but I think she writes great dialogue and I feel like her characters are easy to relate to, you know?

Pinot72: I do. I've read several of hers.

BttyCrokr: What were YOU reading tonight?

Pinot72: Danielle Steel.

BttyCrokr: LMAO!

Pinot72: So...Betty.

BttyCrokr: So…Pinot.

Pinot72: I think it's time for pictures, don't you?

BttyCrokr: We don't even know each other's real first names yet.

Pinot72: Let's do pictures and then we can do real names. Right?

BttyCrokr: I'm nervous.

Pinot72: Why? Are you a hunchback?

BttyCrokr: <g> No. I'm short, but not a hunchback.

Pinot72: That's good. Not a hunchback. Point for you.

BttyCrokr: You're not nervous at all?

Pinot72: Of course I am. But what's the worst that can happen? We're not attracted to one another and that's that. We can stay friends or we don't have to, but we don't know anything really about one another's lives, so we're safe and nobody gets hurt, not really.

Was that cold?

BttyCrokr: LOL! It was a little cool. But you're making sense.

Pinot72: Good. Sense is good.

BttyCrokr: Okay, give me a minute…

I jumped up from my seat and paced around the kitchen, my fingers dug into my hair. "GAH!" I shouted, causing Steve to spring up from a dead sleep and look at me in alarm.

I threw my arms out. "She wants a picture, Steve. Now. What do I do?"

I squinted at him, and I'm sure I almost heard him say something like, "Then send her one and leave me the hell alone."

Opening and closing my fists, flexing my fingers, was a weird way to relax, but it seemed to help just the slightest bit. Staring at the screen didn't, especially since nothing was happening, so I moved into action. As I clicked on my photo folder, I wondered if Pinot72 was having the same mini-breakdown that I was. Probably not. She was way calmer, cooler, and more collected than I was. And she was absolutely right about us not having much to lose; hell, I'd said pretty much the same thing to myself once the photo talk started with LilMinx and then with DrCutie. But saying something and feeling it are two different things and I hated how my hands were shaking as I scrolled through various pictures, trying to find one that cast me in a favorable light, but didn't seem utterly posed and/or goofy.

Josh's wife, Nina, had sent me a handful of pictures snapped during his last birthday celebration a couple months earlier and there was one of him and me that I was very fond of. He had his arm around my shoulders and we both had a healthy (but not incapacitating) buzz on. Our smiles were happy, wide but not too wide, and we were both looking right at the camera. My hair was neat and I had a little makeup on, so I didn't look deathly pale. I'd had the picture framed and it was in my living room, plus I'd given a copy to Grandma, that's how much I liked it.

That was the one. I gave a quick nod, as if convincing myself it was a good choice.

I attached it to an e-mail. I typed in Pinot72's address. I wrote the body of the letter: *I'm the redhead on the left, not the brunette on the right with the five o'clock shadow.*

An eternity went by as I lingered over the send button.

It took nearly five minutes for me to tire of my own indecision.

"Oh, fuck it."

I hit the button, then dropped my head into my hands. "There goes nothing."

Ten seconds later, my computer pinged and an e-mail from Pinot72 came, complete with an attachment. She must have been waiting to make sure I didn't chicken out on her.

I stared, unable to bring myself to click it open. Instead, I sat there and played the wonderful game of What If.

What if she's hideously ugly? (Terribly mean and superficial, I knew, but there it was.)

What if she's drop-dead gorgeous and finds me *hideously ugly?* (Somehow, an even worse thought.)

What if she's perfectly fine, but does nothing for me?

What if she's a fifty-five-year-old pervert named Stan who's been getting his rocks off with me all this time?

"Oh, my God, just stop already!" I said aloud, beyond irritated with my own nuttiness. "Just open the damn thing and get it over with."

Just as I was about to click open the photo, there was a knock at my front door. Well, not really a knock, more like a frantic rapping. A groan of frustration pushed up from my throat as I glanced at the wall clock and noted that it was nearly ten o'clock.

"What the hell?" I muttered as I got up and leaned toward the peephole.

Elena Walker stood on my front stoop, looking just this side of frazzled. My brow furrowed as I pulled the door open. She wore calf-length black sweatpants and a worn-to-the-point-of-falling-apart pink T-shirt.

"Elena? What's the matter? Are you okay?"

"Are you Betty Crocker?" she blurted.

"What?" I looked at her strangely, not really comprehending exactly what she was saying.

"I mean...." She held up a piece of paper. Josh and a short redhead smiled back at me. "*You're* Betty Crocker?"

"I'm..." Then it hit me. Yes, it took several seconds for the obvious to slap me in the face, but it finally happened. *Oh, my God.* My eyes widened and I looked at her in utter disbelief. "You? You're Pinot72? No fucking way!"

She laughed then, a loud, punching sound that surprised me with its heft. "Fucking way," she said, and her use of a dirty word made me tingle all over.

"Wow." It was all I could think of. "Just...wow."

"I know."

We stood there for a few minutes—or a few hours, I wasn't sure which—just looking at each other, grinning.

"So," she began, glancing down at her feet, which I suddenly noticed were bare, her toes polished a deep plum. "Would you be at all interested in grabbing a drink with me sometime?"

"Only if it's sometime soon," was my smooth reply.

She nodded. "Great. That's...that's great. Okay." She jerked a thumb over her shoulder. "I have to get back. Max is in bed and...I can't believe I just left him and ran down the street in the dark with no shoes on to pound on your door. Sorry about that." Another laugh escaped her as she backed down my sidewalk.

"Don't be," I said, unable to keep from grinning. Chewing on my bottom lip didn't seem to help.

"We'll set something up. Soon."

"I look forward to it."

I returned to the kitchen and just stood there, one hand over my mouth, stunned by the night's events. Who'd have thought? Not me. Obviously.

"Holy crap," I said out loud.

Glancing at my computer, I noticed the e-mail and its attachment from Pinot72 were still there, waiting for me to do something.

The picture was gorgeous, a shot taken outdoors. She was looking slightly to the left of the camera lens, as if somebody behind the photographer had caught her attention and she was about to wave. Sunlight glinted off her dark hair, making it look so shiny it was almost blue-black, held back from her face by a pair of black sunglasses perched atop her head, diamond studs twinkling in her earlobes. Her eyes were slightly crinkled at the corners, the beginnings of a smile just forming, and her complexion was so smooth I wanted to reach inside the computer monitor and stroke her cheekbone. Her beauty took my breath away. When I read her e-mail, it made my smile grow even wider.

My name is Elena. What's yours?

chapter thirteen

"Are you effing kidding me?" Josh's disheveled hair did not quite cover the disbelief in his eyes.

"I'm not."

"It's like you're in an effing romance novel or something. This…stuff just doesn't happen in real life."

"Okay, first things first," I said, happy that he was smiling despite his protests and incredulity. "Effing? Stuff? What happened to the good old fashioned fucks and shits?"

"Hey, I don't want my kid running around dropping F bombs on his preschool teacher, you know?" He waggled his eyebrows. "Nina would kill me."

"I didn't think that was your doing," I said with a knowing grin. "You're the king of the potty mouths."

"True. But back to Smokin' Hot Bank Manager…"

"Elena. Her name is Elena."

"Oh, she has a name now, does she?" His wink told me he was just teasing, but I blushed anyway.

"She's always had a name." I tried to focus on my monitor, on the shoe store logo I was creating, hoping to keep things light and not give away the fact that I was just a teeny, tiny bit terrified.

"Yeah, but now you actually get to use it. And maybe even scream it out loud in the throes of passion and ecstasy."

"Funny." Trying to ignore the tingle that shot through me at the thought was more difficult than I expected.

"Are you nervous?"

"No."

"Really? You just felt the sudden urge to make fifty pounds of oatmeal raisin cookies yesterday?" He didn't just have my number, he had it memorized and on speed dial. As if proving his point, he bit into a cookie. "Delicious."

With a sigh, I proclaimed, "I hate you."

"Guess what I've got to do today?" he asked, plowing ahead as if I hadn't spoken.

"I don't know. Jump off a bridge? Dive in front of a speeding bus?"

"Go to the bank." His grin broadened when my head snapped around and he knew he had me, but he kept looking at his computer, typing away. "Want to join me? You could get some cash out of the ATM or something just so you don't look like a stalker." At that point, he looked my way and his eyebrows rose up in question. "Come on. You know you want to."

"I hate you," I said again.

By the time we actually made it to the bank, I felt utterly stupid. I didn't need to go to the bank. In truth, I felt like a love-struck teenager, sneaking around and trying to catch a glimpse of her latest high school crush. The tiny bit of irritation I felt at Josh for having dragged me was way overshadowed by the enormous irritation I felt with myself for allowing him to convince me this wasn't the behavior of a weirdo.

"You're sure you don't want to come in?" he asked once more as he leaned into his open car door, ominous clouds threatening rain behind him.

"I'm sure. I'll be fine right here."

"Wuss."

The door slammed and he headed into the bustling building. I scanned the parking lot around me, wondering where Elena's Accord was parked. Maybe she had a special spot on the other side, her being the manager and all.

Twiddling my thumbs lost its appeal pretty quickly and then it crossed my mind that I had practice with the kids that night. I'd want to pick up some dinner on my way home and my wallet was sadly devoid of cash. I figured I could use the outside ATM and not worry about going into the bank.

I had a twenty-dollar bill in my hand and was reaching for my receipt when she spoke from behind me. Very close behind me.

"Did you get me any?"

The jolt that shot straight to my groin forced my eyes closed for a split second. I held up the twenty. "What a coincidence," I said, turning to face her. "This is for you."

Elena laughed while I tried hard not to stare at her as she stood there, a white deli bag in one hand. She was in full-on businesswoman attire: a deep green pantsuit that beautifully accented the olive tone of her skin. The V of the jacket dipped just low enough to give me a tantalizing peek of collarbone. The scent of rain in the air mingled with her perfume and it took everything I had not to breathe in deeply, not to try to inhale her as a gentle breeze toyed with her hair.

"So," Elena said.

"So," I replied.

She looked down at her pumps, wet her lips with the tip of her tongue and the realization hit me like a slap. Could it be? Did it make any sense at all that she was nervous? Her? Elena Walker, Smokin' Hot Bank Manager and perfect specimen of the human female? Inconceivable!

Still, I was overwhelmed by the sudden urge to rescue her from any discomfort.

"About that drink," I plunged in, surprised to hear my own voice.

"Yeah, about that." The relief that flitted across her face when she looked back up was all I needed to push forward.

"When will you be thirsty?"

She smiled and my gaze traveled to her glossy lips. Honestly, how was it possible for her lips to be that shiny all the time? "What about Friday? I think I'll be thirsty by then. Max is spending the night with my parents."

"Ah, so no curfew for you."

"That's right. I can stay out as late as I want."

"Me, too. As long as I show up for the game on Saturday morning, I'm good." Belatedly, I realized how presumptuous that sounded and hot color flooded my face. "I mean...I didn't mean...um. Ugh." I squeezed my eyes shut.

Thankfully, Elena laughed. Loudly, the shotgun sound of it nearly making me jump.

"Do you know that little Italian restaurant on Main? The new one?"

"That little bistro?" At her nod, I continued. "Want to meet there at 6:30?"

"I'd love to."

Much as I cringed when Josh appeared, it was good timing. Otherwise, Elena and I might have continued to stand there and stare at one another. Which wouldn't have been a problem if neither of us had jobs to get back to.

"Hi there. Josh Bacon," he said as he stuck his hand out to Elena. "Old friend of Avery and longtime bank customer."

Elena was charmed; Josh had that effect on people. She shook his hand. "Elena Walker, *new* friend of Avery and manager of said bank. Thanks for your business. Speaking of which..." She jerked a thumb over her shoulder. "I'd better get back to it."

"Me, too," I said.

"It was nice to meet you, Josh," she said as she backed towards the door. Meeting my eyes, one corner of her mouth lifted slightly. "Avery, I'll see you on Friday."

"I'm looking forward to it."

Exactly four beats went by before Josh turned to me and said, "She'll see you on Friday?"

"As a matter of fact, she will." We headed back to his car just as fat drops of rain began to fall in sporadic spatters.

123

chapter fourteen

Maddie was overdoing it and she knew it. I threw J.T. a questioning look where she sat on a bench watching, and she returned it with a subtle shrug that said, "You know how she is."

It was Wednesday night's practice and I thanked our lucky stars that J.T. had Wednesdays off and that we were only coaching a bunch of six-year-olds. God forbid they'd been high schoolers or the Varsity softball team; we'd have been carrying Maddie off the field on a stretcher.

Despite the pain so obviously etched across her features as she hobbled around, she was gentle and patient with the kids, as always. I tried to help as much as I could, while at the same time sort of staying out of her way and attempting a quiet fade into the background. The kids were used to me, so having me disappear completely didn't seem to be the best path to take. But it was, after all, Maddie's team to coach. I'd done my favor for her and my tenure as the boss was just about up.

I tried not to seem too giddy about that.

Max was up next during batting practice, and as I had done all week, I glanced into the stands to see if perhaps Elena had come by to watch. My reward for such foolish wishing was to catch the eye of Cindy, who looked directly at me and winked. The facts weren't lost on me...the fact that Elena could wink at me and turn my knees to jelly, as well as the fact that Cindy could wink at me and make my skin crawl like I was covered with tiny ants. I suppressed a shudder, gave a wan smile, and turned back to practice. This was the first practice Cindy had attended in quite a while and poor little Max fell right back into his usual pattern. He hit the ball, then immediately whipped his head around to see if his mom was watching. She, of course, was preoccupied with a conversation she was having with another parent in the bleachers.

I had to turn away from the dejected expression on Max's face as he waited for Maddie to set up his next ball. *That poor kid will never give up,* I thought. *He will spend the rest of his life trying to get his mother to notice him.* My heart broke for him; I knew just exactly how futile such a thing could be.

Why have children at all?

It was a question I'd wrestled with for the thirty years since my mother had taken off without me, a question I often wanted to ask her myself. I *did* understand that sometimes there were extenuating circumstances to situations in life and judging somebody without knowing all the facts was never a good idea, but honestly, why have children at all if you were going to pay such little time and attention? It wasn't like Cindy could have accidentally gotten Elena pregnant and oops, now she was stuck with a child she didn't really want. And right there I had to stop thinking, shake my head vigorously, and scrub my brain free of any inadvertent images of Cindy in bed with Elena. She knew a baby was coming. She'd planned on it, had to go through very specific channels.

I shook my head as I watched Max's eyes droop ever so slightly while he tried to be a tough guy. I just didn't understand.

"Okay, why don't you take half the kids over there and work on ball-handling and the rest of us will go over this way and have a little quiz about the rules of the game." Maddie's voice blessedly pulled me away from my swirling thoughts and I was happy to do her bidding.

Practice didn't last much longer after that. As usual, the kids' attention started to wander. We set them free and watched them flutter back to their parents like wild butterflies.

J.T. and I packed up equipment after insisting that Maddie sit the hell down for five minutes and give her knee a break. Her face was pale and her bottom lip had taken up what seemed like permanent residence between her teeth. She was going to end up home on the couch with pain medication and an ice pack; I was sure of it and so was she. But I wisely kept my mouth shut, knowing she'd snap my head off if I dared mutter an "I told you so."

"I'll get the rest of this," I said, waving J.T. away. "Take her home." As she grabbed Maddie's elbow and helped her stand, Cindy approached with a smile.

"Hi there," she said, her perfect white teeth on display.

I hadn't told Maddie about the pass Cindy made at me, so she immediately went into Coach Mode and stuck out her hand to shake Cindy's, pulling Cindy's eyes from me to her.

"Hi yourself. Maddie Carlisle, coach. I don't believe we've met."

For a split second, Cindy looked utterly confused as she took Maddie's hand and gave it a squeeze, introducing herself.

"I was just subbing for Maddie," I explained. "While she had surgery." With my eyes, I gestured to Maddie's bandaged knee. "This is actually her team."

"I see," Cindy said, nodding. The wheels cranking in her head were almost visible as she tried to decide her next move. To ask me out would be to out me, and she was obviously trying to weigh the pros and cons of doing so.

"Which one is yours?" Maddie asked. By the smile on her face, you'd never know her knee was killing her. She was all business.

"I'm sorry?"

"Which kid is yours?"

"Oh. Um, Max. Max is mine." Cindy looked around quickly. Apparently, she didn't know exactly where he was. When her gaze landed on him chatting with Gabriel near the bleachers, she tried unsuccessfully to hide her relief.

"He's a sweetheart," Maddie said. "And a good little ball player. He has a lot of potential. Don't you think so, Avery?"

"Absolutely. He's great." I slid the bases into their sack and busied myself with the rest of our stuff, trying to fade back and let Maddie handle Cindy. I could still feel her eyes on me, but after another minute of meaningless small talk, she took her leave and headed toward the parking lot, Max jogging along quickly behind her like he was worried she might forget him.

"Damn," J.T. muttered when Cindy was safely out of earshot.

"What?" I looked up at her.

"She was *so* checking you out."

I gave a snort and went back to what I was doing.

"Like she wanted to eat you for dinner," Maddie chimed in.

I wasn't sure why I didn't fill them in on my previous experience with Cindy Johnson, but I suspected it was because I didn't want to get into any details about Elena. If I talked about Cindy's sexuality, then Max's other mom might come up and I just wanted to keep her all to myself for a while, selfish as that was. *And*, there was no way I wanted Cindy to know I was ridiculously interested in her ex. *Plus*, I didn't want Maddie to know I'd technically found Elena on Lesbian Link dot com. She'd find that far too satisfying and would never let me live it down. I couldn't have that. So I just shrugged it off.

At that moment, as I put tee-ball equipment away, I almost laughed out loud at the web I was weaving. I didn't want Cindy to know about Elena. I didn't want J.T. and Maddie to know about Cindy *or* Elena. I didn't want Elena to know about Cindy. And I certainly didn't want Max to know about *any* of it. This was the stuff of movie comedies, where somebody inevitably gets bitten right in the ass.

Gee, I wonder who that'll be.

I had to admit to myself, though, that I was grudgingly impressed Cindy had showed a little bit of decorum by not being her previously aggressive self. Maybe I'd misjudged her a little bit? Then, of course, the thought of her and Elena *in flagrante delicto* made my stomach clench and I went immediately back to disliking her.

chapter fifteen

By the time I'd finally been tired enough to go to bed on Thursday night (after baking a lemon bundt cake, an apple crisp, and double-chocolate brownies), I had viciously cursed all manner of gods, clocks, watches, hourglasses, sundials, time zones, and anything else I could think of that may have conspired to make the week drag by as slowly as was conceivably possible. But when I woke up, it was with an enormous smile on my face and a giddy sense of anticipation.

It was Friday.

Knowing I didn't have to agonize over what to wear until later that night was a relief. I put on my Casual Friday attire for work consisting of my favorite pair of Levi's and a V-neck summer-weight sweater in royal blue, and I practically skipped to the office, baked goods in tow.

I'd become pretty good at driving by Elena's and Max's house without gawking like a weirdo, but today I allowed myself the treat of glancing in that direction. It was starting to look lived in, flower pots filled with red geraniums standing on either side of the front stoop like sentries and a colorful flag featuring a pair of bluebirds flapping gently next to the front doorway. Elena had a nice touch, I thought as I turned my car out onto Elmwood and drove to work.

I was in such a good mood, I didn't even bother to cuss out the guy who cut me off so he could turn in front of me at the Twelve Corners in Brighton. I waved and smiled instead, which I think might have freaked him out more than if I'd flipped him the bird.

"I knew it!" Josh hooted with glee a few minutes later. We'd pulled into the parking lot at T. Harrison Jones & Associates at almost exactly the same time, as happened bizarrely often. I'd called him over to help me with all my foil-wrapped goodies, surprisingly not bothered by the smug look on his face that said, *I so have you pegged.* "I knew you'd be nervous about your date and you'd bake your ass off last night. Did you get any sleep at all?" He didn't wait until we got inside, but dove right into the plate of brownies.

"Not much," I admitted. Every time I'd tossed or turned, my brain kicked into overdrive, beating me senseless with thoughts about what I would wear, what I would say, what I would drink, to the point of utter ridiculousness. I couldn't recall ever being so nervous about a date before and the fact freaked me out a bit.

It didn't make me any less excited, though.

With a sigh, I recalled my restless night.

Shockingly, I was able to concentrate on my work for the majority of the day. Tyrell had a friend with a new landscaping company and as a favor (and in return for doing the lawn maintenance on Tyrell's yard, I suspected), he had me designing a look for him. I had no other projects that were under any kind of time constraints, so I spent the day working up a logo for Ladybug Lawn Care, trying to make a ladybug cute and friendly without it being too cartoonish. It came out nice; I was pleased with the shades of red, green, and black and the way they blended. I think Tyrell was happy, too.

"Nice work, Avery, as always," he commended me as he took the color printout with a satisfied grin and told me he'd show his buddy over the weekend.

I sent the various remains of my baked goods home with coworkers. Thank God I work with people who like my sweets or I'd be forced to eat them myself. I'd weigh five hundred pounds, easy.

"I expect a full report on Monday morning," Josh told me as we walked out together. "Unless you want to call me tomorrow…"

"We'll see how it goes," I said, trying my best to act calm, cool, and collected.

"Have a great time." He was sincere as he winked at me and got into his car.

"That's the plan," I murmured.

Once home, I tried not to flit around like some nervous fly-like person. I fed Steve, then took him for a walk as much for me as for him. The day had been pleasantly warm and the sun was still bright as we weaved our way through our development, Steve stopping every ten feet to either sniff something, pee on something, or both.

I didn't mind the stops and starts. They gave me time to breathe in the sweet summer air sprinkled with the scent of fresh-cut grass, and to will myself to relax. I really was being a little silly, letting myself get so worked up.

I was having drinks with a beautiful woman. That's all.

Half an hour later, I completely stunned myself by choosing a suitable outfit for my date on the very first try. I knew Elena would be coming right from work and would probably still be dressed for it. I donned a nice, classy pair of khaki-colored capris, a cream T-shirt, and a short-sleeved, zip-up hooded sweater in this really cool shade of sage green. I toyed with the idea of pulling back my hair, debated with myself in the mirror, then finally did, securing it with a simple clip at the nape of my neck. Simple gold hoop earrings and a chunky bracelet of earth-toned beads that Maddie made me in jewelry class topped off the outfit. A quick touch-up of my make-up was all that was necessary before I stepped into my brown leather slides and surveyed myself in the full-length mirror.

"What do you think, Steve?"

He lifted his head from my yellow flowered comforter and yawned widely, going so far as to allow a high-pitched little squeal come from way back in his throat.

"Perfect," I said as I rolled my eyes. "Thanks for your input. You're always such a fabulous help." I tugged the zipper of my sweater down another inch so the pull lay just below my breasts, and I absently wondered if Elena would be looking in that direction. I hoped so.

One quick nod of satisfaction, a spritz from Liz Claiborne at my throat, a deep stabilizing breath, and I was ready.

Designed to look like a Mediterranean café, the little Italian bistro was called Antonia's. I'd only been in it twice before, but I'd liked the colors, the atmosphere, and the smell. Aromas of garlic, fresh bread, and basil seemed to float by as I walked to the bar and grabbed a seat on the corner. That way when Elena arrived, we wouldn't be side by side, but almost facing each other.

"What can I get you?" His nametag said Jeff and with his bleached blond hair, piercing blue eyes, and almost unnaturally tan skin, he looked anything but Italian. His smile was friendly and his eyes crinkled kindly as he placed a cocktail napkin before me. "I recommend the house Cabernet. Smooth, tasty, and affordable."

"Sold," I said, slapping the polished wood of the bar. I watched as he poured, entranced by the ruby-red, somehow regal shade as it filled the glass.

I was only on my second sip of the wine—Jeff was right about it being smooth and tasty—when I saw her walk through the doorway. The glass in mid-air, halfway to my lips, I watched as she scanned the small interior of the bistro, then saw me. A delighted smile crossed her face and she began her trek in my direction, all black business-suited and sexy. I half-expected her to walk past me and greet somebody behind me, because I couldn't fathom such a beautiful woman wanting to spend time with little old me, but apparently she did. She took the stool I'd saved for her and sat down with a sigh of relief, crossing her stockinged legs and settling in.

"Hi," she said simply. "Whew! What a day."

"Thank God it's Friday?"

"You have no idea. What are you drinking?"

"Cabernet. Try?" I slid the glass toward her and she took a sip. I pretended not to delight in the clear streak of gloss her lips left.

"Oh, that's nice." She gestured toward Jeff, then the glass, and he nodded.

The deep, calming breath she took drew my eyes to the electric blue blouse she wore under the black jacket and I found myself studying her collarbone once again. What the hell was it about that part of her that I found so damn sexy? A *collarbone*? What was wrong with me?

"I had to fire one of my tellers today," she told me, grimacing.

"Oh, Elena, I'm sorry. That's got to suck."

Jeff set her wine in front of her and I told him to put it on the tab I was running. She took a healthy sip. "It does. It does suck. It totally sucks. I didn't want to do it, but she left me no choice."

"Why?"

"She can't seem to tell time. She's received three warnings about being late in the morning and not returning from lunch on time. The last time, I told her just that: it was the *last* time. And then she was half an hour late this morning."

"I don't know if I could do that," I admitted. "I don't think I'm brave enough to fire somebody."

"It's not about bravery. It's about it being in your job description. It's got to be done and you're the man, so to speak. You have to."

"Ugh."

"My sentiments exactly," she said with a chuckle. "That sums it up perfectly." She took another sip of her wine, then cocked her head slightly to the side and studied me. "So."

"So."

"Hi there, Avery."

"Hi, Elena."

"I'm glad to be here with you."

"I'm glad to be here with you after a day like that."

"Tell me about your job." She took her jacket off and slung it over the high back of the barstool. The electric blue shimmered slightly in the dim lighting and was a wonderful complement to her bronzed complexion as she propped an elbow on the bar and her chin in her hand. "What drew you to graphic design?"

"Color," I answered honestly. "It was all about color for me. Some people love words. Some people love the law. Some people love food or politics or cars. I love color."

"Interesting," she said with a gentle nod. "What do you love about it?"

Her eyes took in every expression I made, I could feel them on me and it was simultaneously exciting and nerve-wracking. I wet my lips and tried to explain my passion. "I love the way it invokes a mood. It can draw your eye immediately with its brightness, its volume. It can hide something with its subtlety, make you skim right by and not even notice. It can bring out feelings of happiness, or sadness, or grief, or anger. I took a theater class in college on stage lighting. It was amazing the feelings the lighting director can cause in an audience just by using specific colors or filters for specific scenes."

"Blues and reds?"

"Generally, yes. But more specifically, oranges and yellows and greens. Color affects mood in all kinds of ways, ways we don't even think about. It's pretty cool." At that point, I worried that my babbling might be boring her, but she continued to watch me intently as I spoke. I liked her focus on me. It made me feel warm. Like orange light.

"You probably don't have a favorite color, then, do you?"

"Of course I do."

"Really?" Her surprise was so cute.

"Red. I like red because it says so much, you know? It can scream anger or rage. It can grab your attention with its sheer brightness. Or it can be subtle, more of a brick red, and just make you feel…warm all over. Content."

"That is the most unique description of a color I've ever heard." Elena raised her glass. "To red."

We clinked and sipped, our eyes locked the whole time, a delicious tension stretched between us like taffy.

"How's my man, Max?" I asked, worried that if we stayed silent and staring, I might toss her onto the bar and have my way with her.

"Max is great," she said with the fond smile that parents often get when talking about their children. "He's great."

"You said he's with his grandparents tonight? Your parents?" At her nod, I asked, "Do they live close by?"

"In Webster. They've got a big yard and a pool, so Max spends a lot of time there in the summer. He's done with school next week, so he'll probably be over there a lot more. My mother spoils him."

"That's what grandmas are for, right?"

"That's what she tells me," Elena said. "Do you still have grandparents around?"

"Yep. My Grandma King actually raised me. She lives in one of those new-ish apartments over on Jefferson."

"I know exactly where you mean. Those are nice."

"She likes it a lot." I could sense Elena wanting to ask more, but for some weird reason, I didn't want to talk about my upbringing. I liked hearing about her, so I jumped in before she could formulate her next question. "You have siblings?"

"Three. Two older brothers and a younger brother. You?"

"Only child."

"Oooo, spoiled." She grinned.

"Just a little. And you should talk, being the only girl." I arched an eyebrow, daring her to tell me I was wrong.

She tossed her head back and laughed. "You are absolutely correct. I was spoiled rotten by both parents. And my brothers, though they'll never admit it."

"And I bet they still spoil you."

"They do. And they're so good to Max. Two of my brothers have kids, so Max has three cousins to play with. They're a little older than he is, but they're really good about including him and teaching him the games they like. It's fun to watch." Her smile turned wistful. "Sometimes it seems like yesterday when my brothers were teaching me how to swing a bat or throw a curve ball and now I'm watching *their* kids teach *my* kid the same things and I just shake my head. It's almost surreal, how quickly time goes by. You know what I mean?"

I nodded, trying hard not to blurt out the sentence, "You can swing a bat and throw a curve ball?" I had a lifelong love of all things softball, but imaging Elena in full-on jock attire and smacking a line drive was almost too much wonderfulness to bear at one time. I managed to keep control of myself until the blissful feeling passed a bit.

"So, you were raised by your grandmother?" She emptied her glass and motioned to Jeff for refills.

"Can't slip anything past you, can I?" I joked.

"This isn't going to be one of those dates where I do all the talking—which I'm very good at, I'm sure you've noticed—get home later, and realize I didn't learn a thing about you. So…spill."

Her words were demanding, but her tone was not, and I think that's why I felt safe enough to come near a topic I rarely broached. For whatever reason, I felt secure enough with Elena to open up and talk.

"My mom was only sixteen when she had me," I began. "God, that sounds like the opening line to a young adult novel, doesn't it?"

"A catchy one," Elena agreed.

"Anyway." I cleared my throat. "I don't think she and my grandmother had a great relationship during my mom's formative years. Grandma was very driven, a career woman in the days when career women were often frowned upon. She had a full-time job, had my mom later in life, *and* brought home more money than her husband."

"Wow," Elena commented. "This was what, the sixties? Your grandmother was a woman before her time."

"Definitely. She still is. Very independent. She doesn't like to admit that she's getting older and sometimes needs help."

"And where is your mother?"

"I have no idea."

Elena blinked at me for several seconds. "Wow. Seriously no idea? She just left you?"

The subject wasn't one that got to me emotionally very often, not after thirty years, but something about the sadness in Elena's eyes, the pity in her voice…I swallowed down the lump that threatened to form and gave a curt nod. "When I was four. She just took off and never came back. Last time I heard from her, she was in Colorado. I think."

"And when was that?"

"When I turned sixteen. She sent me a birthday card."

"Jesus, Avery."

"Yeah, well." I gave what I hoped was a nonchalant shrug. That sympathy in her expression was something that never ceased to raise my defenses, forcing me to prove how tough I was, that it was no big deal having my mother run out on me when I was barely more than a toddler. "What can you do?"

Elena's eyes told me she wasn't buying my bravado act, but she was sweet enough not to say so. "And what about your dad?"

"I don't know who he is." I finished my wine in one big gulp. "I'm not even sure my mom or grandma knows." I shrugged again, beginning to look like a woman with some sort of tic. "Hell, *he* may not even know. I don't think he ever came looking for me, but it took me until I was in my early twenties to understand that he may not have even known my mom was pregnant with me."

Elena sighed and shook her head. "I just don't get it." She downed her wine, too, and signaled Jeff. "Do you want to order a couple appetizers?" she asked suddenly. "I need to soak up some of the wine in my stomach."

Her smile was gentle and I agreed. Jeff grabbed us a menu. Deciding quickly and simply on the stuffed mushrooms and a plate of the bruschetta, we put in our order and Elena returned to our conversation without missing a beat.

"I'll never understand how somebody can just disregard their own kid." She held up a hand. "And I mean no offense here. I'm sure there were extenuating circumstances for your mom that I know nothing about, but...I just don't get it."

My brain, of course, immediately zoomed to visions of Cindy paying no attention whatsoever to Max during practice, but before I could silently condemn Elena for being blind or a hypocrite, she stunned me and brought the subject up herself.

"My ex is like that," she said quietly.

"Cindy?"

"You've met her?"

"At practice."

"Yeah? Did she hit on you?"

I looked away, grabbed for my wine, willed Jeff to bring our food.

Elena squeezed my forearm, her touch warm and comforting. "It's no big deal, Avery. It's certainly not new behavior from her."

I shook my head. "She doesn't waste any time," I commented with a bit of a snort, remembering how quickly Cindy had sized me up at one practice, then asked me out the next time she saw me.

"She never did."

I didn't want to pry. At the same time, I wanted to know more. I felt like Elena and I were really connecting, and I wanted to know her on a deeper level, corny as that sounded. "Did she...want Max? I mean, from the beginning?" I crossed my fingers and prayed I wasn't treading on offensive territory here.

"Oh, God, yes. Us having a child was actually her idea."

I stared at her in disbelief as Jeff arrived with our food. We arranged our plates, our utensils, and each took a bite before continuing the conversation. "Seriously?" I asked, trying to reconcile the could-barely-be-bothered-with-her-kid woman I'd seen with somebody who truly wanted a baby, who actually suggested it, introduced the idea into the relationship.

"Absolutely. I wanted kids, too, but I also wanted to wait a bit. I had Max when I was thirty. I would have waited a few more years. But Cindy…no, Cindy wanted to have a baby right then. And what Cindy wants, Cindy gets." That last bit was said with just enough disgust to tell me it wasn't the first time Cindy had wanted something that Elena didn't.

"So…why didn't she have the baby then?"

Elena's answering laugh was bitter. "Oh, she didn't want to *carry* a baby. She just wanted to *have* one. It was a status symbol for her, though I didn't realize that until Max hit the Terrible Twos and she disappeared whenever he got difficult. Her friends were having kids around her, her brother's wife had a baby. She didn't like having the attention pulled away from her, so she figured out a way to get it back." She popped a mushroom into her mouth and smiled ruefully at me. "Of course, it's only after three years of therapy that I've been able to figure some of this stuff out."

I raised my glass. "To therapy."

"Amen."

"Max is a great kid," I said, trying to take away the gray fog that seemed to settle across her face.

It worked. Her smile broke through. "He is. I can't imagine my life without him. And I don't understand how Cindy doesn't feel the same way."

"She's not you," I said simply, because it was simple.

"She didn't even want to be called any variation of Mom. 'Cece' was her idea." She rolled her eyes to show what she thought of that. "I think she was relieved when I told her I was leaving her and I was taking Max with me to my parents' house."

We sat for several minutes in silence, just eating. It was surprisingly comfortable and I felt no squirming need to break the quiet with small talk. When Elena finally spoke again, a fire burned in her eyes as she looked at me.

"That's what I meant when I said I don't get it," she said told me. "The hardest part of all of this is trying to reassure Max that Cindy does love him, that she's not mad at him, that he didn't do anything wrong, that it isn't his fault his other mother is an idiot. I don't know how your grandmother did it. I really don't. She must be one very strong woman."

I'd grown out of pondering it too often, but when I was a young adult and could finally think about things outside of the Box of Me that teenagers and college kids tend to get stuck in, I started to realize how hard it must have been for my grandmother. She never said anything terrible about my mother, but I think she fell back on the old adage, "if you can't say anything nice, don't say anything at all," because she really didn't talk about her much. I began to realize, though, how disappointed she must have been. Here she'd spent twenty years raising what she hoped was a kind, intelligent, responsible girl and what happens? Teenage pregnancy aside, the girl decides one day to leave her four-year-old with her mother and run off, leaving no note, no forwarding address, no numbers, nothing. What is a mother to think about her parenting skills after something like that? It often occurred to me that Grandma must have felt like a failure, she must have been scared, resentful, exhausted, frustrated...so many things and nowhere to vent, nobody to vent to. Still, she took great pains to make sure I didn't hear bad things about my mother from her.

I came up with those all on my own.

"My grandma's the best," I said and I meant it. "She's not all warm and fuzzy, not like most grandmas are. But she gave up so much to take care of me." I shook my head as I was hit by the sheer scope of her sacrifice. "So much."

"Well, looks to me like she did a great job." Elena's smile was genuine and I felt my cheeks warm.

"Thanks. And for what it's worth, I think you're doing a great job with Max, especially since I suspect you're doing most of it single-handedly. It can't be easy."

"It isn't." She stared off into the middle distance as she spoke, her voice soft and full of emotion. "You know, sometimes I wish that Cindy would just go away. That she'd just stop showing up altogether. Isn't that terrible? That I'd wish one of my son's parents to just vanish? But she disappoints him so often...so, so often. How many times can I assure him it's not his fault before he stops believing me? He's such a sensitive kid. And I wish he wasn't. Sometimes, I really wish he'd just toughen up so she can't hurt him so easily." Anguished eyes turned on me, shimmering with moisture. "What kind of mother wishes for her child to be cold and unfeeling?"

145

"A mother who wants to protect that child," I said with conviction. "All of the things you want are the things that might be best for him. That's what moms do; they want the best for their kids. And you know what, Elena? Max is a great kid. He's sweet and he's gentle and he's kind. And he learned all those things from you."

A transformation happened then, as I watched Elena collect herself and blink away the wetness in her chocolate brown eyes. Right in front of me, in an instant, she went from being a simple crush to being a woman I might like to have something with in the future. Something new and intense and wonderful.

It scared the hell out of me.

"You're sweet," she said, obviously unaware of what I'd just witnessed, seeming not to notice the slight trembling of my hand as I finished off my wine. "Thank you. I needed that."

"You're welcome."

"He likes you a lot, you know. It's always, 'Coach King this,' and 'Coach King that.'"

"He may like me, but he *loves* my dog."

Her sharp guffaw startled me, but I was getting used to it. "He certainly does. As long as you stay close by, I won't need to get him his own." The realization of what she'd said hit her then and she busied herself by looking at her watch. "Wow."

Leaning close—I couldn't help myself—I looked at her watch, too. It was after ten. "Wow is right. I had no idea we'd been here for so long."

Her eyes met mine as we sat with our heads only a few inches apart. "Early game tomorrow."

"Uh-huh."

146

A slow smile made its way onto her face and it looked to me like she regretted pulling away as she turned to signal Jeff. I had honestly never seen a sexier woman in my entire life and my whole body began to tingle, like little fingertips were playing over my skin.

We fought good-naturedly over the bill, finally agreeing on an even split. We left Jeff a generous tip and headed out into the Friday night dark.

Smells from the restaurant's kitchen were beginning to dissipate in the air outside, a hint of garlic here, the slight scent of sautéed onions there, mixing in with the cool flavor of the night. We strolled slowly to the parking lot where our cars were parked three spaces from one another. My Jetta came first and I slowed to indicate it was mine. Elena followed me to the driver's side door; I could feel her behind me.

"I had such a good time tonight, Elena," I said, turning to face her. It was all I got out before she kissed me.

My brain registered everything at once—her gentle hands cradling my face, her body pressing me back against the car, the way our height difference made me feel deliciously trapped between Elena's body and my Volkswagen, the softness of her lips on mine, the tang of wine still clinging to her mouth—and I had to focus hard to keep from being completely overwhelmed. Overwhelmed, but in a good way. I wanted to remember everything I could about my first kiss with Elena Walker because I was sure it wouldn't be my last.

It wasn't a demanding kiss, but one of promise, of anticipation. One that was equal parts gentle and insistent. My hands came up to settle on her waist, to pull her hips closer to mine, then to slide up under her suit jacket and feel the smoothly planed muscles of her back beneath the silk of her blouse.

I wanted more and I wanted to slow things down, both at the same time, and I somehow knew that Elena felt the same way. I allowed her to deepen our kiss for several long seconds, relishing the taste and feel of her tongue as it touched mine, before I brought my hands around to her chest and wrenched our mouths apart as gently as I could. One of us whimpered, but I wasn't sure which, and we stood there in the dark with our foreheads pressed together, each of us raggedly trying to catch our breath.

"My God," I managed.

"I'll say."

"My God," I said again and she chuckled. I could feel her playing with the ends of my hair, tickling the side of my neck, and goose bumps of pleasure broke out across my skin. She rubbed her thumb across my bottom lip and it took every ounce of strength I had left in my body to keep from sucking it into my mouth. I was certain that, if she pushed just a little, I would willingly and joyously have sex with her right there in the parking lot on the hood of my own car, and that knowledge both excited and mortified me. Cliché as it was, I'd never felt such sexual compatibility with somebody, ever. Elena and I were going to be a bonfire in bed. I knew it beyond a shadow of a doubt.

Which was exactly why we needed to slow things down. I was afraid such heat would incinerate us both.

My throat suddenly dry, I swallowed hard and tried to find my voice. And some logic when I spoke.

"Early game," I croaked, the reminder the best I could come up with.

"Right." She nodded, which took her forehead from mine. Who knew a forehead could suddenly feel cold and neglected?

"Will you be there?"

Her grimace was full of disappointment, which made me feel the tiniest bit better. "I've got to work."

"Crap."

That made her grin, her teeth gleaming whitely in the artificial light. "If I try, I might be able to catch the end."

"Try hard," I ordered.

"Yes, ma'am."

I don't know exactly why her answer turned me on so, but when she said it, I felt a rush of heat between my legs. I had no idea I was such a hussy. "And if you can't make it…" I trailed off, trying to think of something witty to say, but her hips were still tight against mine and I was having trouble formulating coherent thoughts.

"Don't worry. I know where you live."

Before I could process anything more, she kissed me again, quickly, then backed away. I'm pretty sure I pouted at the loss of her.

I waved feebly as she backed her car out and pulled away, and I brought my fingers to my lips as her taillights faded into the darkness of the night.

"My God," I whispered into the air.

It was another five minutes before I could feel my legs again and was brave enough to step away from my car without worrying I'd collapse into a boneless heap on the asphalt.

chapter sixteen

I saw them arrive with Max, but I would have known immediately who they were, even if they'd come without him.

Elena didn't look much like her father at all. He was a big bulldozer of a man with broad shoulders and very little left of what might have once been sandy blond hair. I could see flashes of her in his smile, though, and her eyes were the same rich brown as his. Her mother, however, was a different story. I could almost hear Grandma's voice in my head, "She looks like she fell off her mother's face." Elena was a carbon copy of the woman, who was strikingly beautiful even in what must have been her late sixties. The shape of her face, the way her eyes were set at a slight tilt, her tall, lean frame; it was all Elena. I felt like I was getting a quick flash of the future any time I looked in her direction. Elena, thirty years from now.

They paid infinitely more attention to Max's playing than Cindy ever had in all the times I'd seen her there. They smiled and cheered and every time Max looked in their direction, Mrs. Walker gave a sweet wave of encouragement. Mr. Walker shot his grandson a thumbs-up more than once.

I tried not to stare into the bleachers at them, but it was hard. Maddie had things under control as far as the team went and I was trying to make myself as unobtrusive as possible, only helping when she asked me specifically, not wanting to step on her toes. I coached third base and then first as the game went on, pleased to see that most of our kids finally understood in which direction to run after they hit the ball. Each time Max was up, he glanced into the modest crowd and my eyes would follow his, my stomach flip-flopping at the jolt of familiarity when his grandmother smiled at him.

Max made contact with the ball every time he was at bat, which I didn't think was a coincidence.

"See my nana and papa up there?" he asked me brightly as he stopped on first base during the last inning. "They're watching me play."

He was so adorable as he stated the obvious to me, I wanted to hug him tightly. I settled for ruffling his hair before I stepped back for the next batter and ordered Max to pay attention. When I glanced over at the Walkers, my heart did a weird little skip as I noticed Elena scootching in to settle between her parents. She caught me looking and gave me a little wave, and I couldn't keep the stupid grin off my face as my cheeks warmed.

Across the field at third base, Maddie arched a brow at me, her expression very clearly telling me she had witnessed that little exchange and was expecting details.

I tried to put my focus back on the game, but my mind drifted a bit. I've always loved the smell of freshly cut grass and I inhaled, taking the scent deeply into my lungs. It was the epitome of summer to me; it's what my childhood outdoors smelled like. Inside it was chocolate chip cookies; outside it was freshly cut grass. I was reminded of how strong the sense of smell is to me as I stood there and watched the end of the game, reveling in the fragrance of the air, knowing I only had a few short months to enjoy it before the autumn chased it away with the completely different, but no less wonderful, scent of crushed leaves.

The game ended, but I was still caught up in the pleasantly comfortable feelings that had distracted me. Feelings of home, of summer, of knowing the gorgeous woman in the bleachers had been kissing me last night. Gabriel came up to me as the teams were cleaning up their gear.

"Hey, Coach King, what was the score?" he asked, sweat glistening across his forehead.

I checked my clipboard. "Seven to five. Us."

"Hey, you guys! We won," he touted as he ran back to his teammates and slapped high fives with the few who were actually listening.

I felt Maddie's scolding look before I actually saw it. "We don't keep score, remember?" she said, shaking a finger at me.

"Oh, we do, too," I argued back. "We just don't talk about it."

"I'm surprised you even know what the score was."

I looked at her, puzzled, and waited for her to elaborate, which she did.

"Who's the hottie in the bleachers?"

"What hottie?" I knew in a nanosecond she wasn't buying my feigned innocence, but she snorted, just to make it ultra clear.

"The one you couldn't keep your eyes off of. The one with the cute little wave."

"She's…" I wanted to say "nobody," but I couldn't do it, mostly because it was so far from the truth. "She's Max's mom."

Maddie squinted towards the bleachers where Elena and her parents were gathering their things. "Wait. I thought that other one was his mom. The one who looked at you like you were a piece of meat and she was a starving wolf."

"Right. She is. This is Max's *other* mom." I watched in excited anticipation as Elena held a finger up to her parents and gave them the universal sign for, "I'll be right back," then headed in our direction.

Maddie gaped at me. "Max has two moms? How did I not know this?"

My smartass answer was stalled in my throat as Elena reached us.

"Hi," she said to me.

"Hey, you," I replied, trying to keep my eyes from roaming over her body. She wore dark dress slacks and a cream silk shirt with short sleeves, obviously having come right from work. A wink of a lacey camisole teased me from the V at her neckline and I seriously entertained the thought of throwing her to the grass and unbuttoning her blouse with my teeth.

"My dad says it was a good game," she commented, interrupting my filthy thoughts. Thank God.

"It was. Max played great," I said. Maddie cleared her throat in a not-so-discreet fashion. "Oh. This is Maddie. Maddie, this is Max's mother, Elena Walker."

"Oh, *Coach* Maddie. Max has talked about you. It's very nice to meet you," Elena said as they shook hands.

"Same here. Your son has quite a lot of potential. Is he enjoying the game?"

"He loves it," Elena said, her smile growing as it always did when she spoke of her son. "He's having a great time. Tee-ball is all he talks about."

"Well, if he keeps it up, I think he'll make a terrific ball player as he grows."

Trying to busy my hands so I didn't look like an idiot, I smiled politely as they talked about baseball and how they each had brothers who played in college. When the conversation stalled, as it almost always does with new acquaintances, Elena said her goodbyes, thanking Maddie, then turning to me.

"I'll catch up with you later?" It was a question, not a statement, and I realized she wasn't sure where the boundaries lay for me there on the field.

"Definitely," I said, putting as much conviction into the one word as I could.

"'I'll catch up with you later?'" Maddie asked as soon as Elena was out of earshot. "What the hell does that mean?"

Hesitation borne from fear of loss swamped me then and I stumbled over an explanation. If I spoke it aloud, would I jinx any chance I had of creating something good with Elena? Was she too good to be true? I was being ridiculous and I knew it. *We've only had one date, for Christ's sake,* I told myself.

"It means…that she lives in my development." I hoped to leave it at that. No such luck; Maddie could read me like a book.

"Okay. And?"

"And…we met for drinks last night."

Maddie blinked at me, torn, I was sure, between excited happiness for me and annoyed hurt that I hadn't told her ahead of time. I could almost see her calm herself down, force herself to speak calmly and not bite my head off.

"And…did you have a good time?"

The smile wouldn't stay tucked away. It blossomed on my face, making me feel a little silly. "Yeah. We had a fantastic time."

"You sleep with her?"

"What? No!" My indignation was real, though I knew the question was to be expected.

"Oh, like you've never gone to bed with somebody on the first date."

I pursed my lips, unable to think of a comeback. "Well, I didn't with Elena."

"Yet," she supplied.

"Yet," I agreed with a wink.

"She's gorgeous."

I nodded as both of us watched her walk toward the parking lot with her parents and Max in tow. After several seconds, Maddie spoke again.

"Did you want to say something about the beauty of that ass, or should I?"

———

Saturday mornings had become a little rough on me. Spending all that time with a dozen over-excited kids, keeping track of the game, answering parents' questions, and trying to stay professional and organized was energy-sucking. Add to that my chat with Elena, my attempts to dodge Maddie's questions, and the anticipation of maybe seeing Elena again that night, and my brain was totally fried.

I read an article once on introverts and it gave me certain facts that I already knew, but had never seen written as public, scientific knowledge. It said that extroverts *gain* energy from being around a lot of people, that they need it. It also said that introverts have energy *drained* from them being around a lot of people and that afterwards, they need to be alone to recharge. I never really understood my need to be away from others, my intense enjoyment of being alone with a good book or a DVD or on a long walk until I read that article. I felt vindicated, strange as it may sound.

I had a friend in college who was the poster child of gregariousness. She was the life of every party, charming, people loved her and wanted to be around her because she was a hoot. She stated to me one day that she was going to make it the mission of her junior year to "pull Avery out of her shell." I suppose I should have been flattered by the attention, but instead it pissed me off. It never once occurred to her that maybe I was perfectly happy inside my shell and had no need or desire to be pulled from it, that just because she was loud and fun and never stopped talking didn't mean there was something wrong with me because I was her opposite. We lost touch not long after that.

Mendon Ponds Park was gorgeous and huge and sprawling, so that's where I took Steve for a long walk later that day to clear my head and regain some of the energy that had been sucked away by tee-ball. I chose one of the lesser-traveled walking paths and clipped Steve onto his retractable leash. I reserved use of it for such walks because he liked to meander and sniff every conceivable thing he came across in the woods, so having extra lead kept me from coming to a complete stop every five feet. When we were in the city, though, I used a good old-fashioned six-foot leash so that I had more control, should Steve decide he'd like to dart after a squirrel or zip across the street to say hi to another dog.

The thing I like best about walking in nature is the ability it gives me to just let my thoughts go. My mind wanders at the same time my feet wander and it's relaxing and it's a relief for me to just empty my head into the quiet comfort of the trees, let my thoughts drift with the breeze that slid through the pine needles like gentle fingers. To say my head was full that day would be to grossly understate the facts. My head was *crammed*, the majority of it being taken up by a stunningly attractive brunette who kissed like a goddess and seemed to be really, genuinely interested in me. I wondered what I had done in some previous life to deserve such riches in this one.

My thoughts turned to Maddie. J.T. had been working that morning, so I'd been Maddie's ride. She was surprisingly reserved and actually kept her questions to a bare minimum as I drove her home. I almost asked her if she was feeling all right, but I was afraid that would be all it would take to open the dam and send her queries flowing out, so I kept my mouth shut and so did she. Which was weird.

Steve and I spent over an hour just wandering, him sniffing and me trying not to think of anything in particular. We got back to the house and I had the sudden urge to make muffins. The realization that I didn't have a clue what the next step was to be sent me flying into the kitchen to work off the nervous buzz. Elena had said she'd catch up with me later. Did that mean she'd call? Should I call her? Would she pop over? Or should I wander down the street?

"You'd think having your tongue in somebody's mouth would warrant you a little leeway in the surprise appearances department," I muttered to myself, but it didn't help me with a solution. Instead, I mixed pumpkin and eggs and flour and greased my muffin pan with cooking spray. As I slid the muffins into the oven, I thought if nothing else, at least my house would smell divine. Though it was more suited for the fall, the scent of warm spiced pumpkin never failed to soothe my soul.

Waiting for that smell to permeate the air, I'd just about worked myself into a paranoid frenzy when my phone rang. I got so few calls on my landline—I used my cell for just about everything—that I didn't recognize the sound right away. Steve cocked his furry head as if he, too, wondered what on earth that strange chime was. The number on the caller ID was local, but not familiar… which meant nothing since I couldn't remember anybody's numbers any longer. Advanced technology was making me stupid. I picked up the receiver.

"Avery? It's Elena."

And just like that, all my stress and worry left me, running off my body like water to pool at my feet.

"Hi," I said, my voice softening all on its own.

"Hey," she replied, her tone mirroring mine.

"I wasn't sure if you had my number." Worry number seventy-five in the past two hours.

"It's on Max's tee-ball schedule. I realize that might be cheating, but I was too embarrassed to admit I didn't get it last night."

"I didn't get yours either, so I think we're even."

Her laugh seemed softer on the phone than in person, but still just as contagious. "Well, I don't know about you, but I was a little…preoccupied last night."

The memory flash that hit my brain made my legs weak and my throat dry. If I closed my eyes, I could almost feel the hard, cold steel of my car against my back and the dichotomy of Elena's warm, soft body pressed along my front. I swore I could still smell her perfume, musky and subtle in the darkness.

"Preoccupied," I said. "Yeah. That's a good word for it."

"Listen, I know this is kind of last minute, but…do you want to come down later? Have a glass of wine with me?" She paused and I swore I could hear her swallow. Could she be nervous? Did she really think I'd say no? "Max goes to bed by eight-thirty. You could come by after that. I just…" She cleared her throat and I grinned. She *was* nervous. "I just would really like to see you again."

"Well, I don't know," I teased. "I need to check my social calendar. I'm a very busy and popular girl, you know."

"I'm not surprised." I could hear the smile in her voice.

"Oh, would you look at that. I just happen to be free at nine o'clock tonight. You're in luck."

"Excellent. Think you can find the place?"

"Let's see…six doors down…hmm. Well, I have Google Maps. I should be okay."

"Let me give you my number in case you get lost." She rattled off her phone number and I jotted it on a magnetic pad on my refrigerator, suddenly realizing that I had her number, too, on my tee-ball roster. Although now, it was official.

"Got it. I'll see you later then."

"Yes, you will."

I hung up with her sexy voice lilting in my head. *Yes, you will.* My legs tingled, as did other parts of my anatomy. God, I was in so much trouble with this one. So. Much. Trouble.

I waited until 9:02 before I headed down the street. I didn't want to be late, but I didn't want to look too eager, either. I could hear Maddie's voice in my head telling me to play a little hard to get. That was difficult to do when I wanted Elena as badly as I did, but I tried my best.

I stood on her front stoop, a plate of pumpkin muffins in one hand, and fixed my hair, fussed with my top, ran a fingertip along each corner of my mouth. Finally, I raised my hand to knock, but the door was pulled open before I could make contact, scaring the bejesus out of me.

"Holy Christ," I blurted.

Elena laughed. "I'm so sorry. I saw you walk by the window and thought I could get to the door before you had to knock." She looked a bit chagrined and I happily wondered if I'd won at the Playing Hard to Get game.

She let me in and I handed over the plate. "I don't know how well they'll go with the wine, but here you go."

"Oh, my God, these smell amazing." She *looked* amazing as I watched her unwrap the muffins. The army green shorts accentuated her skin tone and the pale yellow camp shirt tapered in slightly, hugging her trim waist. She was barefoot and for some reason, I found that incredibly endearing. "I'm eating one now," she informed me as she liberated a muffin from the pile. "You can't stop me."

"I wouldn't dream of it." I had to look away when she closed her eyes and moaned.

"Oh, God," she said, her voice low and almost erotic. "There should be a warning label on these. Sinful. Almost as sinful as your chocolate chip cookies."

I cocked an eyebrow at her. "I believe those cookies belonged to Max."

"Did they?" Her expression was all innocence. "Huh."

I laughed. "I'm glad you liked them."

"Like is not a strong enough word. Max said you made the best cookies in the world and he was right." She held up a bottle of Chardonnay in question and I nodded. "Do you bake a lot?"

"I do. I enjoy it. Helps me relax."

"Well, from what I've seen—and that's not much, hint, hint—you're very good at it."

"Thank you. My grandmother taught me everything I know."

Elena handed me a glass of wine and we clinked, then sipped, watching one another over our respective rims. The lower half of my body was treated to a pleasant flutter. I had come over to visit with her, talk to her, get to know her better, but all I could think about was licking every inch of her body.

"What's your favorite thing to bake?" she asked, yanking me from my thoughts as she left the kitchen.

Following her into the living room, I tried to take in my surroundings without looking like I was doing so. The décor was simple and tasteful, with very little on the walls and a couple of small unpacked boxes piled in a corner. The well-worn sofa was the centerpiece of the room, its fabric a subtle pinstriped pattern of light blue on navy. Pulling out that light blue was a matching armchair, tucked near the fireplace much like mine, inviting you to come sit, get comfortable, grab a book. A squat, cylindrical candle burned gently on an end table, filling the room with cinnamon. Portraits of Max in various stages of childhood graced the shelving unit against one wall.

"Brownies and chocolate chip cookies," I said, picking up one of the framed photos. "Because they're easy, everybody loves them, and I can almost make them with my eyes closed."

"He's two there," Elena said, gesturing to the picture as she sat on the couch.

"He's such an adorable kid," I commented, and I meant it. "I don't know how you haven't just eaten him up by now." Everything about him was dark, even for a toddler. His eyes and eyebrows, his hair, his skin. He looked so sweet and innocent and I had the inexplicable urge to protect him from the world, which scared the crap out of me. I tried to cover by asking, "What ethnicity are you? Italian? Latina?"

"My mother's Greek."

"That was my next guess."

"People think I'm lying when I tell them I'm Greek because Walker doesn't exactly scream Mediterranean."

"No, and neither does your dad. What's your mom's maiden name?"

"Giakomopoulos."

163

"Okay, *that* screams Mediterranean. And I've seen your mother. You look just like her." I shot Elena a quick glance, then returned my focus to the shelves. "She's gorgeous."

"Thanks. One of my brothers is also dark like her, though not as dark as I am. My other two brothers are lighter, like my dad."

"And Max looks like you."

"He does. I was pretty proud of that." She grimaced in self-deprecation and it was somehow a charming expression on her. "Does that make me bad?"

"Positively evil." I finished my perusal of the pictures, then turned back to her where she sat alone on the big, blue couch. A gentle pat on the cushion next to her was all I needed to get my feet moving.

"So tell me about your day," she said, sitting back, pulling her legs up to fold underneath her body. Cradling her temple with a hand, her elbow braced on the back of the couch, she studied me intently. As I mirrored her pose, I wondered at how I could feel so relaxed and comfortable with her, and so utterly anxious at the same time. It didn't seem possible.

"Well, let's see." Trying hard not to gulp my wine, I took a small sip. "After the game, I took Maddie home."

"Have you been friends with her long?"

"Ten years?"

"That's pretty long. She seems very nice."

"She and her partner, J.T., are great. You'd like them." I was sure she would. There wasn't much *not* to like about Maddie and J.T. They'd like Elena, too. I was positive. "Anyway, J.T. was working today—she's a cop—and Maddie still doesn't feel confident enough to be driving with her knee like that, so I took her home." Elena's fingers found the ends of my hair and toyed with them gently as she listened.

"I just love the color of your hair," she said, almost to herself.

"Thank you."

"It's like…copper, but with more red. And it's really soft."

"That's because I use ridiculously expensive shampoo."

That made her chuckle. "What else did you do today?" She continued to play with my hair and I continued to try not to notice. I was completely unsuccessful.

"Then Steve and I went for a long walk at Mendon Ponds."

"Oh, my God." Elena laughed that sudden sharp laugh and I couldn't help but smile at the sound. "Steve is all Max ever talks about. You need to bring him over."

"Ah, so you're just using me for my dog, is that it?" I teased.

We were close. Very close. I could smell the wine on her breath, and again, that musky, very subtle perfume that I was coming to think of as *her* scent. I attempted to show some tact as I inhaled it deep into my lungs.

"Oh, no," she said, her voice throaty. "I was thinking of using you for much more than that."

The fact that we were sitting was a blessing. A short woman cannot, in any way, shape, or form, be nonchalant or subtle about kissing a woman who's taller when they're both standing up. It's just not smooth, nor is it suave. You have to get up on your tippy toes and hope you don't fall over before you reach her lips, and she sees you coming a mile away.

165

So sitting was good. She looked at me expectantly and I knew in an instant that she was letting me make the moves this time. And I appreciated it. The tip of her tongue peeked out to wet her lips and that was all the prodding I needed. Closing the gap between us, I pressed my lips to hers, taking great pleasure in the tiny little gasp that escaped her.

From there, it was all softness and warmth, which gradually became heat, well on its way to fire. Our wine glasses miraculously moved to the coffee table without spilling a drop, our mouths never leaving each other's. I wanted to touch every part of Elena, and at the same time wanted to go as slowly as possible. My body was aflame and everywhere she touched me I felt tiny little landmines explode under my skin. My fingers acted of their own accord, deftly unbuttoning her camp shirt while my tongue was deep in her mouth, exploring her, delving into her, giving her a sample of what the future might hold for us. Only when I felt her hands cupping my backside, her palms sliding up and down my bare thighs, did I realize I'd maneuvered myself so I straddled her lap, suddenly, magically taller than her, in command and in control and absolutely relishing it.

Her bra was white lace and somehow seemed terribly appropriate. It only made her skin look darker, more tan, a deeper bronze. When I pulled back to look, the sight of her stole the breath from my body. Chest heaving, eyes dark, lips swollen, blouse hanging completely open and displaying small, round, lace-covered breasts. I could barely hold back my groan of arousal.

"My God, you're beautiful," I whispered, and wondered if I'd ever meant anything so sincerely in all my life.

I took her mouth with mine once again, running my fingernails up the heated skin of her stomach. She squirmed beneath me, grabbed my head, fisted her hands in my hair as she pushed her tongue into my mouth, threatening to pull control of the situation right out from under me like a braided rug. I was having none of that and I let her know it by dipping one hand fully inside the cup of her bra. I kneaded a handful of flesh firmly in my palm, groaning as I felt the hardened pebble of her nipple pushing into my skin.

I had no idea how many times the little-boy voice called "Mom" from upstairs before it reached my ears. Elena heard it first, of course, and wrenched her lips from mine, holding me away from her mouth by my hair, which she still had clasped in her fingers.

"Wait," she whispered, and had to say it a second time to get my attention.

Both of us sat still, the only sound in the room that of our uneven breathing, me sitting in Elena's lap, my hand still inside her bra, and my own panties uncomfortably damp. Seconds ticked by and I thought we might be home free.

"Mommy?" Max's voice came again, louder this time, and it had the effect of cold water being thrown on us. Our eyes met and Elena's were filled with apology as I extricated my hand. Clumsily, I rolled from her lap and flopped into a sitting position on the couch. Elena stood, buttoning her shirt as she headed for the stairs. Max called her again.

167

"What's the matter, honey?" she said as she climbed.

Leaning my head back against the couch, I blew out a frustrated breath and tossed my arm over my eyes. How in the world had I forgotten about Max? What the hell was I thinking, practically undressing Elena in her own living room when her son was just upstairs? He could have walked right in on us; we certainly wouldn't have noticed. What was the matter with me? I was acting like a teenage boy on his first date, jumping at the first opportunity to get into her pants. Didn't I have more control than a fifteen-year-old?

I was still irritated with myself when Elena came back down. Before I could utter a word of apology, she beat me to it.

"I am so sorry," she said, her voice barely above a whisper. "He had a nightmare."

"Poor little guy," I said. "Is he okay?"

"He's fine." She waved a hand at the stairs. "But it's going to be a while before he gets back to sleep, so…" Her voice trailed off and she waited for me to catch up, which took longer than it should have.

She wanted me to leave.

"Oh. *Oh.* Oh, okay. Sure. No problem." I stood, feeling a little jittery and kind of stupid, unable to comprehend exactly how, not three minutes prior, I'd had Elena's breast in my hand and now she was quietly ushering me out the door.

"I'm really sorry, Avery," she said, still keeping her voice down, telegraphing to me that she didn't want Max to know somebody else was in the house.

I matched my volume to hers. "It's no big deal. I'm fine." In truth, I had no idea how I felt. Everything had happened so fast.

"Mom?"

"I'll be right up, honey," she called over her shoulder in the direction of the stairs. Looking back at me, she promised, "I'll call you."

"Okay."

She grasped my chin and gave me a quick peck on the lips.

And then I was on the front stoop.

The door clicked shut, but my head kept spinning.

chapter seventeen

"What's the matter with you? Are you getting sick?" Grandma laid her hand against my forehead, then each cheek. "You've got dark circles under your eyes."

As always happens to me when something is on my mind, I slept like crap. No matter how sandpaper-like my eyelids became as I lay in my bed the previous night, my mind just wouldn't give me peace, replaying the evening over and over, my body repeatedly turned on, then shut down, until the sun began to peek over the horizon and I finally forced myself downstairs for much-needed coffee.

"Too much chocolate before bed, Grandma. I didn't sleep well." Not the whole truth, but not a total lie either. The empty container of Ben & Jerry's New York Fudge Brownie in my kitchen garbage can could attest to that.

"You're sure? Maybe you should go see Dr. Garber."

"I'm fine."

"You don't look fine."

"Gee, thanks."

"Drink your tea." Grandma brushed my hair away from my face in a gesture so sweet it almost brought tears to my eyes. She was never a touchy-feely person when I was growing up, but once I moved out and began living on my own, for some reason she became more so. She hugged me hello and goodbye, touched my face, straightened my clothes. It freaked me out when it first started happening, simply because it was so...*not her*. But it wasn't long before I grew to like it. Who doesn't like to be touched by somebody who loves them?

She looked at me with such worry in her green eyes that I almost blurted out the entire story of my previous night, from beginning to end. Deciding that might be too much for her, I patted her hand.

"I'm fine, Grandma. Really. The ice cream did me in. I just need a nap and I'll be good as new. Stop worrying." To change the subject, I asked, "Hey, how's Mr. Davidson?"

A pretty pink tint blossomed on her cheeks and she glanced down demurely into her empty teacup.

I feigned a gasp. "Grandma! What have you been up to? Have you been a bad girl?"

A playful slap caught my upper arm. "Stop that," she scolded me. "We've just had dinner together. That's all. He's a very nice man."

I grinned at her as she spoke, and for a split second she looked young again. And happy. "I think that's great." I took my cup into the kitchen, preparing to head home. "Maybe the three of us can have dinner together some time. Then I can tell you if he gets my stamp of approval."

Grandma's laugh was musical, like the higher, tinkling keys on a piano, and it echoed in my head long after I'd closed her door behind me and was driving myself home. My mother may have been cold and unfeeling, but I loved my grandmother with all my heart. I tried hard to remember the last time she'd had a date. Obviously, at eighty-five years old, she wasn't exactly playing the field. But I wasn't stupid and I knew she sacrificed a big chunk of her social life by raising me.

I vaguely remembered a man when I'd been in elementary school. Jim? Joe? Something with a J. I think Grandma saw him for quite a while, but she was very discreet. He never stayed over, not that I was aware of, but he took her to dinner a few times a month and they spent some evenings together. At the age I was, of course, I was all absorbed in me, me, me, so I probably paid little attention. To this day I can't pinpoint when he stopped coming around.

When I was in college, there was a neighbor who lived across the street and a couple houses over from Grandma's, Mr. Samuels. I was pretty sure he was sweet on Grandma and she seemed to like him quite a bit, too. I never asked for any details and she didn't offer any and I felt a little funny prying into her love life, so I left it alone and just assumed. Mr. Samuels passed away a year or two after I moved into my own place. Grandma never said anything other than what a shame it was, but she was quieter than usual for several months.

And since then? Nobody that I could recall...until Mr. Davidson.

I was still grinning about the whole thing when I pulled into my driveway and let myself into my house. So what if Grandma was eighty-five? Did that mean she didn't deserve to have somebody to love?

"Of course not," I said aloud to Steve as I ruffled his ears and kissed the top of his head. He yawned.

I love Sundays. Lazy, relaxing Sundays. My favorite day of the week. I always began with a visit to see Grandma. But after that, the day was mine. I could read a book for the rest of the afternoon. I could tend to my houseplants, maybe arrange some flowers outside, depending on the season. I could go to a movie or rent one. I loved not having to be anywhere at any time. Sundays were mine.

This Sunday in particular my mind was not going to sit idle, and I decided I needed something to occupy it. Steve was basking in the periodic sunshine on the back patio, so I headed upstairs to the second bedroom, which I used as an office. On Friday, Tyrell had given me the bare bones of our next big project—redesigning the logo and tag line for an existing beverage company in the area—and I made myself comfortable at my desktop and worked on that for a while, sorting through colors, shapes, and ideas to see if anything popped up at me. I settled on a cool lime green/bright orange color combination, but the design itself eluded me. I gave up and headed downstairs for a something to drink.

Though gray with ominous clouds moving quickly overhead, the day was warm and had warranted the screen door instead of the glass one. As I descended the stairs, I thought I heard murmuring coming from the back yard. A sight that would have made me groan three or four weeks ago instead brought a smile to my lips. Max knelt in the grass, wearing denim shorts and a Spongebob Squarepants T-shirt. He had one arm draped over the short fencing, and he scratched the top of Steve's head. Steve, of course, was loving every minute of it and soon rolled over to offer up his belly for a rub. Laughter bubbled out of me at his antics; I couldn't believe he'd let a six-year-old win him over so easily.

Without stopping to consider why I was happy to see the boy, I slid the back door open.

"Hey, what's going on?"

Max looked up and grinned at me, and I got such an unexpected glimpse of his mother in his face, it was as if she had poked me in the ribs. "We're just sitting here," he said matter-of-factly.

"Well, you know, I was thinking..." I tapped my forefinger against my lips as though contemplating something very important. "It feels like a day that needs chocolate cupcakes. Don't you think so?"

His eyebrows raised and he nodded, his head bobbing rapidly enough to flop his bangs into his eyes.

"I could use a little help from an assistant chef," I added, suddenly feeling like I wanted nothing more than to spend some time with him and wondering what the hell was wrong with me. "You up for it?"

"Okay," he said, scrambling to his feet, his excitement obvious. I helped him over the fence and we headed inside, Steve following right behind Max, tail wagging and eyes bright.

"First, we need to call your mom and let her know you're here. We don't want to get in trouble like we did last time, do we?"

"No way."

"Okay." I picked up the handset and asked if he knew his number. Surprisingly, he did. I helped him dial and then let him have the phone.

"Mommy? Hi. I'm at Coach King's house. We're gonna make cupcakes! Chocolate ones!" He paused. "I'm not. No, I promise I'm not."

"Not what?" I whispered to him.

"Making a noose of myself," he whispered back.

I could hear Elena's voice in the handset saying, "Nuisance. *Nuisance* of yourself."

"Tell her if she comes over in an hour, she can have a warm cupcake and a glass of milk." I winked at him and he repeated my words.

When he was finished, I pulled one of my kitchen chairs over to the counter for Max to stand on. Folding down the top of my extra apron a couple times, I tied it around him, explaining, "If you're going to be my assistant chef, you've got to look the part." The pride on his face told me he liked that idea.

I got ingredients out, batching them on the counter. His eyes scanned them.

"Where's the box?" he asked.

"What box?"

"The box the cupcake stuff comes in."

After a second or two of brow furrowing, I realized he meant the box of cake mix. "Oh, no, little man. We make this from scratch."

"What's that?"

"Well, I don't exactly know why it's called 'from scratch,' but it means we use all our own ingredients and we don't use a boxed mix. A boxed mix is really just a lot of this stuff here," I waved a hand over my ingredients, "put together ahead to save you time. But my grandma always told me that scratch is better. A box is faster, but scratch tastes better."

I don't know that he understood my explanation, but he gave a curt nod and looked ready to begin.

I set the chocolate and butter to melting in a double boiler on the stove and then helped Max crack eggs and measure sugar into the mixing bowl. I even managed not to cringe when he stuck his thumbs through the shell and got egg whites all over the counter.

"What's your mom up to today?" I asked him, trying to be nonchalant in my questioning as we watched the KitchenAid go to town.

"Cece's over. They're fighting." His eyes never left the bowl.

"They fight a lot?"

He shrugged.

"What were they fighting about?"

He shrugged again.

"Max?" I squatted a little bit so I was level with him. "Hey. Look at me." He did, reluctantly. "You know Mom and Cece love you very much, don't you?"

This time it was just a half-shrug. "I guess."

"No," I said firmly, hating the uncertainty in his eyes. "No, there's no guessing. They *do* love you. You're the most important thing in the world to them."

"They yell a lot," he said softly.

"At you?"

"No, at each other."

I blew out a frustrated breath for him. I hated the idea of Cindy yelling at Elena. Did she yell back? She didn't seem like a woman who raised her voice often, but I knew it was not uncommon to partner with somebody who could bring that out of you. And was it even possible to explain something like this to a six-year-old? Max may have seemed wise beyond his years at times, but he was still a little boy, and there were things about his moms that he just didn't need to know.

"You know, Max, sometimes grown-ups don't even know they're yelling. Sometimes, after we've been together for a while, we get so used to yelling that we just do it all the time. And it doesn't necessarily mean we're mad at you or each other or anybody else. We're just loud because we think that's the only way the other person will hear us. We have to learn how to be a little calmer, a little quieter, that sometimes people listen better when you don't shout at them."

He seemed to absorb this, roll it around in his little head. "Maybe I should tell 'em next time. Tell 'em not to yell so much."

"Maybe you should." I put my arm around his shoulders and gave him a little squeeze. Part of me felt bad for him, having to deal with his moms. Another part wondered what it would be like to have your parents around, even if all they did was argue all the time.

We left that topic and focused on the cupcakes. Max was adorably precise in his measuring of flour and cocoa powder, taking an exorbitant amount of time to get them just right in the measuring cups, an almost equal amount ending up on the counter, on the chair, on the floor. My own patience with him surprised me; I somehow managed to keep my hands to myself and let him do the work. I also somehow enjoyed it. We finally got all the ingredients mixed together and then slowly added the melted chocolate.

"We don't want to stir this in, we need to fold it," I told him.

He looked puzzled. "Fold it?"

"When you stir something fast, what actually happens is that you're taking all the air out of the batter. That's what makes it smooth and dense. When you fold something, you're keeping the air in, which makes the batter fluffy and light. We don't want this batter to be smooth and dense or it won't bake right. We want it to be fluffy and light. So folding is really a fancy way of saying stirring really slowly and really carefully, from the bottom and over the top, like this." Damn if the kid wasn't hanging on my every word. I showed him how to fold and then let him do the rest. His concentration was so deep, I wondered if his face might turn red from the intensity. It took an effort on my part, but I forced myself not to chuckle at his determination.

He did a great job, I had to admit.

His next task was putting paper liners in the muffin tin and then I poured the batter and into the oven it all went.

"Now for the best part," I said and handed him a clean wooden spoon. "My grandma always said that my payment for being the assistant chef was that I got to lick the bowl."

Max's eyes lit up so brightly, I was surprised there wasn't light pouring out his ears. "I *like* your grandma."

That earned him a ruffle of the hair, then I set him up at the table with the spoon, the bowl (in which I'd left a bit of extra batter to make it worth his while), and a smile. I used heavy cream and chocolate chips to make the frosting while he licked happily, chocolate outlining his mouth as if he were a clown who'd used brown makeup for his smile instead of red.

There's nothing quite like the smell of warm chocolate and it only took about fifteen minutes for my kitchen to emanate the scent. Max was savoring every last drop of the batter, taking his time to make it last. When the knock on the door came, he hadn't budged from the table.

"Hi, there," Elena said with a smile. She wore black workout pants that reached just below her knees, a turquoise tank top, which gave me a mouthwatering view of her shoulders, and white Nikes with ankle socks. She was beautiful and I tried not to look at her chest, tried to forget that I'd had my hand in her bra the night before, tried to ignore how warm and perfect her flesh had felt cradled in my palm.

She squatted down to give Steve a scratch, then turned into the kitchen where her son was doing his best to cover himself in cake batter. She burst into laughter.

"We made cupcakes," he said proudly.

"Yeah? Did you get any batter in the cupcake pan or just all over your face?"

"Mom," he said, drawing the word out, its tone saying she was embarrassing him, and went back to the bowl.

I peered in. "Huh. That might be able to go right back into the cupboard. I might not even have to wash it."

Max giggled adorably and Elena took his hand to help him off the chair. "Come here, you. You're a mess. Let's wash your face and hands before you get chocolate all over Coach King's house."

I watched as Elena wet a paper towel and cleaned her son. I picked things up and moved them to the sink, trying hard not to inhale deeply whenever Elena's scent hit my nostrils. How could one woman smell so divine all the time?

Max took up residence at his usual spot: in front of the oven door, watching the cupcakes bake. Steve sat down next to him and they looked like a Norman Rockwell painting. I shook my head with a grin and turned to find Elena watching me.

"Three more minutes," I said, hoping my sudden nervousness didn't show in my voice, "and you can have a cupcake and some milk. If you've been a good girl." I winked.

"I'm really sorry about last night," she said, her voice barely audible. I got the clue that she didn't want to talk about it in front of Max (who was carrying on a conversation with Steve), and I felt a little hamstrung, not sure what was okay to say and what wasn't. I gave her an unconcerned grimace-shrug-dismissive wave combination, the universal sign for "it was no big deal."

I must not have been all that convincing to Elena, because she jumped in with, "We can talk about it later, if you want to, but I just wanted to say I'm sorry."

The timer saved me from having to come up with any kind of reply. I liked having something to do that kept me from squirming under Elena's gaze. In a couple minutes, I had all three of us set up at the kitchen table with deliciously warm cupcakes on plates, dripping melted frosting, and glasses of milk all around.

It was very domestic and I was shocked to realize how comfortable I was with the arrangement.

"Okay, buddy, time to go. Let's let Coach King have the rest of her Sunday in peace."

"Oh, wait," I said. Quickly, I slapped some frosting on six of the cupcakes and put them in a square Tupperware container that was deep enough to allow me to snap on the lid without smashing the contents. I handed the container to Max. "Remember? Assistant chefs share in the fruits of our labor."

"Did your grandma say that, too?" he asked, his face serious.

"She did." I walked them to the door. "See you later."

"See ya, Coach," Max said over his shoulder as he ran ahead down the sidewalk.

181

"Bye, Avery. See you soon." Elena's voice was low, almost intimate as she tossed me a little wave. "Max, you wait for me, please," she said, raising her voice to Stern Mom level.

"Bye," I said, and watched them go, trying to understand the swirling emotions in my head, while at the same time, trying to ignore them.

chapter eighteen

"I still can't believe you didn't tell me about her, that I'm just now hearing about all of this." Maddie could pout with the best of them and she seriously worked it that Friday night at dinner.

"All of what?" I'd talked quite a bit about Elena once Maddie prodded me. At the same time, I tried to downplay how taken I was with her but apparently, I hadn't done a very good job.

"You *like* this girl. It's obvious. Why didn't you tell me sooner? I don't understand, Avery." She pouted some more. "My feelings are hurt."

J.T. was in the kitchen doing the dishes. She could hear the conversation just fine and hadn't leapt to my defense, so I could only assume she was miffed at me, too.

I sighed, knowing she'd get it out of me sooner or later. "I was mad at you, Maddie. Did you forget that part? You crossed a line with me and I was angry with you."

Maddie's furrowed brow told me she wasn't quite following. I sipped my coffee and gave her time to catch up. When she did, it was glaringly apparent, her eyes widening in shocked realization, which quickly turned to smug delight. I sighed.

"You met her on Lesbian Link dot com, didn't you? Didn't you?"

"Yes. I did. Are you happy now?" I heard J.T.'s snort from behind me.

"When are you seeing her again?"

"I don't know yet."

She looked at me as if I had just sprouted a third eyeball in the middle of my forehead. "What do you mean, you don't know yet? Call her."

"I have. We've been playing phone tag."

It was the truth. The week had been near-chaotic for us both as far as work went. Josh and I were working like crazy to keep up with the promises Anita made to her biggest client, a large grocery store chain. Elena had been wooing not one, not two, but three potentially huge clients for her bank and by the time each of us got home, our brains were fried and we wanted nothing more than to fall into bed.

To sleep, unfortunately.

"She has to woo clients?" Maddie asked, sounding as surprised as I had been when I'd gotten Elena's message on Tuesday.

"Apparently."

"Huh. Who knew?"

I shrugged and sipped my coffee.

"Don't try being all nonchalant with me, young lady," she then said, slapping lightly at my arm. "You can't pull off nonchalant and you don't fool me."

"I'm not trying to fool you, Maddie. I'm just…a little confused."

"About what?" She turned serious, gave me her I-want-to-help face, which filled me with warm affection for her.

Putting my feelings for the situation with Elena into words was harder than I thought. The weird push/pull I felt from her was so new to me; besides that, it had only been a week or so. And then there was Max. I had no idea how I'd become so attached to him. I wished Josh were there with his magical ability to find just the right words for any occasion.

"You're right. I like her. I really like her. And I adore her son. I'm just not quite sure yet what she wants." I detailed my previous Saturday evening for Maddie, right down to me abruptly ending up outside the front door. "She apologized to me on Sunday, but frankly, my head was still spinning a bit from the sudden change in the weather, if you know what I mean."

Maddie appeared to choose her words carefully, which told me something wise was about to leave her lips, something I probably should have seen already. "Sweetie, she has a child."

"Yeah, and he's a great kid."

She tried unsuccessfully to hide her smirk. "You don't like kids."

"Well, I like *him*."

"And you know he's always going to come first for her, right? That's part of being a mother. And if Elena is smart, she probably doesn't introduce the people she dates to him right away."

"He already knows me."

"As his coach, not as his mother's girlfriend. From what you've told me, he's still dealing with the separation of his parents, and that's never easy on a kid. I'm sure Elena doesn't want to complicate it for him by bringing you into the picture."

She said it gently, I think so as not to make me feel stupid. She wasn't telling me anything I didn't already know, but actually hearing her say it out loud was kind of...weird. I'd never dated somebody with children before, so this was new to me, even if it was common sense.

"Yeah," I said again, but this time let it all sink in. With a resigned sigh, I said, "You're right."

"I think you just need to relax, sweetie. Don't sweat it, you know? Take your time with her. Date for a while and don't worry so much. Enjoy just being casual. I know I'm probably being a moron for trying to tell a lesbian to slow down in her pursuit of another woman, but you know what I mean. Just relax and take it one day at a time. It'll be easier on everybody involved."

Maddie's words twisted and rolled around in my head. The only solid fact I could come up with was that Elena and I had done much more groping at one another than we'd done talking. Not that we hadn't talked, because I really enjoyed our date at the bistro the previous Friday. But since then, my common sense had been blinded by my libido, and more than anything, I wanted to rip her suit off and have my way with her.

I needed to put that desire on a shelf for a bit, I decided. That'd be a good start. I was going to slow things down and get to know her, let her get to know me.

—

Tee-ball for little kids has the shortest season in the history of mankind, so our last game was the next morning. It was great, a lot of fun, and I was pretty sure the kids were going to miss it. I knew I was happy it was almost over, but I did think I'd miss it just a little bit. I decided not to tell Maddie.

School had ended the previous weekend and we were missing a couple of kids whose parents had planned vacations in advance, but for the most part we had a full team. And we won. Not that I was keeping score or anything.

I did scan the crowd once or twice, no sign of Elena. One of her messages during the week said she was going to try her best to catch the end of the game, but she had so much paperwork to catch up on the chances of her actually making it were slim. So while I was disappointed, I wasn't surprised. Cindy had dropped Max off earlier—just dropped him off; she didn't even get out of her car—and I assumed she was coming back to get him.

No sign of her, either.

Out of the corner of my eye, I caught Max also scanning the crowd, his face etched with disappointment. I had played softball in high school, and though I was sure Grandma came to every game she could manage, it wasn't many. She had a job and our games started right after school and most of the time it was just too hard for her to make it to the field in time. I knew this, but I scanned the bleachers at each and every game anyway. When I failed to pick her face out of the crowd, my disappointment was palpable and I imagined my expression was pretty close to the one on Max's face at that moment.

"Come on, buddy," I said to him, putting my arm around his small shoulders. "It's time for ice cream and pizza."

Maddie called it her tee-ball tradition. On the day of the last game, she sent J.T. off during the second-to-last inning to pick up the sheet pizza she'd preordered from Ziti's Pizza Emporium, along with the cooler of ice cream bars that Mr. Ziti himself always threw in on the house. Then she fed her team until they were stuffed to the gills, the whole time telling them how awesome they were and how much she would miss them. She really did have a way with them; they listened to her praise attentively even as they shoved pepperoni-dotted squares into their mouths. I faded in and out on her speech a little as I watched each kid, but then I tuned back in.

"...and I'd like to really, really thank Coach King for helping us out this year."

Shouts of agreement pierced the air as the kids cheered for me, clapping and laughing. I was horrified to feel my eyes well slightly. I nodded and smiled widely, not trusting myself to speak and thankful that the kids were too young to expect such a thing. I scanned from child to child, feeling an inexplicable fondness for them. Brittany Number One, Brittany Number Two, and Isabella were eating delicately and chattering like ladies who lunch. Gabriel, Max, and Mikey were reliving the last two innings, insanely proud of themselves. Katie and Jordan had a pile of dandelions on the bench next to their paper plates. Less than two months earlier, most of them hadn't even seen each other before and the majority of them hadn't the first clue how to play ball. I helped make them into a team and I had to admit there was something crazily satisfying about that fact.

One by one, parents packed up their kids and took them home. Soon all the pizza was gone, the equipment packed into J.T.'s truck, and only David, Mikey, and Max were left.

"You go on," I said to Maddie and J.T., knowing they had plans for the afternoon. "I can hang here until they're all gone."

"You're sure?" Maddie asked.

"Absolutely. Go. Have fun."

With a wave and thanks, they pulled out, leaving the four of us alone at the field. Then Mikey's mom came and left me, David, and Max. Then it was just me and Max.

"She said she'd be here," he said with a little-boy huff.

"Who?" I wanted to clarify so I knew with whom to be irritated. A glance at my watch told me it was after one. We'd made certain the parents knew the game would be finished by noon and we wanted an extra half hour to feed and congratulate the kids. By 12:30, every parent should have been there, every kid ready to go home.

"Cece." He sighed when he said her name, like he wasn't really surprised. "She dropped me off and said she'd be back before the game ended."

"How about we give her a call? See where she is?"

"Okay."

"Do you know her number?" I asked, pulling out my cell. Maddie had taken all the paperwork for the team, so I had no numbers available to me.

"Um…" He squinched up his face, his expression saying he was thinking really hard.

Nothing.

I knew I could easily drive him home with me, but I realized that might be construed as inappropriate. What if Cindy showed up after all and I've taken off with her kid? *She probably wouldn't even notice,* the devil on my shoulder sneered.

I did have Elena's number.

After an annoying internal debate, I punched the buttons and listened as the phone rang.

"Hey, you." She sounded happy to hear from me and I tried hard not to smile, lest Max wonder why I was grinning like a big dork while talking to his mommy.

"Hi there. Listen, I'm really sorry to bother you at work. Max is still here with me."

Elena's voice dropped to a low, nearly emotionless tone. "Has Cindy not picked him up yet?"

"That's right."

"Son of a bitch."

"It's okay. We're fine. I just thought you should know."

"I'll be right there. Thanks, Avery."

The line went dead before I could reply; I was sure she was fuming in her office, angry beyond belief at her ex and I didn't blame her one bit. I snapped my phone shut and looked at Max. "Mom's on her way."

For the next ten minutes, we sat in the bleachers. Max wasn't in a conversational mood and I sat quietly with him.

Elena pulled into the parking lot and practically exploded from her car. She stomped over to the bleachers, her face tinted a light pink.

Max stood and gathered his things, but wasn't looking at either of us.

Elena took a deep breath. I walked with them to her car. "Thank you, Avery." The sincerity in her voice was profound and I nodded.

"No problem. He's good company." I ruffled Max's hair. "Nice game today, buddy."

I'm not sure how long I stood there, watching the dust from their departure dissipate into the air. Longer than I should have. If I'd left sooner, I would have been gone before Cindy's Lexus pulled into the parking lot.

She eased up next to me and powered down her window. Dark sunglasses shaded her eyes, so I couldn't tell where she was looking, but I could feel it.

"You're an hour late," I snapped, not looking at her.

"I am?" She sounded honestly bewildered and I felt something inside me snap. I stopped and turned to face her.

"Doesn't it bother you at all that all the kids are gone? That your son is not here? Do you have even a clue where he is?"

One shoulder lifted. "I assume you called Elena and she came to get him. No big deal."

"Not to you, apparently," I scoffed and resumed my path toward my car.

"What's that supposed to mean?" she called after me.

"Really? You don't know what that's supposed to mean?" I whirled on her. "It means that maybe you should try paying as much attention to your little boy as you do to your Blackberry. I happen to think he deserves it, but you evidently disagree."

Her face hardened; I could tell that even without the benefit of seeing her eyes. She raised a hand and pointed a finger at me. "Don't you judge me," she said through clenched teeth. "You are in no position to judge me."

I stood staring at her as the tinted window hummed up and she peeled away, her tires throwing pieces of gravel. I thought about the countless times in my life when I'd tried in vain to understand why my mother didn't care enough to take an interest in my life.

"On the contrary," I muttered. "I'm in *exactly* the position to judge you."

chapter nineteen

"Oh, wow. I love this color." Elena ran a hand along the wall of my hallway leading into the living room as if hoping to take in the essence of the deep khaki. "It's so rich. It reminds me of chocolate milk."

Swollen pride is unbecoming, I know this, so I tried hard not to show how much her compliments meant to me. "Rich" was exactly the word that had come to mind when I decided on the wall color for my living space. At first I worried it might be too bold, too much of a statement, looked too much like dirt. But as soon as I finished rolling it onto one wall, I knew it was perfect. Add in my taupe couch and throw pillows in various earthy shades, and it ended up being a very warm, inviting room I was proud of.

"Thanks," I said. "I was happy with the way it turned out."

My smile was wide as I watched her slowly wander the room, running her hand over furniture, picking up framed photos to study. It was July fourth and Max was staying the weekend with Elena's parents, who were taking him to see some fireworks on one of the Finger Lakes. When Elena told me she was free, I jumped all over the chance to have some alone time with her, some time to talk and get to know her. Of course, my promise to keep my hands to myself for at least a few hours seemed like a distant memory as my eyes roamed over snug pair of denim shorts. Tearing myself from the view, I slid a bottle of wine from the rack tucked in the corner.

"Cabernet all right?" I asked.

"Perfect. Is this your grandmother?" She held up a silver-framed black and white photo of a sophisticated, poised young woman from the forties.

"Yep," I answered from the kitchen as I operated the corkscrew. "She was working her first clerical job then."

"Impressive." She replaced the frame and scanned others. "A woman before her time, you told me."

"I think my grandma invented that term." When I returned to the living room carrying two glasses of wine, she was running her fingers over another framed photo. This one was much smaller and I kept it tucked in the back of the others; I was surprised she'd found it.

"Is this you and your mom?" Her voice was quiet, as if she wasn't quite sure what my reaction would be.

I peeked around her shoulder, not needing to see the picture to know which one she held, but feeling the irresistible urge to peek anyway. "Yeah."

"My God, look how adorable you were."

I snorted, any anticipatory tension disappearing.

"No, really," she stressed, then made goo-goo sounds at the picture. "Look at those chubby little thighs and that red hair. I bet your mom wanted to eat you up."

"Yeah, well." I looked carefully at the young woman with the toddler, something I didn't allow myself to do often. She was quite pretty and she was actually smiling, the sun glinting on her light hair, her cheek pressed against mine. The scene seemed as close to happy as anything I could find or remember about the two of us since then. "I think..." I cleared my throat. "I think this was before she started feeling...I don't know...trapped? I was two here. She didn't leave for another two years."

Elena's long, thin fingers caressed the toddler's face. "I can't imagine how hard that must have been for you."

"I was young. I don't remember much."

Carefully, she set the photo back where she got it and turned to me. Taking a glass of wine from my hand, she asked gently, "Why do you do that?" There was no accusation in her voice, no irritation, just curiosity.

"Do what?" I knew exactly what she was asking, but I feigned confusion anyway. It was a defense mechanism for me, almost second nature. After nearly thirty years of habit, I didn't even think about it.

"Brush it off like it's no big deal." Her hand slid down my arm and she linked our fingers.

I shrugged.

We sat on the couch facing one another. "You don't have to pretend with me," she told me. "That's all I'm saying."

"I know," I said. And I did. But I felt an irresistible urge to change the subject, so I raised my glass. "Here's to an easier week than the past two have been."

"I'll drink to that."

We clinked and sipped. It was a holiday, but both of us had gone into work for a few hours. I could only speak for myself, but I figured if I got some things out of the way I could focus more on the time I had with Elena.

"Did you get things done today?" I asked Elena as we relaxed into the couch. "I thought bankers were supposed to have it easy...bankers' hours and all that."

She snorted. "I always laugh when I hear somebody talk about bankers' hours. They've obviously never spent a day in my shoes."

My arm was stretched across the back of the couch and I could touch her hair. The strands were soft and silky and I tried not to let that distract me. "So, what exactly are the duties of a bank manager?"

She squinted, obviously trying to find a good starting point. "A typical day could consist of off-site meetings that might be run by my manager or by other business partners like our business banking, investment and insurance division, or training department. Sometimes I have appointments with current business customers to help them maximize their relationships with us. That's a good way to get referrals to other business clients, by the way, so I try to schmooze a little bit, take them to lunch or whatever."

"I've always thought of a bank's customers as people like me."

"Unless you run a business, it probably wouldn't cross your mind."

"What else do you do?"

"If I'm in the branch, I might open accounts for new customers or field complaints from old ones."

"I've seen you handle those. Nicely done, by the way."

She seemed pleased as she went on. "I have administrative duties like coaching my staff, having one-on-one meetings, taking care of audit concerns, and introducing new products, services or promotions to them."

"And you've got to be the woman with the numbers."

"I have combinations, keys, and alarm codes," she confirmed with a nod.

"You rule."

"I do."

We grinned at one another, very comfortable in the silence. A zap hit me low in my abdomen when I realized that her eyes had settled on my mouth. Then, as if *she* were the one who'd been zapped, her gaze snapped up and she blurted, "Tell me about your job. What's it like to work for an advertising company?" She took my hand in her own, effectively untangling my fingers from her hair, and held onto it.

I poked the inside of my cheek with my tongue. Was it possible she was doing exactly what I was doing? Trying to keep things verbal rather than physical, at least for a little while? I didn't ask; I didn't want to embarrass her if I was wrong. Or if I was right. Instead, I sipped my wine and focused on answering her question.

"Well, first one of our account reps lands the client. For us, that's usually Anita. She, Josh, and I all work together. Anita handles the client, I do the logos and colors, Josh is the word man. So, Anita lands the client and then Josh and I will usually sit in on a meeting with them to see what it is they have in mind for their project or new product or company in general. After that, Anita, Josh, and I sit down together and brainstorm, based on what we all heard from the client. Josh and I usually try to come up with four or five different ideas to pitch to Anita, who usually whittles them down to two or three. Then she takes them back to the client."

"Is it hard?" Elena asked, tilting her head to the side. "To give a client what they want?"

"It can be. Totally. Especially if the client isn't sure what they want. Those are the toughest accounts. Or they know what they want, but they can't seem to verbalize it, so you give them what seems like a dozen different ideas and they tell you it's just not quite right. The color's off or the words sound funny or whatever. Ugh. Makes you want to scream. Luckily, it doesn't happen often. The three of us make a good team and usually at least one of us can find whatever wavelength the client happens to be on."

"That has to make you feel good. When you and your client are on the same page."

"It does make me feel good. So does being with you."

Her burst of laughter surprised me, but she quickly tried to cover and tightened her grip on my hand as I reflexively tried to pull it away. "I'm sorry. I'm sorry. I promise I'm not laughing at you; I'm laughing at the look you just got on your face."

"What look?"

"The one that said, 'Oh, my God, did I just say that out loud?'"

Heat flamed my cheeks, but I couldn't hide a grin because she was absolutely right. I'd been thinking how good it was to just be near her and the next thing I knew, the words had flown from my mouth likes rocks from a slingshot. "Oh, crap."

Elena tried to hold my gaze, but I was too self-conscious and looked down at my lap, feeling more exposed than I was comfortable with. Her fingertips under my chin brought my eyes back up to hers. Her voice was just above a whisper.

"Please don't be embarrassed, Avery. Being with you feels good to me, too."

"Yeah?"

"Definitely." She paused and wet her lips with the tip of her tongue. "Do you think we've done enough talking now?"

"Definitely."

It was so easy to become lost in her kiss. My brain couldn't decide what to focus on: the unbelievable softness of her lips, the hint of wine on her tongue, the gentle yet possessive way she cradled my jaw in her hand, or the alarmingly hot wave of excitement that washed over me. All of that was overshadowed suddenly by her other hand as it slid into the hair at the nape of my neck, gripping my head and pulling me closer.

More. It's all I could think as I tasted her mouth, felt her tongue, pushed my own against it. *I want more. And more. And more.*

It wasn't clear to me how long we kissed before we were startled apart by Steve as he jumped at the sliding glass door, wanting out. I glared at him as my chest heaved.

"Jesus, Steve. Timing, buddy. Timing is everything and yours just sucks." I turned to Elena, who was breathing just as heavily as I was, and who had hooded eyes and swollen lips, and it was all I could do not to dive at her and rip all her clothes off. I gestured to Steve with a cock of my head. "Let me just…put him out. Then he'll be set for the night."

"Okay. Good. I was just going to ask you anyway if you have a bed."

I opened the door for Steve and I'm sure my grin was lopsided as I replied, "Why, yes. I do have a bed. Why do you ask? Would you like to see it?"

Her stare was so concentrated and passionate, I was surprised I didn't burst into flames right then and there, leaving a big scorch mark on my carpet.

"Actually, I'd like to get in it," she told me. "Naked. With you. As soon as possible."

I was unable to reply to that, as my heart leapt into my throat and every drop of moisture in my body shot straight to the crotch of my panties. I let Steve back in without looking at him, shut the door and locked it, crossed the room to grab Elena by the hand, and tugged her up the stairs behind me.

It wasn't quite a full moon, but the night sky was clear and the moonlight cast a sexy, cool blue tint through my bedroom window. I left the blinds up and the lights off and turned all my attention to the beautiful woman next to me.

My fingers had the hem of Elena's cotton T-shirt and had pulled it up and over her head before I even realized what I was doing. Mentally vowing to slow down and enjoy the whole process of undressing her, I tossed the shirt to the floor. She bent forward to kiss me, but I held her back, my hand pressed to her sternum.

"Wait," I breathed.

She stood still and allowed me to unfasten the fly on her shorts, let me push them down her legs. She stepped out of them and paused, letting me set the pace. I took a step back from her.

"I just...just let me look at you."

Breathtaking didn't begin to describe her, and I hoped I wasn't drooling all over myself as I took her in. Surprisingly, the simple white bra and pink and white striped panties only added to her casual sexiness, and even in the dim light, I was awed by her. I roamed her body with my eyes, wondering if she could feel it, feel how much I wanted her. I took in every inch of her, from her bashfully smiling face down the long column of her neck to her freckled shoulders, lingering on her modest breasts and anticipating what they'd taste like, the color of her nipples and their hardness against my tongue. I knew I'd be dipping into that belly button as I held onto the slight roundness of her hips and I had every intention of going lower, wanting to feel those long, sexy legs draped along my back as I buried my head between her thighs.

It was hard to tell in the faint light, but I thought a tremble rippled through her.

"Avery." Her voice caught, not much more than a murmur. The sound of my name was like a caress, and I swallowed hard. Stepping closer, I used one finger and placed it against her lips. She kissed it sweetly and her eyes never left mine as I dragged it over her chin, down her throat, between her breasts, along her tummy, and over the front of her panties. Her gasp was very slight, but sexy as hell, and I could tell she was trying hard to keep control of herself. I retraced my path back up.

"You are the most beautiful thing I have ever seen," I said quietly, and I'd never meant anything more in my life.

I couldn't keep my mouth to myself any longer. I pulled her head down to mine and I kissed her then. Hard. With purpose and intention, conveying with my lips and tongue and teeth exactly what I wanted to do with her. What I wanted to do *to* her. For hours.

Two steps backwards, her legs hit my mattress and she was down, on her back with me crawling up her body, my destination being that sweet, hot, wet mouth of hers. Despite my intention of slowing things down, they seemed to speed up instead. I barely remember scrambling out of my own clothes, though the excited gasp that escaped me as I removed Elena's bra is burned into my memory. The warmth, the smoothness, the taste of her skin is magnificently clear to me. She dug her fingers into my hair as I moved along her body, sampling every inch of her with my mouth, dipping my tongue into her navel and moving slowly lower. She was tall, but rather slight in build, and my smaller hands fit to her like a sculptor to clay, as if I wasn't only touching her, but molding her, pressing and sliding my fingers and palms along her bronzed skin, stroking her as I would a piece of art, gently, reverently, and with immense awe.

The first touch of my tongue to her center sent her hips up off the bed, a quiet, strangled cry emanating from her throat. It was nearly the end for me as I felt her heel press into the small of my back and the fingers of one hand fist in my hair to direct me, to pull me in more snugly. She was sweet and tangy and salty and I seemed to know just what to do, how much or how little pressure to give her, when to slow down or to speed up. It was as though I'd been making love to her for years and I was stunned by our compatibility. I shifted slightly so I could reach up and cup her breast without taking my mouth from her. I rolled her hardened nipple between my fingers and she stifled a groan, whispered my name, pushed herself harder against my tongue. And then she tipped over the edge.

She made very little sound as she came, but every muscle in her body spasmed and I half-expected to be missing a chunk of hair when she finished, though I didn't mind; the pressure was delicious. Tightly grasping her hips, I stayed with her, stayed pressed to her hot, wet flesh, until her climax subsided and she gently tugged my head back from her.

Ragged breathing was the only sound for several minutes and it filled the room. I lay with my head on Elena's stomach, her fingers twisting my hair softly as we recovered. Heat radiated from both our bodies and the musky scent of sex permeated the air.

"Wow," she finally said.

I grinned against her skin. "I'll say."

"That was absolutely amazing, Avery. Good God."

I turned my head so I could look at her face. "You have the quietest orgasm I've ever heard," I said with a chuckle.

She laughed. "I have a child. That's a sound he doesn't need to be woken up by. Ever. Believe me, I know." The grimace that followed told me she'd heard more than necessary when it came to the sex life of her parents and I laughed with her.

I propped myself on an elbow and gazed at her skin as my fingers played across it. I traced the fine, barely visible scar that cut across her abdomen and through her pubic hair. "Max was a C-section?"

"Poor little guy was all wrapped up in his umbilical cord. He almost strangled himself."

"Were you scared?"

"Terrified. Here I'd done everything necessary to prepare. I'd gone to Lamaze classes, read every book I could get my hands on, I was all ready to take on natural childbirth. I was in the hospital all of an hour when my ob/gyn realized she had to go in and get him. I knew nothing about C-sections. Not a thing."

"Yikes."

203

"It was a pretty stressful ordeal." She stroked my hair back off my forehead. "Luckily, everything came out fine."

I nodded, still enamored with the lightly pinkened flesh, still running my fingertip over it and absently wondering if the doctor had even a moment of regret before taking a scalpel to such perfect skin.

"Hey, come here." She tugged gently at my hair. When I was face to face with her, she whispered, "Enough talk. We're not finished. Kiss me."

Never one to disobey a direct order from a beautiful woman, I did as I was told. In a matter of a few mere seconds, I was on my back, Elena was stretched out above me, and her fingers were everywhere. It was a blur of sensual pleasure, nothing solid, just waves of pure bliss as she ignited my skin with her mouth and her tongue and her hands. When her fingers pushed into me, hard and knowing, I had no reservations about noise and I cried out her name, grasping blindly for my headboard, needing something concrete to hold onto, to ground me. She pulled out slowly, thrust back in with determination, and I heard a rumble in the distance, followed by colors behind my closed eyelids. I lifted my head and realized with disbelief that the local Independence Day fireworks display had begun, viewable out my bedroom window over the trees, as they are every year.

Elena glanced over her shoulder as the next burst hit, filling the room with green light. I could see a wickedly amused smile spread across her face as she turned back to me.

"Well, isn't that apropos," she stated, then refocused her attention on my body. My head slammed back onto my pillow as her hand resumed its movements and her mouth fastened onto my breast, the hot, wet suction sending me into oblivion in a few short, heavenly moments.

There were actual honest-to-God fireworks as I came.

We lay in the aftermath of our lovemaking, in the aftermath of the fireworks, in the aftermath of the feelings racing through my bloodstream. Catching our breath, we were quiet and not uncomfortable. My head rested in the crook of Elena's neck, the sound of her heartbeat a muffled thump-thump beneath my ear. She drew lazy circles with her fingertips on my shoulder and I did the same thing on her belly. We weren't done. We were far from done. I could feel it. My body still thrummed with the excitement of being so close to her skin and I could almost hear her soaking up the energy for another go around.

I couldn't remember the last time I wanted somebody so badly. Or so constantly.

"Why are you single?" she asked suddenly, softly.

"I'm sorry?" Her question took me by surprise.

"I'm just wondering why a successful, intelligent, sexy woman like you hasn't been snapped up. I mean, look at you. What the hell is wrong with the last person you were with? Is she blind? An idiot?"

"I could ask the same questions about you," I pointed out, flattered beyond belief.

I felt Elena give a little shake of her head. "No. You already know my story. My ex *is* an idiot. Tell me about yours."

"Lauren."

"Lauren." Elena seemed to try the name on for size. "What's wrong with her?"

For some reason, I thought about the idea of karma and decided I should be nice. After all, our problems weren't all Lauren's; I was equally, if not more so, to blame. "I wasn't in love with her."

It was a simple statement, not a lie. It was almost all of the truth.

"Ah."

"I thought I was at first. And when I realized I wasn't, I tried hard to be. She's a sweet girl. She's really very nice."

"So you broke her heart." She didn't accuse, just stated a fact.

I sighed. "Yes, I did. It was pretty awful for a while, but she deserved better."

"Has she found it?"

"Not yet. I don't think. We still talk on occasion. She calls once in a while to say hi. She's really—"

"Very nice," Elena finished for me, a grin in her voice.

"She is," I replied, feeling just a touch defensive, but playfully so. I lifted my head and looked into her eyes. It was dark and late and I couldn't see much detail, but I held her gaze for a long moment and she didn't look away.

"I don't do this kind of thing with just anybody, Avery," Elena whispered, the sound sending a pleasant shiver tingling across my skin.

"Do what kind of thing?" I propped my head on my hand, my elbow next to her ear, and studied her face in the dark, ran my fingers lightly across her throat.

"Fall into bed after two dates. Have an inability to carry on a conversation without thinking about..." She trailed off.

"Sex?" I finished for her teasingly.

"Yes. Sex." She looked away then, fiddled with the edge of the sheet, and her voice became even softer. "I don't have casual sex, Avery. That's what I'm trying to tell you."

She swallowed audibly and turned back to meet my eyes. "It means something to me."

The warmth that spread through me then was like a pleasant version of a hot flash. My blood warmed, my skin flushed, and I felt almost high with giddiness. I wanted to jump up and do a little Snoopy dance around my bedroom, but I somehow managed to leash my inner geek and stay calm. Instead, I smiled down at her, let my fingers play over her lips, so soft to the touch.

"It means something to me, too."

And this time when I kissed her, when she kissed me, it was different. It was deeper, both physically and emotionally. We took our time, explored and looked into one another's eyes. I wanted to touch every single part of her body. I wanted her to feel me everywhere. We melded and sweat and pushed and stroked and groaned and filled each other. And hovering in the room with us, hanging in the air like a mist, was the unmistakable promise of a possible future. This time when I pushed Elena to her limit and then nudged her off the precipice, when she said my name on a guttural moan, I closed my eyes in bliss and felt tears stinging behind my eyelids. Her ragged voice, her hands in my hair, her body arching into mine, it filled me up, made me feel whole, made me feel invincible.

Hours later, we rested, drifting in and out of sleep as dawn broke over the horizon out my window. I lay in bed on my side, Elena's warm body curled behind and around me, spooning me so perfectly it was almost surreal. Her leg was tucked snugly between my thighs, pressed up into my own wet heat that I now worried might be never-ending. Her arm wrapped around me, under my own arm and against my chest where I clasped it with my hand, brought it to my lips and kissed the knuckles softly. I could hear and feel her gentle, even breathing near my ear, and smell the scent of arousal and foreplay and raw, primal sex that hung suspended in the air, wafting like remnants of a dream. I breathed it, took it into my lungs, into my body, until I could not only smell it, but taste it. Feel it. And I knew. Beyond a shadow of a doubt, I knew.

It meant something.

chapter twenty

Grandma looked tired, but happy to see me. I tsked at the dark circles her eyes.

"Aren't you sleeping well?" I asked as I unwrapped the banana bread I'd baked the night before.

She waved a wrinkled hand dismissively as she put the kettle on for our tea. "I've had a bad couple of nights," she said, clearly trying to allay any worry I might have. "It happens. I'm fine."

"Well you look exhausted. Don't you have an appointment with Dr. Garber coming up soon?" I seemed to recall her saying something to that effect not long ago, but I wasn't sure. I suggested to her once that she let me keep a copy of her schedule, things like doctors' appointments, dentist appointments, hair appointments, so that I could help her with transportation, but she would have none of it. She didn't want to "burden" me, she'd said, with driving her all over the city. I was also sure part of it was stubborn pride. She'd stopped driving three years earlier when her eyes were giving her trouble, but she was always able to find somebody in her complex to get her where she needed to go. No matter how much I argued that she was no bother at all, she only used me for a ride as an absolute last resort. She hated "interfering" in my life.

"I went last week. She said I'm fine, just getting old."

I snorted. "She did not say you're just getting old."

"That's what she meant."

"Grandma..." The expression on her face told me to let it go, so I did. I may have been thirty-four years old, but my grandmother could still shoot me a look that made me feel eight again.

Once we settled at her small table, she seemed to cheer up a bit.

"Grandma," I said quietly. "I met someone."

Grandma studied my face. "You met someone," she repeated, not quite following.

"Uh-huh. The mother of one of my tee-ball kids."

"Oh, you *met* someone." She studied me with those green eyes and I squirmed, as I always did when I felt like she could see right into my head. "So, tell me about her."

"Well, we've only been dating for a short time," I began.

It might seem weird that I would talk to my eighty-five year old grandmother about my love life, but she was all I had in the world and I'd always wanted to be completely open with her, even when that maybe wasn't the best course of action. I'd hesitated coming out to her when I was twenty, but my first girlfriend had broken my heart and I was a physical and emotional wreck; I wanted the loving arms of my grandmother, the only mother I'd ever known. My lesbianism wasn't something she took to immediately and we rarely talked in-depth about the subject of homosexuality. I think it was just something that was taboo to her when she was young, but she did her best to try and understand. I wouldn't say she'd been supportive, but she never made me feel...abnormal or like a disappointment to her. We simply didn't talk about it. It was a fact, but we didn't discuss it much, so to have her asking about Elena in detail was somewhat surprising for me. "She's absolutely beautiful. Her mother's Greek."

In Upstate New York, in Rochester specifically, ethnicity is a very important part of people's background. Italian, Greek, Jewish, whatever, they're part of a person's identity. Everybody knows their heritage. Both Grandma's and Grandpa King's ancestors were from across the Atlantic, Grandma being Irish and Grandpa being Scottish, I was taught this at a very young age. So telling Grandma that Elena was half Greek was not just a way of describing her physical appearance, but of telling a bit about her upbringing, the morals and values of her family, or at least of her mother.

"Greek, huh? What does she do?"

"She's the branch manager of the bank over by that new office building near Church Street."

"And you've been…seeing this girl?"

I smothered a smile at her carefully chosen words. It was important to her that she didn't seem like a relic, that she seemed almost hip, using the correct phrases and such.

"I have."

"How long?"

"Not long. A couple weeks. We're both really busy, so we haven't had a lot of time to spend together. But we've managed."

"I can tell by your face that you like her."

"I do." I studied my tea, still unnerved after so many years that Grandma could read me so well. "I like her a lot."

Grandma nodded slowly. "And she has a child?"

"Yes. A son. Max. He's a great kid. He helps me bake."

She chewed some banana bread thoughtfully. "And you're okay with that."

My eyebrows dipped to just above my nose; I could feel them. "Okay with him helping me bake? Sure."

"No, Avery, okay with the fact that this woman you like so much has a son."

I shifted in my chair. I couldn't help it. I was feeling eight again, with her eyes boring into me like she could see every thought in my head. "Why is everybody so concerned about her having a kid? First Maddie and now you." I sounded more defensive than I'd meant to, something that irked me.

Grandma raised one eyebrow. It was a very clear variation on a line that went something like, *We know you better than you know yourself, so stop playing dumb with us.* "I can't speak for Maddie, of course, but it was less than two months ago that you sat at this very table and told me how much you didn't like kids, how bad you are with them, how much you were dreading coaching that team."

I scratched at a spot on my neck and looked off into the living room, unable to meet her eyes. "I know."

"Coaching a team of kids and helping to raise a kid are two very different things."

"I didn't say I was going to marry her, Grandma." I tried to make light of things and shot her a goofy grin, but as usual, Grandma could see right through me. She didn't say it, but I could tell she was just humoring me.

"All right, Avery. If you say so. I just wanted to make sure you're aware, that's all."

"I'm aware," I said, relieved but somehow not. "Believe me, I'm aware."

"Good. Now, when do I get to meet this…what's her name?"

"Elena."

"Oh, that's pretty. When do I get to meet this Elena?"

I smiled and cocked my head slightly, surprised. She'd never asked to meet one of my girlfriends. I'd always brought it up because I knew the whole idea of my sexuality made her uncomfortable. "You want to meet her?"

"You like her." It's all she said, but it was the second time she'd said it and it spoke volumes. Grandma *did* know me better than I knew myself.

"I'll find out what her schedule's like and we'll set a date, okay?"

"Let me know. I'll cook a pot roast."

⁓

Dating somebody with a child was damn hard. Or harder than I was used to anyway. I tried to be cognizant of the fact that I probably shouldn't just go walking down the street and knock on her door every evening.

Which is exactly what I wanted to do.

All the time.

We settled for the telephone after Max went to bed, and once in a while she'd catch me online at home while I was working on whatever project was up next at the office. Work would always go by the wayside then and I'd end up chatting with her until it was way past my bedtime. She was as witty and fun online as she was in person. She was also damn sexy. More than once I ended up breathless, sweating as I sat in my desk chair with my hand in my own pants like some porn-addicted male. Luckily, it was more exhilarating than embarrassing.

It was new for me to be dating somebody that I couldn't spend time with every day...or at least every other day. I am, after all, a lesbian and that's what we do. We move right in, figuratively and literally. I wanted to be with Elena all the time, but I stepped carefully because of Max. I had to let her set the pace and it was a little maddening at times. Our work schedules, plus Max, didn't allow time for us during the week after the Fourth. That Friday, she and Max headed to Niagara Falls for four days with the family of one of her brothers. It was a trip they'd planned the previous winter and I could tell she was looking forward to it. I was gracious and understanding and told her to be careful, have a good time, and call when she got a chance.

Steve and I spent that weekend taking a couple of hikes and watching a few movies on cable with me trying not to think about how much I missed Elena, how it had been over a week since I'd seen her, and how badly I wanted to be in Niagara Falls with them.

I was in my office just after lunch on Tuesday when my computer beeped for an incoming e-mail. I could feel the grin split my face as I read:

Hey, Gorgeous –

We're back, safe and sound from Canada. I just wanted to let you know and I figured if I did it this way rather than calling you, I could be a good girl and unpack, get some laundry done, and catch up on my work messages. I know if I use the telephone, we'll end up talking for hours. Not that you're not

preferable to laundry, but I really need to get it done. You know
what I mean. I'll call you tonight and we'll catch up, okay?
    Hope you're having a good day at work.
    Elena
    PS: I missed you.

I, of course, could focus on nothing other than the fact
that she'd called me gorgeous and the postscript. It had
been nearly a week and a half since I'd last seen her. Since
I'd last touched her. Images bombarded me, images of her
naked body beneath me, her naked body on top of me, the
feel of her lips, her hands, the sound of her near-silent
climax. I couldn't shake free. I felt like a drug addict going
through withdrawals.

Later that evening, I was tucked neatly in my kitchen,
an unseasonably balmy breeze blowing in from my open
windows. July can be very hot and very humid in
Rochester, but that evening was almost cool and the gentle
wind made the wind chimes hanging near my patio tinkle
prettily.

The knock on the front door startled me, and Steve,
too, apparently, as he sprang up and whacked his head on a
chair leg. His bark was quick, a staccato stab in the quiet
air and it made me jump.

"Shh," I told him as I went to the foyer. "Relax,
buddy."

I turned the knob and Elena burst through the door
like a gust of wind. She used me to close it, turning me by
my shoulders so my back was flat against the wood.

"I only have a couple minutes," she said breathlessly,
her face only inches from mine. "My dad's fixing the
kitchen drain and he's letting Max help him and they both

215

have their heads under the sink, so I snuck out because I just couldn't wait any longer to see you." She took a breath and smiled at me. "Hi."

"Hi," I said, equally breathless. My head was spinning.

"God, I missed you." My head thumped against the door as she crushed her mouth to mine, no preamble, no gentleness or lead-in. Just a full, deep, and thorough plundering of my mouth with her tongue, her hands gripping the sides of my head, and oh, my God, I was in absolute heaven. I kissed her back, pushing against her, then pulling her closer, the only sounds in my foyer being our heavy breathing and the soft smacking of our lips.

Stopping for air, she rested her forehead against mine.

"So," I panted. "You're home, huh?"

"I am, but I've got to get back before the boys notice I'm missing." Pulling back so she could see my face, she asked, "What are you doing on Saturday?"

"Nothing," I answered, too fast, then nearly rolled my eyes at myself. "Wow, how about that for playing hard to get?"

She grinned. "My parents are having a cook-out. I want you to come with me and Max."

I blinked at her. Meet her family? Wasn't that a big step? "You do?"

"Yeah. My brother says I talk about you too much and I'd better bring you home soon so they can all meet you. You up for it?" I thought I sensed the slightest bit of anxiety on her face. Did she really think I'd say no? "Max will stay at my parents' that night, so we'll have some time just the two of us later."

"Are you enticing me with the promise of sex?"

"Damn right, I am. What do you think? Will you come with us?"

"Only if you'll come to my grandmother's with me for pot roast on Sunday."

We stood looking at each other. Neither of us said it in so many words, but this was a big moment. This was the two of us telling one another that we thought we had a future together, that we wanted a future together. It was exhilarating and exciting and frightening and I could feel my palms begin to sweat.

"Deal," she said and we both breathed sighs of relief.

"What about Max?" I didn't know how to ask if he knew his mother was not only dating somebody who *wasn't* his Cece, but somebody who *was* his tee-ball coach, or even how much he understood about what "dating" actually meant.

"We've been talking. A lot," she said. "And we'll talk some more." I must have grimaced or something because she caressed my eyebrow with her thumb as if trying to smooth away any apprehension I might have. "Don't worry," she whispered. "It'll be fine. I've got to get back." She kissed me sweetly once more and was out into the night before my head had stopped whirling. "You look fabulous, by the way," she tossed over her shoulder as she scooted quickly down the sidewalk. "I'll call you later."

Only then did I have a chance to even look at her body, to appreciate the sway of her hips and the way the calf-length yoga pants hugged her ass like a lover's hands. The breeze rustled her hair and I realized I could still smell her coconut shampoo as it hung in the air of the foyer.

As if she knew I was watching, she turned back when she got to her own sidewalk and gave me a little wave, then disappeared into her house six doors down.

I closed my door and leaned back against it with an enormously satisfied sigh, thinking I'd just been hit by Hurricane Elena. Bringing my fingers to my lips, I touched them, closed my eyes, and could almost feel her mouth on mine. I could still taste her, a little sweet, a little salty.

I was in love.

chapter twenty-one

Having grown up in a very quiet, sparsely populated household with one television set, my favorite escape had been to find a peaceful corner and read a book. So it was pretty easy to see how Elena's family might overwhelm me.

There seemed to be dozens of them—though in reality there were probably only ten or so—and they all talked at the same time. I was reasonably sure that nobody was actually listening to what anybody else was saying. After the initial onslaught, though, I found it sort of amusing and sat back to observe.

The day was sunny and hot, a typical July afternoon in Upstate New York. I sat at a picnic table in the shade next to Elena's sister-in-law Carrie, and watched the four kids run around the yard as I sipped iced tea. Carrie and Elena's mother—whose name was Maria—were discussing fresh herbs versus dried ones. I got the impression Carrie was new at cooking and was picking Maria's brain for all the information she could get.

"What about you, Avery?" Maria asked, catching me off-guard. "Do you cook?"

"I bake."

"Yeah? What do you bake?"

I gave a half-shrug. "Mostly cookies. Cakes. Nothing fancy."

"Don't listen to her, Mama." The bench sank slightly as Elena took a seat next to me. The warmth of her hand radiated through the skin of my knee and I smothered a grin of delight. "She makes incredible cookies. Incredible. Ask Max."

Maria nodded. "Well, Max *is* a world renowned cookie expert. Do you have children?"

"I don't. I have a dog." I wondered how much Elena was catching, sitting right next to me, but chatting with her sister-in-law. It was clear to me that Maria was feeling me out, possibly trying to decide if I warranted her approval as an acceptable match for her only daughter.

"Dogs are wonderful, but not quite the same as having kids."

Duh. "No. No, they're definitely not the same."

"Do you want to have children of your own?" she asked, and I almost choked on my sip of iced tea.

"It's never really come up." Even I was shocked by how easily the fib slipped from my lips.

"Mama, will you stop interrogating her please?" Elena's voice was soft and gentle, but had a firmness to it. So she *had* been listening.

"What? I'm not interrogating her, we're just talking." Maria pouted and I saw a quick flash of Max that made me smile. "Right, Avery?"

"Mama," Elena warned her mother before I could answer.

Maria snorted and waved a hand dismissively at her daughter. I got the distinct impression they bickered like this often, it was part of their life and hard feelings were rarely, if ever, present. Elena went back to her conversation with Carrie, but squeezed my knee, then stroked the back of it with her fingertips. The jolt that was sent straight to my groin surprised even me. I cleared my throat and took a large slug of my iced tea. I was pretty sure there was a subtle, satisfied smirk on Elena's face as she listened to Carrie talking about her hair stylist.

Despite the noise and endless activity, I liked Elena's family a lot. Her parents seemed to be sweet, genuine people who welcomed me into their midst. Her father, Ed, was quiet compared to the rest of the gang and stayed rooted to his spot at the grill most of the day, though he shook my hand with sincere pleasure to "finally" meet me. I threw Elena a look that said, *"Finally?"*, but she pretended not to see it. Her brothers teased her mercilessly, but I also got the impression they were extremely protective of her. Her older brother Jason corralled me into a seemingly endless conversation about my job and though he didn't come right out and ask me, I was pretty sure he wanted to find out if I made a respectable salary. But he was nice and funny and I didn't mind spending the time bantering with him.

The other thing that was endless was the food. Along with constant cookies and chips and various nibbles, there was the cookout itself. An interesting mix of traditional American summer barbecue fare like hot dogs, hamburgers, and potato salad, and some Greek dishes, such as a feta-and-spinach couscous, bite-sized *spanikopita*, and the sticky, sweet, crazy delicious baklava Maria made from scratch. I tried hard not to make a pig of myself, but it was heavenly and after my second piece of dessert, I made her promise to one day teach me how to properly construct it, having never been able to get it right on my own.

221

We finally left Max around nine o'clock and he hardly noticed. Two of his cousins were also staying overnight at Ed and Maria's, so he was much more interested in catching fireflies than coming home with his mother.

Once shut safely in Elena's car, we both heaved big sighs of relief, then burst into laughter.

"Holy crap," I said.

"It wasn't so bad, was it?"

"Is your family ever quiet?"

She made a thinking face and pursed her lips. "Um… no." She started the car and pulled out onto the street, heading us in the direction of home. "Really, though, was it bad?"

The authenticity of her worry was adorable and I patted her bare leg. "No, sweetie, I had a great time. I like your family a lot."

"Oh, good." She seemed genuinely comforted by my reassurance.

"There was one thing that was bad, though."

"There was? What?"

"You." I slid my hand slowly up her thigh, happily watching her throat move as she swallowed. I'd been dying to touch her for the past several hours—since she'd begun her teasing of me, which she'd continued throughout the day—and I couldn't wait any longer.

"Me?"

"Yes. You." I shifted so I was close enough to speak in her ear as she drove. I kept my voice low, a little sexy. "What were you trying to do to me, pawing at me under the table with your mother right there? Give me a heart attack? Make me slide off the picnic bench? Hmm?" I pushed my hand between her legs, roughly clamping against her, feeling the heat radiating from her center right through her shorts. "You'd better get us home quickly or I'm going to have my way with you right here in this car while you're driving." I punctuated my threat with a quick flick of my tongue against her earlobe.

"Jesus Christ," she said with a hiss and pushed down on the gas pedal a little harder. "I hope I don't drive us off a cliff."

"So do I. It would be a shame for you to die before I can finish what I've started."

We got back to my place in record time and I have no idea how because I was too busy sucking on Elena's neck to keep track of our progress. She'd barely shifted the car into park before I was around to her side and pulling her out. The leftovers her mother had sent home with us would just have to wait; I dragged her up the walk, fumbling with my keys.

Once inside, I gestured up the stairs with my chin.

"Go. Now. I'll let Steve out and be right up." Her face was flushed as she nodded, but no sooner had she reached for the banister, than I said, "Wait." Grabbing her face with both hands, I kissed her. Hard, deep, and with purpose. Then, forcibly pulling away, I said, "Okay. Go. I'll be right up."

Elena seemed to sway on her feet slightly before turning and heading upstairs. I felt a twinge of satisfaction in knowing I could undo her the same way she undid me.

A little surge of guilt hit me for not giving Steve a little more attention, but I had pressing matters awaiting me in my bedroom and I promised him I'd make it up to him as I grabbed a couple treats from his jar and lured him upstairs with them, depositing them on his dog bed in the corner of the room.

There's something indescribably breathtaking about having a beautiful woman naked in your bed, waiting for you. I stood at the foot, just looking at her and wondering how the hell I got so lucky. The yellow of the comforter and the sage green sheets were the perfect complement to her skin tone and dark hair. Her cheeks were still flushed and she gripped the sheet in her fingers, her deep plum nail polish matching the bedding nicely.

"My God, you're sexy," I breathed.

Her expression shifted, telling me she'd liked the comment. "Get over here."

"Bossy little thing, aren't you?" I peeled my clothes off, my eyes never leaving hers.

"You ain't seen nothing yet."

Our lovemaking that night was every bit as intense as it had been the first time, but it was also something else, something different. Something more. We caressed and teased and groaned and arched, sweat-slicked skin against sweat-slicked skin. We battled for the position of top, making a mess of the bedding, Elena winning out most of the time (not that I minded having that beautiful body above me). I tried hard to focus, to be sure every detail… each smell and taste and sound…was burned into my memory, for I knew—*I knew*—this was a turning point in my life. I don't know how and it's kind of a corny thing to say, but I felt a shift in my world that night.

Elena on top was a sight to behold. Holy good God. Her body was stunning as she straddled me, sleek and lean, her breasts small, her hips rounded. I grasped her waist, slid my hands down to her thighs, and as she straightened up, basically sitting above me, I couldn't help thinking how utterly, gloriously female she was. It took my breath away —or so I thought until I dipped my hand between her legs and she arched with a groan, tossing her head back—and the rest of the air left my lungs.

Knowing I'd created the wet heat around my fingers spurred me on and I picked up the pace, reaching for her breast with my other hand, kneading it as I bent my own legs and braced her back with my knees. She fell forward, catching herself on her hands so she was on all fours over me, and still I kept my rhythm. Our faces were only inches apart, as she turned her head slightly and sucked in a breath through her teeth, telling me how close she was.

"Come on," I coaxed her. "Come on, sweetheart. I've got you." She rocked against my hand and I could hear her fingers digging into the pillow on either side of my head.

"Yes..." she said, her voice barely above a whisper. "Oh...Avery..."

"That's it. Come on. Let it go. I've got you..."

Her teeth clacked together audibly and her entire body seemed to tighten. The orgasm tore a groan from her throat as I pulled her down on top of me and slid my fingers inside her, gasping with joy at the feel of her muscles convulsing around me. She buried her head in the crook of my neck.

"God, I love you," she ground out as the last contraction hit and left her as wrung out as a wet towel.

It didn't surprise me; I'm not sure why. I think I'd felt it coming. I know I was feeling the same way. So I replied simply, "I love you, too, baby," and pressed a kiss to her temple. Straightforward. Effortless. Uncomplicated. I have no idea how, but there it was.

We straightened our legs out at the same time, dropping them flatly to the mattress like weights, and we chuckled as we lay in a panting heap for several long moments.

Elena pushed herself up on an elbow so she could look me in the eyes. Despite the darkness of the room, I could see the strength of the gaze.

"I do love you," she said quietly.

"I know." I kissed the tip of her nose. "And I do love you, too."

"Do we need to talk about…you know…exclusivity?"

I cocked my head a bit. "What do you mean? Like me not seeing anybody else and you not seeing anybody else?"

"Exactly. I know it's kind of fast, but…" Her eyes darted away as her voice trailed off and it occurred to me that she was embarrassed.

"Are you just an old-fashioned girl, Elena?" I teased gently, giving her a little squeeze.

When her eyes came back to mine, there was an intensity to her gaze. "I don't want you to be with anybody else." She wet her lips and dropped her voice to just above a whisper when she continued. "I don't want anybody else touching you like this."

If I could have melted into a puddle, I would have, absolutely. And the slightly possessive quality of her voice sent a pang straight down between my legs where it rested. And throbbed.

Bringing my hand to her face, I informed her, "I don't want anybody else touching me like this either." And then I pulled her in for a mind-blowing kiss to seal our pledge and start things heating up all over again.

It was close to three o'clock in the morning by the time we lay in each other's arms, lightly dozing and as spent and breathless as marathon runners. But my mind wouldn't settle, for some reason. Maybe I was afraid if we actually went to sleep, I'd wake up to find it had all been a dream, that Elena was still and forever out of my reach, that I'd been standing in the lobby of the bank, fantasizing all this time.

"So, what have you told Max about us?" I asked her. Yep, the wee hours of the morning, after endless, limb-melting sex, and I wanted to chat.

I felt Elena chuckle against my shoulder. "Where on earth did that come from?"

I shrugged. "Just wondering."

"Well, I explained to him that Cece and I are not going to be together again, which I think is hard for him because I get the impression Cindy lets him believe it's a possibility."

"But it's not, right?" I tried hard not to sound like a child, but I didn't succeed.

Elena pressed her lips to my neck. "No," she whispered. "It's not."

"Okay."

"Then I told him that Mommy doesn't want to be alone forever, that she does want to share her life with somebody. I told him that 'dating' meant I was looking for that person. And that I've been dating the same woman for a little while now and I wanted to know what he thought of her."

I swallowed, suddenly nervous over the outcome, as if the conversation with Max hadn't taken place yet and there was a chance he'd put the kibosh on me. "Did you tell him it was me?"

"Yup."

"What did he say?"

"Cool."

I waited for her to elaborate. Nothing. "That's it? Cool?"

"That's it. And 'cool' is a pretty positive response coming from him."

It was true. I'd heard him say it more than once, so I should have been relieved. But I'd never been in the position of having somebody *other* than the woman I'm dating have a say in our relationship. It was kind of weird. I let it sink in and I nodded as it did. "Okay. Good. That's good."

"It *is* good."

"It must be hard for you."

"What do you mean?"

"I mean, just about everything you do, you have to take Max into consideration. It must be hard."

"It's just part of being a parent." I felt her shrug.

"Still. It must be tough." I absorbed that for a few seconds before all kinds of questions began to zip through my head, like a fleet of biplanes pulling giant signs behind them. I turned my head to look at Elena's face. "What's the hardest part about being a mom?"

Her brow furrowed. "Hmm. I'd say it's probably the constant negotiation on rules because they change as your child grows, so there's this ebb and flow based on Max's abilities at any given time. Things as simple as bedtime or how much TV he gets to watch."

I nodded. Made sense.

She jerked. "Oh, wait. I know." Her gentle laughter shook the bed. "You have to be the grown-up. You know what I mean? Your kid can push your buttons like nobody's business and sometimes he gets you. He gets you bad. And you're tired and you've had a crappy day and he's just pushing, pushing, pushing. It's easy to let him pull you into some kind of argument where you're *both* acting like kids, sniping back and forth and making zero progress. But you have to take a step back and be the adult, even if you piss him off. Or worse, break his little heart. Sometimes that really sucks, but you have to do it."

"For his own good."

"Exactly."

"God, how many times did we hear that when we were growing up?" I smiled as Grandma's voice filtered through my brain, telling eight-year-old, very upset little me that whatever she'd decided it was for my own good.

"You know what's the absolute scariest thing in the world about parenting?"

"Tell me."

"The first time you hear your own mother's voice coming out of your mouth."

I laughed. "Do you remember it?"

"Like it happened this morning. Max was two and he wanted a cookie and he'd had, like, a dozen or something ridiculous, and I told him no more. And he kept asking why, but none of my explanations were good enough for him. So the next time he asked why, I snapped and told him, 'Because I said so, that's why!' Oh, my God, Avery, I was horrified. I clamped both hands over my mouth and just stood there. *Horrified!*"

I squeezed her tightly, grinning. "Ah, the old 'because I said so.' A classic, truly. My grandmother said it all the time."

"It *is* the quintessential Mom Answer."

"Without a doubt."

We chuckled a little more and eventually quieted, snuggling closer, our limbs entwined. I fell into a sated, restful sleep during which I dreamed of baby bottles, soft yellow chicks, and plastic tee-ball bats.

Weird.

chapter twenty-two

Grandma was, of course, charming on Sunday afternoon. I smothered a smile as I chewed a bite of her melt-in-your-mouth pot roast. My grandmother was always pleasant and polite, but she had an 'extra charm' button reserved exclusively for incredibly good-looking men, Mr. Davidson, and apparently, Elena.

"This is delicious, Mrs. King," Elena said sincerely. Speaking of charming. If Elena didn't meet with Grandma's approval, there was no hope for me.

"You're very kind, Elena. Thank you." Grandma speared a chunk of potato with her fork. "Now, your son—Max is it? How old is he?"

I was pretty sure I'd already given her this tidbit of information, but I appreciated her making conversation with Elena.

"He just turned six two months ago."

"And will you have more children?"

I've been chewing and swallowing my food for the better part of three decades, but that didn't prevent me from snorting pot roast up my nose as I choked on a mouthful. I was sure I saw a trace of amusement in the way the corners of Elena's mouth turned up ever-so-slightly, but she thankfully didn't look my way as she answered.

"Well, it will depend on a lot of different factors, but yes. I think I'd like to have another child."

"You would?" I asked before I could stop myself.

She nodded and smiled, then forked a baby carrot into her mouth.

"Good to know," I said, more to myself than either of the other two.

"Avery doesn't think she's good with children, but I keep trying to tell her she's wrong."

"*Grandma.*" I covered my eyes with one hand.

Elena's shock of a laugh cut through the air as Grandma replied, "I'm just telling her the way it is, that's all." Her smirk told me she knew exactly what she was doing.

"Your grandmother's right, Avery," Elena told me. "You're very good with kids. That tee-ball team loves you. Max thinks you're the coolest thing since video games."

"Well," I said, playing with my meat. "I *am* pretty cool. That part's true."

She pushed at me playfully and we got off the subject of kids for a while. Thank God because I just wasn't ready to get into a deep discussion about it, but I didn't want Elena to know that. I managed to shift the topic to Mr. Davidson. Then we talked about the financial industry, television, and cleaning products for the kitchen. In that order.

All in all, the visit was a huge success and I could tell by Grandma's enormous smile and the way she hugged Elena and told her to be sure and come back soon, that she'd been won over.

I smiled all the way home.

I dropped Elena off at her own house so she'd be there when her parents dropped Max off. She didn't want to leave me, but thought she'd better spend some mommy time with Max. I felt the same way; I didn't want to be away from her, but I knew I'd neglected Steve all weekend and he could probably use some mommy time as well. We kissed goodbye in my car, barely able to pry ourselves away from one another before clothing was in danger of being removed. Elena breathlessly pushed herself out the door of my car and I nearly ended up with my face on the passenger seat as I tried to stay with her. She gave me one last peck on the lips.

"I'll call you later," she said as she backed away.

"'Kay."

I watched her go inside, then blew out a huge breath, my cheeks puffing with the effort. I was exhausted, my thighs ached, and my nipples were sore.

Life was good.

Later that night, Steve and I lay in pooped-out piles in the living room after a long romp through the park. We were watching TV, Steve stretched out on the couch next to me and actually allowing me to cuddle with him, when Maddie called.

"Are you in love?" she asked in response to my hello.

"What?"

"I've been calling you all weekend, at all hours, and you didn't answer." I vaguely recalled a distant memory of the phone ringing a couple times and then realized I hadn't checked my voicemail.

"Oops. Sorry about that."

"The only time you don't answer *at all* is when you're having sex. And you only have sex when you're in love. So…are you in love?"

"Yes." There was no point in arguing with her; she knew me too well, and if I tried to lie, she'd only annoy me until she pried the truth from me. Besides, she was right on all counts. And it felt good to say it. Silence filled my ears. "Hello?" I said, wondering if we'd been disconnected.

"I'm still here. I just didn't expect you to admit it." Then she laughed.

"I know from experience that hiding things from you is futile."

"Damn right. So…details?" Her hesitation was very slight, but I understood it. After all, she was my best friend and I'd barely told her a thing about Elena, so I wouldn't have been surprised if Maddie was angry. But she didn't seem to be and she listened to me blather on and on about Elena, how wonderful she was, how great I thought we were going to be together, and how incredible the sex was. It didn't take long at all for her to loosen up, let her reservations go, and ask me questions, some of them filthy. It felt like everything was back to normal.

Except I was no longer single.

And did I like the sound of that.

The next week flew by and before I knew it, it was Thursday. I hadn't seen Elena all week, but we talked on the phone every night. There was a part of me that felt some frustration at having my beautiful girlfriend a mere six doors down and not being able to touch her, but at the same time, I liked the pacing. I felt like we were really getting to know one another through our phone calls. After all, we both knew that if we were in the same room, we'd end up naked and panting within a matter of minutes, so the phone calls ended up being a good thing for the relationship, forcing us to talk rather than, well, fuck. At least, that's what I kept telling myself.

Josh came into the office late on Thursday and when he finally arrived just before lunch, he waved around a small photo of what looked to me like some kind of splotch. He dropped it on my desk.

"Take a gander at that," he said, his chest all puffed out like a proud peacock.

I squinted at it. "An amoeba?"

He swatted at my arm. "No, stupid, it's an ultrasound picture. Of my kid."

"You fathered an amoeba?" I couldn't help it. It was fun.

"You know, getting laid on a regular basis hasn't made you any nicer." He tried to snatch the photo away, but I held it out of his reach.

"Okay, okay. Show me."

He pointed out what little detail we could see at fifteen weeks—which wasn't much. But he was so cute and so proud that I just listened and nodded while he went on and on.

"They usually don't do an ultrasound until twenty weeks or so, but Nina wanted to get one now so she could check on dates and stuff, just to be sure."

"And?" I asked. "When's the magic date?"

"We're due February tenth."

235

I loved that he was using 'we' instead of 'she.' It was cute.

"Well, then, you've got..." I consulted my calendar. "About six months to get your shit together. Think you can manage?"

He flopped down into his desk chair as if his bones had all suddenly disappeared. "I have no idea. But I don't have a choice either, so I guess I've got to say yes. Right?"

"That's the spirit," I said with a smile. "Seriously, you're going to be a great dad, Josh. No worries."

"From your lips to the big man upstairs," he said, pointing at the ceiling.

I worked steadily through lunch on our latest project, trying out several different shades of burgundy/maroon/ brick red before finally settling on the one I thought would work best for the banner our client was having printed. They were a burger chain, but not fast food, per se. They were a well-known establishment in the Greater Rochester Area called Ziggy's and they made the most outstanding cheeseburger I have ever eaten in my entire life. And I'm not even that big a fan of burgers. But Ziggy's Ultimate Cheeseburger was just that and I actually salivated a bit as I thought about one. I cocked my head as I looked at the Ziggy's logo on my computer screen, and thought of their kid-friendly atmosphere—the fun cups with the squiggly straws, the coloring page placemats, the free balloons. Without allowing myself time to back out, I picked up my phone and dialed Elena's cell. I didn't like calling her office phone, even though she said it was okay to do so. I figured if she was busy with work she'd let her cell go into voicemail, but if her office phone was ringing, she might feel obligated to pick it up and I didn't want to interrupt.

"Hey, sexy," she answered, her voice a low hum that swept through my body like a wave of warmth.

"God, how do you do that with two words?" I asked, bewildered.

"Do what?" she asked, pretending to play innocent.

"Like you don't know. How's your day, sweetheart?"

"Crazy busy and flying by. Yours?"

"The same. Listen, would you and Max maybe want to go to Ziggy's tonight for dinner? It'd be fun." I held my breath, knowing full well that this was the first time I'd suggested all *three* of us spend some time together.

"Oh, my God, we'd love it. *Max* would love it." Elena sounded very happy and that, in turn, made me very happy.

"Great. Why don't you two just come down to my place when you're ready? That way, Max can see Steve, too. Okay?"

"That sounds great. Can't wait to see you."

By seven o'clock that night, we were seated in a red vinyl booth at Ziggy's. Elena and I sat across from one another and Max was next to me, coloring away on his placemat depicting talking burgers and dancing fries. I got a little mushy inside when he said he wanted to sit by "Coach King." I shot Elena a look that said we were going to have to teach him my first name.

"I need ketchup," he said as I handed him his fries, drawing the words out irritatingly.

"What was that?" I asked, cupping a hand to my ear. "I thought I heard a high-pitched whining sound."

Max tried to smother a grin, but wasn't quite successful. "Can I have ketchup on my French fries, please?"

georgia beers

"Why, yes. Of course you may have ketchup for your French fries. What a nice, polite young man you are." I poured ketchup onto his paper plate. "Tell me when." We went through the same drill with his junior cheeseburger and then I helped him lay a napkin in his lap and we each bit into our burger at the same time, grinning like goofballs at each other. When I looked up, Elena was smiling at me with an expression on her face I couldn't quite define.

"What?" I asked her around a mouthful of food.

"Nothing." She shook her head and popped a fry into her mouth. "I'm glad you suggested this."

"Me, too."

"Me, three!" Max said, punching a fist into the air.

Ziggy's had a clown in-house that night and when I waved him over to our table, Max was in awe. The clown did that thing where he twisted balloons together until they resembled a poodle or a Dachshund or a hat, me wincing the whole time, as I'm always sure the damn things can't possibly hold up to such manhandling and will pop loudly at any moment and give me a freaking heart attack. But of course there was no popping and Max ended up with a giraffe made of yellow latex. He was a very happy kid.

It was nearly eight thirty by the time Elena looked at her watch and announced it was time to head home.

I pulled into their driveway twenty minutes later. A quick glance in the back seat showed Max dozing in his booster chair, his giraffe held lovingly close.

"This was so much fun, Avery. Thanks for…just thanks."

238

"Hey, I had a blast. And frankly, I'm a little jealous *I* didn't get a balloon animal."

Her fingers were gentle as she cupped my chin as kissed me sweetly on the mouth. At that point, I felt I was getting to know her body pretty well, but I was always surprised by the softness of her lips and I sighed a little as I sank into her.

"Ugh. Kissing. Yuck!"

We both jumped at the sound of Max's sleepy voice. My eyes must have registered my panic because Elena gave my face a loving caress as she laughed. "You won't always feel that way, pal," she said to her son. "I promise."

I got out and went around to the back, helping Max out of the car and pulling out his chair as well. I waited as Elena popped the locks on her own car and took the chair from me, tossing it into her own back seat as Max ran to the front door of the house.

"What do you say to Avery, Max?" she asked.

"Open the door, Mom," he said, jiggling the locked knob.

"Max." The Mom Voice.

He jiggled the doorknob again.

Elena tossed me a look before continuing with, "Max, what do you say to Avery? I'm not going to ask again. Next time, TV privileges are gone."

He sighed, clearly annoyed, and muttered a less than enthusiastic, "Thanks, Coach King." I assumed he was tired.

Elena shrugged an apology. "Thanks, Coach King."

I grinned at her and returned to my own car, really wanting to follow her inside, but not wanting to push. She would tell me when she felt comfortable enough for me to be there again with Max home; I was confident of that, and I thought tonight had been a big step.

At home, I took care of Steve, checked my voicemail and settled down to watch a little television.

I sat for a long while paying no attention to what was on the screen, thinking about the evening as well as the past several weeks. Was it possible I'd been wrong about myself all this time? That not only did I like kids, but kids liked me? And that I was *good* with them? Where had my certainty come from that I was not cut out for child-rearing? The answer was pretty simple, really: my own childhood. Instead of focusing on the wonderful job my grandmother had done raising me, I'd chosen to zero in on the fact that my own mother abandoned me, as if it were some sort of genetic predisposition and I was doomed to the same fate. I'd just never had a reason to look beyond, to go deeper.

I thought about Max. I thought about the kids on my team. I thought about Elena telling my grandmother that she'd like to have another child. The image of her pregnant, her belly swollen and her skin glowing and her smile radiant…it was beautiful. Sexy, even. And for the first time in my entire life, I began to wonder what kind of mother I'd make. What kind of mother I'd *really, truly* be.

And it didn't scare me.

chapter twenty-three

The next couple weeks went by quickly and smoothly. Summer was coming to a close and I felt the urge to look behind me, wondering if I'd missed it.

Elena and I—and Max—had fallen into a nice routine and we did a lot together. We went on a picnic, we hiked with Steve (which was less of a hike and more of a short, zigzagging jaunt with a six-year-old tagging along), we went to the movies, and we visited both Elena's parents and my grandmother more than once. We were slowly settling into being a happy little family unit and I was enjoying myself more than I could have imagined.

It was a Wednesday evening and Elena was hosting her monthly book club at her place, so Max was at mine helping me make oatmeal raisin cookies. His help had become such a regular occurrence that I bought him his own Dora the Explorer apron to wear while we baked. So he stood on a chair next to me in his bright yellow apron with half a cup of raisins and waited patiently for me to give him the go ahead, tossing one into his mouth every so often.

Max's face lit up, his eyes sparkled animatedly. "Did you see my lunch box in the catalog from the mail yesterday?"

"I did," I told him, knowing he was referring to an ad flyer he'd seen.

"It's so cool. I really want that. Cece is supposed to take me to get my new backpack for school." He grimaced. "Mom says 'don't count on it,' though." Then he sighed as only a little boy can.

I made a mental note to ponder talking to Elena about watching what she said in front of Max with regard to Cindy. I knew she got incredibly frustrated by her ex's lack of participation in Max's life, but I also knew it didn't help Max to hear about it. He was only six. He didn't understand how justified she was.

"Okay. Dump 'em in." He tipped the raisins into the bowl and I slid it in front of him. "Stir it up." I knew he wouldn't last. His little hand wasn't strong enough to stir the heavy batter for long and he got bored pretty quickly, but he gave it a whirl.

"We talked about you," he said, his dark brows furrowed with concentration.

"Who talked about me?"

"Me and Cece."

"Yeah?" Now this was interesting. "You didn't give away any of my secrets, did you?" I poked him playfully in the ribs.

"You don't have any secrets," he protested, giggling. "She wanted to know if you're nice."

"She did?"

"Uh-huh. She asked if you were nice to me and I told her how you take me and Mom places all the time and that we have fun. And I told her how cool Steve is."

At the mention of his name, my dog lifted his head from where he was dozing under the kitchen table and blinked at us.

"And what did Cece say to that?" I felt awful, pumping him for information yet again, but I couldn't help myself. I was utterly shocked that Cindy gave a shit who was hanging around her son. Shocked in a good way.

"She was glad." Max shrugged as if it didn't really matter.

"Well, I'm glad, too. You know I'm only nice to you because you're a great assistant chef, right?" I poked him again and he squealed. "If you were a lousy assistant chef, I'd toss you in the closet and keep you there until Mom came to get you." I poked him some more, delighted at how ticklish he was.

He laughed and squirmed himself right off the chair, and once I let up, he lay on the kitchen floor, panting and adorable. I got a big spoon out of the drawer. Once he caught his breath, he reclaimed his spot and we filled two cookie sheets with fat drops of raisin-spotted batter. I was even able to accept that they weren't all uniform in size, that Max's were all over the place, and soon the house smelled of warm oatmeal cookies.

It was nearly nine thirty by the time Elena arrived to pick up her son. He was crashed on my couch, the Disney Channel on mute on my television, Steve curled up near Max's feet. She stood looking at him for several moments, her face a portrait of a mother totally in love with her child. She looked gorgeous.

After a few minutes, she joined me in the kitchen where I was wrapping up a big plate of cookies for my assistant chef.

"How was book club?" I asked her, my voice low.

"Great, as always. You should join us."

"Then you wouldn't have a babysitter," I pointed out with a half-grin.

"But I'd have you sitting next to me." She pulled me into a hug. I wrapped my arms around her warm body and took in the scent of her: coconut shampoo and the warm, sweet scent of her body spray. "And I wouldn't have to miss you."

Our kiss started gently enough, her soft lips finding mine. As always, it was so easy to just slip into it, to lose all sense of time and space and just float in her arms. I slid my hand up her arm and into the silky hair at the nape of her neck. In response, her tongue darted into my mouth and I could taste the wine she'd had during book club... something red and peppery. We moved almost unnoticeably until my back hit the edge of the counter and Elena's hands dropped lower to cup my ass. I reluctantly pulled my lips from hers, halting her progress with a hand on her chest.

"Elena," I said softly as a warning.

"Christ, I can't wait for this weekend," she whispered, nipping my jaw. "I am this close," she held her thumb and forefinger scant millimeters apart, "to propping you up on this counter and taking advantage of you right here among the kitchen utensils."

I blushed and smiled simultaneously. "Just hold off for two more days, baby, and if you're good, maybe I'll let you smear cookie dough on me and lick it off."

Elena grinned wickedly. "Promise?"

"Sweetie, you can have anything you want from me. Don't you know that by now?" I gave her a quick peck on the lips and extricated myself from her grasp…not because I wanted to—the idea of her "taking advantage" of me did nothing but send my arousal through the roof—but because Max was in the next room and I couldn't imagine trying to explain to him why Mommy and Coach King were naked and groaning on the kitchen counter.

Elena took a deep breath, exhaled loudly, and then shook out her body as if waking up from a trance. She straightened her clothes, wiped the corners of her mouth, and gave a curt nod. Obviously, Mom was back on the scene, which I found endearingly amusing. She scooped Max up in her arms—he barely opened his eyes—and I got the door for her.

chapter twenty-four

"So, where are you guys going?" Maddie asked me early Saturday afternoon. I hadn't spoken with her in over a week and it felt wonderful to catch up.

"Alexander's. Elena's never been and you know how much I love it."

"And how are things going with you and the Greek goddess?" Maddie teased, using her newly minted nickname for Elena. I was bringing her and Max to Maddie and J.T.'s for dinner the following week, so she was easing up a bit on the "why haven't we met her?" accusations she'd been e-mailing me on a regular basis. And no, the tee-ball games didn't count, she'd informed me in no uncertain terms.

"Slow and easy. But it's okay."

"Slow and easy isn't always a bad thing," Maddie said and I could almost hear her wink.

"She's worth the wait, believe me."

"Oh, I believe you. I haven't seen you this goo-goo since...since...wow, I don't think I've ever seen you this goo-goo over a girl."

I couldn't help but laugh at Maddie's choice of adjective. "I'm not *goo-goo*," I protested. "You make me sound like I'm three. I'm just really..."

"In love."

"Well, duh. Yeah. But it's more than that. Somehow. If that makes any sense."

"Are you trying to tell me Elena is The One with a capital T and a capital O?"

She wasn't mocking me, not really. She was trying to keep it light, but I could tell she seriously wanted to know if that's how I felt about Elena. I tapped my forefinger against my lips as I pondered honestly. "Yes. I think she very well might be."

Maddie was quiet for a moment. When she spoke, her voice was gentle. Pleased. "I'm glad to hear that, Avery. I'm very happy for you. I knew you'd fallen hard for this woman, but I wasn't sure exactly *where* on the scale, you know? I can't wait to meet her."

A knock on my front door hurried our goodbyes. "We'll see you on Tuesday," I said.

I was surprised to see Elena when I opened my front door. I set the phone down on a side table as I smiled widely. "Well, hello there, gorgeous."

She was dressed casually, but was no less sexy than usual, in low-waisted jeans and a deep green tank top. I, too, was casual in a pair of old boxer shorts and a Duke Women's Basketball T-shirt, but I paled in comparison. She was delectable.

Elena stepped into the foyer and directly into my personal space, one eyebrow arched mischievously and a predatory gleam in her eye, each of which sent a pang of arousal straight down between my legs. She took my face in both hands and kissed me, hard and rough, pulling a moan from my throat while kicking the door shut behind her.

"I'm sorry," she muttered between kisses as she spun us around so my back was against the door. "I know you've got things to do today. So do I. But I just dropped Max off at my mother's and I was thinking about us spending time together later and I couldn't wait to get my hands on you. If I don't get this out of my system, we'll never make it to the restaurant tonight." She stopped and looked me in the eyes. "I hope you don't mind."

I tried to meet her gaze, but my own eyes had swum out of focus from the intensity of her kiss, and my breathing was ragged. I think I managed a shake of my head and a sentence fragment or two. "No. Don't mind. Don't mind at all." Something like that. I pulled her face back to me and she took my mouth with hers again, stopping the kiss only long enough to pull my shirt over my head and off. Her hands slipped behind my back and with a quick flick, my bra was unfastened. She yanked that off, too, and filled her hands with my breasts.

Her touch was not gentle, it was demanding. And bossy. And possessive. And I couldn't remember the last time my panties became so damp so fast. God, it was easy with her. *I* was easy with her. She could take me from zero to sixty in about four seconds. I moaned loudly and the back of my head knocked against the door when she fastened her mouth onto my nipple and bit down, then sucked me in hungrily. I lost all sense of time while she went back and forth from one breast to the other with her tongue, her teeth, and her fingers. Just when I thought I seriously might spontaneously combust, she stood back up and kissed me again and her tongue pushed into my mouth at the same time her hand dipped into my shorts and underwear. We both groaned at the contact.

"Oh, my God, you're so wet," she whispered against my lips.

"It's what you do to me," I replied honestly, then raised my right leg and hooked it around her hips to give her better access. I was slightly off balance and gripping her shoulders tightly, and I wasn't terribly comfortable in this position, but I didn't care. I just didn't want her to stop touching me.

Elena didn't disappoint me, but instead gripped my right thigh with her hand, lifted it higher, and held it, helping me balance, while at the same time pushing us both hard against the door and setting up a rhythm between my legs. I held on for dear life and tried not to scream in pleasure and delight so as not to bring any neighbors running to my aid. The foyer filled with the sound of our labored breathing and the recurring beat of my shoulders against the door.

"I love you," I murmured in Elena's ear as she drove me higher, the pitch of my voice climbing as well. "Elena. God, I love you." The edge was in sight now, I could feel its rapid approach. "Oh, yes. God, yes."

"Like that?"

"Just like that."

"Yeah?"

"Oh, yeah. Oh…" I clamped my jaw shut and groaned through my teeth as colors exploded behind my eyelids like fireworks.

"There it is," Elena whispered, her lips next to my ear and her sexy voice intensifying my climax as she kept her hand moving against my hot and swollen flesh. "That's it, baby. That's it. Just for me. All for me." She held on tightly, keeping me upright as I rode out the contractions, panting and whimpering and wondering how the top of my head hadn't blown off.

"Oh, my God," I said breathlessly when the last spasm had left me boneless and Elena's hand slowed and then stopped, but still pressed tightly against me. "Dear God. I've got to…down…"

And together, we slid down the door and dropped like a discarded towel onto my foyer floor, breathless, satisfied, and utterly wiped out.

"Holy crap," I finally said after several moments of waiting for my vision to focus once again. "That was…holy crap."

"Thanks for wearing the easy access shorts."

"Hey, whatever I can do to make your life simpler. Is this ambushing me at the front door going to be a regular occurrence? You've done it twice now."

"It might be." Elena chuckled and tightened her arms around me. "Should I apologize for the lack of warning?"

"Absolutely not. I'd reward you for your element of surprise if I could move any of my limbs. Or feel them."

"I love you," Elena said a few moments later before we began the difficult task of untangling ourselves from each other and attempting to stand.

Five minutes later, she was gone and I was still standing in my foyer, braless (not that anybody would notice) and wearing my T-shirt inside out.

Steve wandered by at that moment. He stood and seemed to study me, then turned and went back into the living room.

"Hey. Did you just judge me?" I asked defensively, glaring at his retreating backside.

251

Alexander's was filled to capacity with its usual Saturday night crowd, but we had a cozy little table for two in the corner and as far as I was concerned, there was no crowd. Just Elena, in her drop-dead gorgeous little black dress with a plunging neckline that made me salivate as I imagined running my tongue along the V made by the fabric. I indicated her cleavage with my eyes.

"Nice dress."

"I thought you might like it." The expression on her face was mirthful as she sipped her Pinot Noir.

"Like it? I'm not sure I'll be able to think about—or look at—anything else." Changing my voice to a serious note, I added quietly, "You look beautiful, Elena."

I was pleased to see her cheeks flush a delicate pink. "Thank you. You're looking awfully gorgeous yourself, you know."

Though I wasn't showing nearly the skin Elena was, I had chosen an emerald green silk blouse and left it unbuttoned lower than I usually dared. I'd paired it with a new pair of black dress slacks and black strappy sandals with a slight heel, and I'd pulled my hair back into a gold clip, leaving the escaping strands alone, hoping they looked sexy rather than messy. I was reasonably sure, judging by the look of desire on Elena's face, that I'd pulled it off.

"I just want you to know on my way out earlier today, I had to caress my front door in fond memory." I winked at her. "I'll never look at the foyer the same way again."

"Maybe we should plan on changing the way you look at *every* room in your house."

"And then in yours."

"I'll drink to that." She held up her wineglass and we clinked.

The evening went on like that, regular conversation peppered with sexually infused flirting, and God were we good at it. I often had to stop and remind myself that this was the very same untouchable, unattainable bank manager I'd been ogling for months. I had been so sure she was out of my league and now here we were, sitting together at dinner talking quietly and teasingly about all the filthy things we were going to do to each other when we got home. It was almost surreal and by the time we were handed dessert menus by the waiter, I was so excruciatingly wet I half expected to slide out of my chair and end up under our table on the floor at any given moment.

I didn't need to open the dessert menu. I knew I was getting the chocolate cherry cheesecake.

"I'm going to have the crème brulee," Elena informed me. "I almost always order that when it's available."

"Your favorite?"

"What's not to love? Hot and sweet outside, warm and creamy inside..." She let her voice trail off and sipped her wine, looking smugly satisfied at what I was sure was a dopey (possibly drooling) expression on my face.

"Jesus Christ," I muttered, grabbing for my water. "You're going to be the death of me yet."

Our desserts arrived quickly and I tried hard not to scarf mine down like a starving person. My mind was stuck in an endless loop, like a skipping record, and all I could think about was taking Elena home and getting my hands, my mouth, my tongue underneath that black dress. There would be no quiet climaxing tonight. Oh, no. I was bound and determine to wring some serious noise out of her.

"Avery?" The voice surprised me because it wasn't Elena's. I wrenched my gaze from across the table and looked up to see my ex, Lauren, standing over me with a smile. There was something in her eyes—a glint? a glare?—that came and went so fast, I almost missed it. "I thought that was you. Hi!" She bent down and gave me a hug, which I returned awkwardly.

"Hi," I said to her. She was smiling widely, her eyes were bright, and she looked...I couldn't come up with a word. But it made me squirm.

"Hi there." She glanced in Elena's direction.

"Oh, God, I'm sorry. Where are my manners?" I nodded across the table. "This is my...date, Elena Walker. Elena, this is Lauren Gardner."

"I'm Avery's ex," Lauren added, though I figured Elena had probably put two and two together just using the name. They exchanged greetings and shook hands politely.

"I can't stay long...my date's in the ladies' room."

"Your date, huh?" I said teasingly, hoping to allay the weird feeling I had. The mention of a date was promising.

"Yeah, she's great. I met her at my ob/gyn's office. She's the receptionist there. Can you believe it?"

I shook my head. "Leave it to you."

"And I'd seen her quite a bit because...drum roll...I'm pregnant!" She all but squealed her news, causing several other patrons to glance our way. I didn't mind, though. She was so ecstatically happy about it and her glee was contagious.

"Lauren! That's terrific. Good for you."

"You know, it's also gotten me thinking about a lot of past stuff," she said, sobering a bit, the glint returning.

"Past stuff?" *Uh-oh.*

"I owe you an apology, Avery."

"An apology? No, you don't. Absolutely not." *Please don't say it.* I waved a hand at her, hoping to brush the whole subject away like so much dust, and I couldn't bring myself to look in Elena's direction, for fear she'd see the panic on my face.

"Yes, I do. I shouldn't have tried to force you. If somebody doesn't want to have kids, it isn't fair for the other person in the relationship to try to change their mind. I know that now."

And there it was. I wanted to stop her from talking, but the look on her face told me she was doing exactly what she'd come to our table to do. I just sat there while she did more damage, injecting a tone of genuine understanding into her voice. I never expected that she'd want to hurt me; I thought we were friends, sort of. She had to know Elena had a child; it was a small community. Why else say this stuff?

"You were so adamant about not ever wanting kids in your life, about having no desire to be a parent, and I never took the time to understand. I mean, kids are a ton of work. A ton. Believe me," she babbled on, "I'm just starting to get that. You told me time and time again that you didn't like kids, you'd never wanted them, that they'd ruin our relationship, and you were right. Just because you loved me didn't mean you'd love having a child, even if it was mine. Or ours. I should have listened instead of fighting with you endlessly and making you the bad guy for simply being honest with me. You know? I'm really sorry about that."

I'd tuned out about halfway through her diatribe, the moment when I felt Elena go perfectly still across the table from me. All the delicious food I'd consumed during the previous hour threatened to make a reappearance as my stomach turned nauseatingly.

"Ooo, there's Kristy," Lauren said, her gaze locked across the room and a glowing smile on her face. "I've got to run, but it was so good to see you and I'm glad we cleared the air. It was nice to meet you, Elena." She winked at me, the bitch, and she was gone.

When I finally had the courage to look across the table, Elena was studying what was left of her crème brulee. She didn't eat any more of it.

The waiter brought the check and I gave him my credit card before he could walk away. We needed to talk about this, but not here, not in a restaurant full of people and not at the table across which we'd been discussing which articles of clothing were coming off first. That conversation suddenly seemed a million years ago.

The night was beautiful—balmy and comfortable—but we walked to the car in silence. I wanted to give Elena time to absorb all the information she'd been thrown, and at the same time, I wanted to *stop* her from absorbing too much. The bottom line, though, was that I had no idea what to say. I was damned either way. Either I'd broken up with Lauren because she wanted children and I didn't, even though I'd led Elena to believe otherwise. Or I'd lied to her and let her believe that's the reason I broke up with her, which was just cruel.

There was no good way out of this and I knew it.

I wanted to kill Lauren.

"Elena..." I began as we got into the car.

256

She held up her hand, not looking at me. "Just...don't talk to me for a minute. I have to think."

Her tone was low and brittle, like ice splintering under my feet. I swallowed down the acid that kept rising into the back of my throat and keyed the ignition.

We drove the fifteen minute trip in silence and it felt like hours. I kept opening my mouth to say something, but again, I had no idea what and I'd close it again. Elena stared out the passenger side window and said nothing, her mouth a straight, inexpressive slash across her face, telling me nothing other than she was not happy.

A tiny bubble of relief floated to the surface when she followed me into my house and I was grateful she didn't just leave. I let Steve out back, shut the sliding glass door and turned to face the music.

Elena was gazing off to her right, shaking her head very slightly back and forth.

"Elena, please look at me." My voice shook, which annoyed me.

"Why did you break up with Lauren?"

It was a straightforward question, and yet the answer was so complicated. I wet my lips and grimaced as I searched for the right words.

"It's a simple question, Avery. Why did you break up with Lauren?"

"It wasn't working," I said, hoping Elena didn't think I sounded as lame as I did. "I wasn't in love with her and she deserved better. I told you that."

"Did she want children?"

"Yes."

"Did you?"

There was no good way to answer that. "No." At her snort, I quickly amended, "Not with her."

"And now you've suddenly changed your mind?" She pinched the bridge of her nose between her thumb and forefinger. "God, I'm an idiot," she muttered.

"You are not an idiot."

When she finally looked at me, her dark eyes snapped with an anger I never expected. "I have a child, Avery."

"I know that."

"Well, apparently, you don't *understand* it."

What? "What the hell is that supposed to mean?"

"He always comes first. Do you get that?"

"Of course I get that."

"Do you? The woman I spend the rest of my life with is going to end up being another mom to him. Do you get *that?*"

"Yes. You said yourself that I was good with him, that I took good care of him."

"You did. And he's been an angel most of the time when he's been around you, but that's not always the case. What about when he's sick? What about when he throws a tantrum? What about when he's being a little brat? What about when he lies or hurts himself or is just plain crabby?" She paced around the room as she spoke, gesturing wildly with her hands and arms. "It's not all fun and rainbows. It's not all puppies and tee-ball games. What about when he's throwing up in the middle of the night or when he breaks something of yours or when he just flat out doesn't listen to you?"

"What are you talking about?" I asked, bewildered, but trying hard to follow her logic. "You've lost me."

"I know." She nodded and I didn't like the look on her face then. "God," she yelled at the ceiling. "I never even asked you if you wanted a kid. I just assumed. And you let me! I am *so stupid*! I even told you I wanted another one and you didn't say anything. Did it never occur to you it might be a subject we should discuss?" Then she went from yelling to muttering, rubbing angrily at her forehead with her fingertips. "I let you into Max's life. I introduced you to my family. On assumption. All on assumption. Blinded by my hormones, like I'm a fucking teenager. I am *such* an idiot. Jesus Christ, what a mess."

"Wait, wait, wait," I blurted, holding my hands palms forward like a crossing guard stopping her at the corner. A sense of panicked foreboding was settling on my shoulders and I couldn't shrug it away. I inched closer to her, but she took a step back from me. "What are you saying?" I asked her, trying not to sound as terrified as I felt. "We've got something good here, Elena." My head was pounding, my stomach churning dangerously. "I love you. And you love me."

She looked away and rolled her lips in, biting down on them. When she looked back at me, her eyes were wet. "I am a mother. First and foremost, that's what I am. My son comes first; he has to. Max will always come first."

"I know that."

"No, I don't think you do."

"Elena, please don't do this. Please."

"I'm not doing anything, Avery. It's already done."

I stood frozen as she picked up her bag and her keys from my side table and walked out my front door. I'm not good in an argument. I've never been able to debate. I can't think quickly enough to get my points across. At that moment, I wanted to scream to her to stop. I wanted to throw myself to the floor and wrap my arms around her ankles like a toddler. I wanted to beg her not to leave, to talk to me, to let me explain, to give it a chance.

But she was too stubborn to stop and I was too destroyed to move.

Instead, I stood there and watched her leave, fairly certain I could hear walls crumbling around me.

chapter twenty-five

I fell into such a state of depression, I could barely function. I vacillated between being angry at Lauren for wreaking the havoc she had, at Elena for giving up so easily, and at myself for not fighting harder. I was embarrassed that it was all affecting me so intensely after only a few weeks with the woman, but that didn't help me drag myself out of bed. I pretended I had the flu and called in sick to work. Nobody questioned how I'd gotten the flu in the middle of August. I spent most of the week in bed with the comforter pulled up over my head, hoping the world would all just go away or maybe the blackness would swallow me whole and I could simply disappear.

I missed Elena so badly, my chest ached.

The Sunday after our dinner, I faked my way through a very quick visit with Grandma, telling her I had a project I needed to get home and work on. I don't think she believed me, but she didn't press the issue. Then I called Elena's number over and over and over again for hours. After filling up her voicemail completely on both her home phone and her cell so I couldn't leave any more messages, I screwed up my courage and walked down to her door. Her car was gone, so I left a note asking her to please call me. She didn't.

By Sunday night, I was out of my mind with frustration. I tried calling again and this time, she answered. She spoke before I could say anything, her voice like steel, hard, cold, immovable.

"Stop calling me, Avery. Don't call me. Don't come down here. I don't want to see you. Do you understand?"

The click sounded in my ear before my words hit the air. "No, I don't. I don't understand."

I crawled into bed then and only got out to relieve myself and let Steve relieve himself.

Nearly four days went by.

By noon on Thursday, I was so disgusted with myself I wanted to punch somebody. The anger started to set in and, though I'm not an angry person by nature, feeling pissed off was infinitely better than feeling devastated. I dragged my sorry behind out of bed, wrinkling my nose at my own noxious scent, and wondered how Steve hadn't chewed his way through a wall just to get away from me.

I muttered my way through a peanut butter and jelly sandwich, forcing it down where it sat like a rock in my stomach, and letting my anger surface and bubble over, wondering aloud how Elena could just end it like that, without allowing me any sort of explanation, without wanting to hear another word from me. True, we'd only been together a short time, but I thought it was pretty clear—to *both* of us—that we had something special. For her to just slam the door on any possibilities seemed cold and selfish to me and I deserved better.

That conclusion, of course, did nothing to make the hurt go away.

After a shower, some much-needed shaving, and some clean clothes, I felt the tiniest bit better. I tossed Steve in the car and took him to Mendon Ponds, where we wandered through the parks for more than two hours.

I've always found nature to be rejuvenating for me. Something about being among trees that are decades and decades old creates an awe in me that I can't quite explain. It makes me feel small—not in a bad way, but in a way that helps me to understand how precious every moment is. The songs of the chickadees, nuthatches, and cardinals added to my gradual relaxation as Steve and I tromped through the woods, him with his terrier nose to the ground and me with my wondering eyes raised to the skies. I breathed deeply, willed my body to relax, and told myself that I'd be okay.

Then I went home and baked a batch of sugar cookies and a chocolate pound cake.

I had phone calls to return, mainly to Maddie. I'd cancelled Tuesday's dinner with her on the fly on Monday, not wanting to get into details because I was too much of a wreck at the time, but she'd left six messages since then and I really needed to call her back before she had J.T. and her buddies banging down my door to make sure I wasn't hanging from my shower rod.

"Where the hell have you been?" she practically shrieked into the phone. Damn Caller ID. "Are you all right? I've been worried sick."

"I'm alive. I'm fine. I'm just not ready to talk about it," I said as soon as she stopped to take a breath.

"Girl troubles?"

"Are there any other kind?"

She sighed loudly in my ear—for my benefit, I'm sure. "I really want to ask you what the hell is going on, but I know you. You're like a clam. The more I poke at you, the tighter you close yourself into your shell."

"I promise to give you details soon, all right? I really just…need a little more time to lick my wounds."

"That bad, huh?"

"I'll call you this weekend," I said. "Give my love to J.T."

I felt the tiniest bit better after that. Now Maddie knew I was hurting, but she also knew I was okay. Josh was the other one who was wondering about my state of mind. He knew it was extremely rare for me to blow off one day of work, let alone four. But I just wasn't up for any more chit-chat or dodging of questions. I'd go back to work tomorrow and see him then. I was suddenly exhausted and wanted to crash in my bed. Steve and I took care of our nightly business and then I headed upstairs to bed with two cookies, a glass of milk, and the remote: the exciting and riveting life of a single girl.

Tomorrow, I'd try to wedge myself back into my old life, my life prior to Elena and Max, before I began thinking of them as my future. Somehow, though, that old life seemed impossibly far away.

⸻

"Man, that sucks. I'm really sorry, Avery." Josh flipped his hair out of his eyes and I could tell by the look on his face that he didn't quite get what had happened between Elena and me (I wanted to tell him to join the club) and that he wasn't sure what to say. Just like a guy.

I shrugged, tried to make light of things, which was hard when my eyes insisted on filling with tears at inopportune moments. "Yeah, well, what can you do?" I turned back to my monitor and he turned to his and as we sat with our backs to each other, I said, "Tell me how Nina's doing."

He took the cue that I wanted him to change the subject and he ran with it, rambling on about Nina's weird craving for baked potatoes with chives and bacon bits on them, despite the fact that she didn't like bacon. Or chives. He regaled me with stories of their weekend trip to Home Depot to pick a paint color for the baby's room and how they stood there for over an hour and finally brought home enough chips of different shades of green to wallpaper at least one wall. I only half-listened, but it was good to hear that life went on, that some things were still the same, that Elena hadn't completely shattered everything I considered normal by simply walking out my door. I shook my head, hoping to dislodge those thoughts, and allowed myself to get angry again that I'd let her get so deeply into me in just a few short weeks. I was far too easy and I vowed not to let that happen again. I'd be stronger next time.

Next time.

Yeah, right. I snorted.

"What?" Josh said, stopping his storytelling.

"Oh, no. Nothing. Not you. I was...thinking and got annoyed."

He squinted at me. "You're not even listening to me, are you?"

"Yes! Yes, I am. I promise. Bacon bits. Chives. Green paint. I'm with you." I made a rolling gesture with my hand. "Please. Continue."

He eyed me skeptically, but dove right back in and moved on to the shopping for a crib story. I made sure to listen more closely this time.

By early afternoon, I knew I was going to make it through the day intact. I only had to excuse myself to the ladies' room once to deal with tears that wouldn't blink away, but I pulled it together and went back to work.

"How about a drink after work?" Josh asked. "It is Friday, after all."

"That sounds fabulous." The relief in my voice made me wince. "Steve will be fine for an extra hour or so." I'd gone home at lunch to let him out, so I didn't feel guilty about grabbing a cocktail after work. Besides, I thought I could use one. And I also thought I deserved one. I glanced at the clock. Three more hours. I could do it.

We were each focused on our projects when my cell phone rang, making us both jump, then chuckle as we saw each other startled. I squinted at the screen, the number one that seemed vaguely familiar, but that I couldn't pinpoint.

"Ms. King?" A female voice. Stern. Professional.

"Yes."

"This is Sandra Johnson from the residences on Jefferson." Grandma's assisted living complex. "We need you to come by right away."

My heart leapt into my throat. "Is everything okay?" I asked, my voice shaky. "Is my grandmother all right?"

"We really need you to come by immediately, Ms. King. We'll give you details when you get here."

—∽∽—

266

My grandmother had passed away in her sleep on Thursday night.

A lot of large medical terms were tossed my way, but they bounced off me like I had an invisible force field surrounding my body and landed on the floor at my feet. Grandma had basically had a heart attack in her sleep and never woke up. End of story. She was dead. That was really all I needed to know.

Josh had followed me and stood with me now, which I barely noticed, as I'd gone into some sort of zombie-like state of catatonia. Sandra Johnson was the consummate professional, quietly and thoroughly explaining to me that Grandma had missed her weekly bridge game with her coffee klatch and one of them had come looking for her. When she didn't answer the door or the phone, her friends became worried and contacted the staff. They let themselves in with a passkey and found my grandmother, still peacefully tucked into her bed. I listened, but didn't respond in any way other than nodding. Josh kept his hand on the small of my back and looking back now, I'm sure he was half-expecting me to faint right there in my grandmother's living room and was bracing himself to catch me. Honestly, all I could feel was nothingness. I was numb. My grandmother was gone. I had no family left.

I was alone.

Sandra Johnson gave me her card and explained that they would take care of Grandma's body, get it to the right people. She also gave me the card of the funeral home my grandmother had listed in her paperwork and told me the funeral director would contact me when he was ready for me. Apparently, there were legal matters that had to be taken care of by Sandra Johnson on behalf of the residence.

I nodded some more, then turned to Josh and asked him to take me back to my car.

As I passed Grandma's couch, my hand seemed to reach out all on its own and grab onto the knitted afghan she and I had made together one winter, before she knew I was all thumbs and she actually thought she might be able to teach me how to knit. We'd used all the colors of the sunset…flaming oranges and deep crimsons and rich pinks. I pulled it into my arms, bundled it up like a ball and pushed my nose into it, inhaling all the scents that reminded me of Grandma—Jean Nate bath splash, freshly baked cookies, her Aqua Net hairspray. I tried to imprint them into my memory, knowing I was going to lose them before long. Lose them forever.

I was an empty shell.

That's the best way to describe how I felt and how I acted for the rest of that day. Josh was worried about me and wanted to follow me home. I told him I'd be fine, that it was a short drive. He followed me anyway; I could see him in my rearview mirror a couple of cars back. When I turned onto my street, he kept going. I made a mental note to thank him later.

I kept waiting for some dam to burst inside me. When it didn't, when I continued to wander around like an automaton, I began to wonder if Elena had sapped all the emotion out of me. My grandmother deserved more, but I had nothing. I felt barren.

Lemon cookies were sharp, loud, they burst with flavor. I thought maybe they would help. I began pulling together the ingredients I'd need, measuring flour and baking soda, grabbing butter and eggs from the fridge. I zested a lemon into a small glass dish, feeling a microbe of relief at doing *something* to keep myself busy so I wouldn't simply float off into oblivion like a child's lost balloon.

When the dough was all mixed and I was lining my cookie sheets with parchment paper, there was a small knock on the sliding glass door. Max smiled crookedly and waved at me, his little hands pressing fingerprints all over the glass. Steve stood beside him, tail wagging, looking proud as if to say, *Look what I found wandering around back here!*

I took a deep breath and crossed the room to let him in.

"Hi, Coach," he said, smelling of little boy and the outdoors.

"Hi, buddy."

I turned and headed back into the kitchen, he and Steve following me.

"Whatcha doin'?" he asked.

"Making cookies."

"Need help?" He seemed less animated than usual, a little subdued.

"Sure."

I went back to my mixer while he pulled a chair over to the sink and climbed up to wash his hands.

"Cece's over," he said, even though I hadn't asked. He wiped his hands on the dish towel, then slid the chair around to the other side of me. "They're arguing, so I came here." It was all the explanation I needed and all he intended to give.

Apparently not having learned my lesson the first time, I didn't ask if his mother knew where he was. I didn't tell him he should call. I didn't want to think about Elena, plus Max was quiet and I was honestly grateful for

269

somebody else's presence, so we worked together in silence, both in our own mental worlds. He watched as I rolled a small ball of dough in the bowl of sugar and then he followed suit.

Once we filled up the cookie sheets, I made another batch of dough and we repeated the process all over again. When my kitchen table was covered with four dozen cooling lemon cookies, I mixed up the ingredients for thumbprint cookies, which were my grandma's favorites. I rolled the dough balls in the chopped walnuts and gave Max a quick demonstration of how to push his thumb down into the middle to create a little crater in each one, then fill it with a tiny taste of jam. We used raspberry and strawberry preserves, again my grandma's favorites. He worked hard, concentrating on his job and not saying much at all. He was the perfect baking partner and I loved him for it.

When we'd added the thumbprint cookies to the lemon cookies on the table, I searched for the recipe for Grandma's second favorites, the ones she simply called "chocolate balls." Max stood by the table, munching on a lemon cookie, and as I started putting ingredients into the mixer, I could feel his eyes on me.

"Coach?" he asked quietly, as if afraid his voice might break something in the air.

"Hm?"

"Why are we making so many cookies? Are you having a party or something?"

"No." The sad chuckle I gave held no energy and no humor. "No parties."

"Then why?"

I stopped what I was doing and stared into my mixing bowl, watching the silver beaters fuse a handful of items into one smooth combination. Then I said, very softly, "My grandma died last night."

I didn't look at him. I simply stood there, my hands bracing my body against the counter, thinking, *Why on earth would I say that to a six-year-old? Elena was right. I know nothing about kids.*

And then I felt it.

Max wrapped his small arms around my waist and hugged me tightly, his cheek pressed against my side. I imagined it was the only way his young brain knew how to convey what he was feeling: sympathy. I swallowed the lump in my throat and put my hand gently on his head.

"Thanks," I whispered to him.

"Welcome," he whispered in return.

We went back to work.

After two batches of chocolate balls, I finally sent Max home, not wanting him to get in trouble and not at all ready for the wrath of Elena, should she have to come looking for him again. I wrapped up an enormous plate of cookies and sent them with him, then watched from my front stoop until he was inside his own house.

I'm not sure how long I stood in the kitchen in my flour-covered apron, surveying the mess, trying to decide what to make next. As long as I kept baking, I felt strangely connected to Grandma. It was weird and ridiculous and I knew that, but I was afraid to stop, afraid to let that last, tenuous thread slip through my fingers. At the same time, I was virtually exhausted, at least mentally. Who knew it was just as grueling to hold your emotions at bay as it was to be overwhelmed by them?

I was counting the eggs I had left, trying to decide how many snickerdoodles I could conceivably make before I had to make a trip to the grocery store when there was a staccato knock on the front door. Four quick raps, like the person on the other side was anxious to have the door opened. I closed my eyes and sighed, not wanting to deal with any neighbors, salespeople, Jehovah's Witnesses, girl scouts. I stood quietly and didn't move, bringing a finger to my lips to shush Steve, who'd lifted his head from the kitchen floor, ears pricked up.

The knock sounded again in the same rhythm.

"Damn it," I muttered as Steve jumped up and barked. I wiped my hands on my apron as I entered the foyer. When I opened the door, I couldn't have been more surprised.

"Avery." Elena stood there, no trace of the anger or pain I'd seen on her face the last time she'd been here, no ice in her tone as she said my name like the last time I'd spoken to her. She stepped inside and before I could say anything, she lifted a hand to my face and stroked my cheek so gently my eyes filled. "Baby, I'm so sorry. Are you okay?"

That was it. That was all it took. As if my protective walls were made of sand and Elena's voice was the tide coming in, they simply disintegrated. There was no loud crashing sound, no shocked feeling of destruction. The barrier around my emotions was simply there…and then it had slipped away. All the pain, all the sorrow came pouring out as I crumpled, Elena's arms suddenly around me, holding me, trying to cushion my descent with her body and we ended up on the floor, a tangled mass of limbs.

I cried like a child, missing my grandmother so badly I thought I might just shatter into a million pieces, never to be repaired. Elena held me and rocked me and whispered comforting words as her lips pressed to my hair, to my temple, as her arms wrapped tightly around me. I fisted her shirt in my hand and let it all out, sobbing against her chest and feeling such a sense of loss, I wondered if I'd ever recover.

I have no idea how long we sat there. I think I'd started to doze a bit because the next thing I knew, Steve was curled up beside me, his little body warming my hip. I petted him absently and as he lifted his head and looked at me, I had a flash of something almost…human in his eyes, like he knew exactly what was going on and he was comforting me the only way he could. I scratched behind his ears and tried to offer a reassuring smile. I think I fell short.

"Hey, let's get you to bed," Elena said softly. "You need to rest. Come on."

She somehow managed to stand up and pull me up, too, without letting me lose contact with her body. Her arm tightly around my shoulders and holding me close, she walked me up the stairs and to my room. In my zombie-like state, I was barely able to operate. I have very little recollection of Elena undressing me or helping me into a T-shirt and pulling back the covers on my bed.

"Steve," I croaked.

"I'll take care of him. Just lie down. I'll be right back."

She left the room, calling my dog with her. I remember hearing the sliding glass door open and close a couple times. Then I thought I heard Elena's voice, but I wasn't sure. My body felt like lead and my eyelids were lined with sandpaper and didn't want to stay open. I turned on my side and my gaze fell on the 5 x 7 framed photo of Grandma and me on the day I graduated from college. Tears blurred my vision and I buried my face in my pillow so I couldn't see the picture.

Sleep must have claimed me for a while because the next thing I remember was Elena crawling under the covers with me. It was fully dark out now and she smelled of dish soap and toothpaste. She spooned up behind me, wrapping me in the warmth of her embrace.

"What about Max?" I asked, worried about her leaving her son home alone, not registering that she'd never do such a thing.

"He's fine. Cindy's got him."

"What? What about—"

But she interrupted me. "We have a lot to talk about and we'll get to that." Her lips grazed my ear in a sweet kiss. "But for tonight, I'm right here."

"Why?"

"Because you need me."

"I do."

I was surprised by my own sleepy admission and I wasn't so tired and emotionally wrecked that I didn't understand what she was doing for me or that it didn't make everything between us magically better. I wanted to grab onto her comment that we had to talk, but my brain was too fogged with grief and exhaustion. I was simply thankful and chose not to look beyond that, at least for the moment.

"Elena?"

"Hm?"

"I don't know what to do. I mean...about a funeral or any of that. I have no idea what to do."

"It's okay." I could feel her breath against my hair in the dark. "We'll figure it out together tomorrow."

"Okay." I let the relief wash over me, so much better than the sorrow. But the funny thing about sorrow is that it never quite goes away. It just hides for a little while and then pops back up like a spot of grease you thought you washed out. "Elena?"

"Hm?"

"I'm all alone now." I sounded eight years old and I knew it and I didn't care. It was how I felt.

"No, you're not." Elena's arms tightened around my worn out body and battered soul. "You have me."

I wanted to think about that, to ask her exactly what she meant, to tell myself she was just trying to make me feel better. But my mind couldn't hang on to any individual thought. They floated away like balloons on a sunny day as grogginess overtook me and I fell into a deep, dreamless sleep.

chapter twenty-six

Maria Walker turned out to be a godsend in the days that followed. Elena called her on Saturday morning and said only one thing: "Mama, Avery and I need your help."

She was on my doorstep within an hour, gave me a lengthy, heartfelt hug that almost started my waterworks up all over again, and took over like the best of personal assistants. Coming from a Greek family whose size and scope I couldn't even begin to fathom, she'd been through dozens of wakes and funerals and knew exactly what needed to be done.

The two of them went with me to Grandma's apartment. I wasn't sure I was ready to go in, but Elena was right: if Grandma was as organized as I always claimed she was, she probably had files with her final wishes, a will, etc. Turned out she'd already made arrangements with the funeral home of her choice, the one whose card Sandra Johnson had given me previously. She even had a burial plot, of which I was completely unaware, that she and my long-lost grandfather had purchased over thirty years earlier. She would be laid to rest next to her own parents, which gave me some sense of comfort.

Maria helped me go through Grandma's clothes, for which I was grateful because it would have been easy to simply stand in her closet for hours and smell each and every item, becoming lost in sense memory. I chose her emerald green suit, which she not only loved, but looked smashing in. She had matching low-heeled pumps to go with it, so I grabbed those, too. Maria reminded me to also select undergarments, which was kind of weird. Even as a child, I don't remember ever going through my grandmother's underclothes or seeing her in less than a slip and pantyhose. I must have looked a bit hesitant because Maria cheered me up by telling me the story of when her older sister Angela's husband passed away and she forgot to bring his underpants to the funeral home. The thought of her husband entering the Great Beyond while going commando really didn't sit well with Angela and she'd turned teary-eyed to her brother, Stavros, who sighed and went into the men's room to take off his own BVDs, which he then donated to his sister's late husband.

I'm not a religious person at all, but I was thanking any gods who would listen for my grandmother's amazing sense of planning. She had everything written out for me, right down to the hymns she preferred to have sung at her service. I don't remember much about the wake on Monday or the interment on Tuesday. I shook endless hands and withstood countless hugs from elderly people I knew and many I didn't. The entire staff of her residence home came by to offer their condolences. Grandma's coffee klatch/bridge club members were devastated and pulled me into one emotional hug after another as they wept. I smiled (I think) as best I could and I managed not to break down in front of my grandmother's friends. Elena stood by my side the entire time, whisking me away if she thought I needed some air, zipping me to the restroom if she suspected I might crumble.

The thing I remember most, odd as it sounds, is the numbness. For the most part, I remember feeling nothing. I wonder if that's your brain's way of protecting you and helping you get through such difficult procedures; maybe it just shuts off any and all feeling so you can survive the day without going to pieces in front of strangers. Whatever the reason, I was grateful. I'd spent much of the weekend mourning so that by the time the wake arrived, I didn't think I had any moisture left in my body to cry out.

Grandma's casket was all set to be lowered into the ground as the brief service at the cemetery ended. She was well-loved, as evidenced by the dozens of people gathered around the gravesite and I felt a deep sense of pride. The day was sunny and beautiful, balmy but with the distinctive scent of leaves and earth in the air, warning of the impending fall. It was my favorite season and Grandma's as well, and I was suddenly very sad she would miss it. I blinked back the mist that covered my eyes. Apparently, I did still have some moisture left.

My fingers were warm, as they'd been entwined with Elena's for the entire service and I'd never been so thankful for something solid in my entire life. I felt like she'd been giving me strength all day, channeling it through our hands like an electric current. She tugged me off to the side so that others could step to Grandma's casket and pay their final respects. I let out an enormous breath, knowing that the worst was past and that now we'd just go back to Grandma's apartment complex where they had a buffet set up in the common room. Elena must have read my face because she pulled me into a hug, squeezing me tightly and murmuring to me to hang in there a little longer, that it was just about over.

I was burrowing into her embrace, inhaling the wonderful smell of her, when I felt her body stiffen slightly. I lifted my head from her shoulder and looked up at her face.

"What?"

"I'm not sure, but…" Her voice drifted off and I followed her gaze back toward my grandmother's plot where people were slowly sifting away. A woman stood there with her back to us, maybe ten or fifteen feet from where we were. Her hair was an unremarkable shade of brown, pulled back into a chignon at the nape of her neck. She was petite, maybe five three or four, and was dressed smartly in a black suit and simple black pumps.

"Who is that?" I asked, my voice a whisper even as a strange feeling uncoiled slowly in my stomach, like a snake preparing to strike.

I felt rather than saw Elena shake her head. "I'm not sure…" There was something she wasn't saying, but rather was waiting for me to catch up.

The woman pulled a handkerchief from her black clutch purse and pressed it to her face, then gently placed a single white rose on the casket. When she turned around and I could see her face, my breath caught in my throat and I felt as if my heart suddenly stopped beating.

Though I didn't look a lot like her, there were certain unmistakable similarities. Our cheekbones were set the same. Our eyebrows slanted upwards at identical angles. The bow-like shape of her upper lip was very much like mine.

"Oh, my God," I heard Elena whisper behind me as the woman stopped in her tracks less than six feet away, her tear-filled hazel eyes widening. Her smile was friendly and sad at the same time. She took one tentative step towards me and stopped, like she was afraid to get too close.

"Hello, Avery," my mother said, her voice gentle, unfamiliar yet part of me.

I had no words. The hell with words, I had no air. I stared, partially in disbelief, but also with some semblance of relief, as I'd known somewhere deep down inside my soul that this would happen one day.

I simply blinked at her. It was all I could manage.

"You're..." She studied me, her eyes still wet. Now, instead of sorrow, they shone with happiness, with pride. "You're so beautiful. God. I mean, I knew you were, but seeing you in person like this..." She searched, finally settling on, "You look just like your grandmother," which was, of course, exactly the right thing to say in that moment.

I swallowed and I think I tried to speak, but nothing would come. I just stood there like a mute idiot. Elena, bless her heart, stepped in for me and held out her hand, keeping her other one still linked with mine.

"Hi. I'm Elena Walker."

My mother shook hands with her and if she was surprised by our linked hands, she didn't show it. "It's nice to meet you, Elena, though I wish it were under better circumstances. I'm Samantha Carter."

Elena nodded, reclaimed her hand, and stood beside me again, her grip on *my* hand tightening as I stood silently, trying to digest the sudden appearance of Samantha Carter—my mother—after thirty years of absence. I wondered if there were hidden cameras somewhere, if this was simply one big cosmic joke being played on me by some higher power. Maybe I was being Punk'd.

"Look, I know this must be very weird for you," she said.

I was glad to see Samantha Carter's smile held a slight awkwardness. I didn't want to be the only one who felt like she was suddenly in the wrong dimension.

She opened her clutch purse and took out a small piece of paper, folded in half. "This is where I am. I'd love to get together and talk, but I understand that you might need some time to think about it. Your grandmother said you were very smart and very stubborn, just like somebody else she knew." Her smile was sad and her eyes filled. "I have to go. Avery…"

She lifted her hand and I think she wanted to touch me, but thought better of it at the last minute (for which I was grateful), her arm dropping back down to her side. "I'm very sorry about your grandma. She loved you very much."

As one tear spilled over, she turned and walked quickly to the parking area, leaving me standing there filled with too many conflicting emotions to count.

━━

Silence.

Blessed silence.

I wondered if there was anything so wonderful as I flopped down onto my couch that evening after having changed out of my funeral attire and into shorts and a T-shirt.

"I hope the house doesn't catch on fire," I said absently as Elena puttered in the kitchen.

"What do you mean?"

"I don't think I have the energy to get up and escape. I'd just lie here and let myself fry."

Elena came in chuckling and handed me a glass of wine.

"Oh, you are a goddess," I said as I managed to wiggle into a semi-sitting position and take the wine from her.

"You probably say that to all the girls."

"Only the ones with nice asses who bring me wine."

She lifted my feet and set them in her lap as she sat. "What a day, huh?"

"Welcome to Understatement 101," I snorted as I reluctantly zeroed in on the one thing I'd been trying to keep from surfacing. I shook my head slowly. "I can't believe she showed up out of the blue like that." My brain tossed me an image of Samantha Carter's tear-filled hazel eyes.

"It wasn't exactly out of the blue, honey. Her mother died."

"Yeah, that's another thing I'm having trouble with." Samantha Carter had said, *Your grandmother said you were very smart and very stubborn, just like somebody else she knew.* It was pretty obvious by that statement alone that Grandma and her daughter had been in contact. I thought about the small scrap of paper she'd handed me that contained her home address, phone number, and e-mail address. "How could Grandma not tell me she knew my mother was in Syracuse all this time? An hour and a half away and I had no idea. And how long did Grandma know? Always? Why wouldn't she tell me that?"

283

"You could ask your mother," Elena suggested quietly.

"Yeah, maybe I'll add that to the list of things I've wanted to ask her for the past three decades, starting with what kind of mother abandons her four-year-old?" I sighed and took a too-large gulp of wine.

We sat quietly for long moments. I leaned my head back on the arm of the couch and closed my eyes, my thoughts swirling around in my head like a daiquiri in a blender. Elena kept me silent company and when I opened my eyes again, she was looking at me.

I stared back at her.

Her gaze stayed on me as she sipped her wine, as if she was trying to read something in my face. "What are you thinking?"

"Well, let's see," I said, pursing my lips and debating. "I'm thinking I'm exhausted and I'm sad and I miss my grandma terribly already. I'm also thinking that I'm ecstatic that this day is over. I couldn't take one more hug from a distraught elderly person without suffering a breakdown. I'm thinking I'm going to put Samantha Carter into a box and give myself a break on that front, at least for tonight because I just don't want to think about it any more. And…" I sipped my wine, realizing suddenly that yes, I was going to go there. "I'm wondering what you're still doing here." I said it lightly; I wasn't angry, but I was intensely curious.

Elena gave a slow nod, gazing into her wine glass with what seemed like great concentration. Several moments went by and I really started to think she wasn't going to respond at all, when she said quietly, "I was a jerk."

"You were?"

"That night. After we saw Lauren in the restaurant."

284

"Oh. Yeah. You were. Not as big a jerk as *she* was, but yeah."

She set her wine down on the end table and covered my bare feet with her hands, kneading them as she spoke, her focus on them. "It's just...I started to worry. About Max. About myself, too, but mostly about Max. It's been so hard, you know? To be the nurse when Cindy gives him yet another boo-boo on his heart. A little piece of mine breaks off every time I have to make an excuse for her, every time I have to explain to him that it's just how she is, that he didn't do anything wrong, that she *does* love him. I'm terrified of bringing somebody else into his life that could end up breaking his heart all over again."

I wanted to say something, but at the same time, I was afraid to break the spell she seemed to be under. Instead, I watched her and I waited.

"And then I met you," she went on, glancing at me and favoring me with a small smile. "And you were amazing and you were beautiful and I was lost..." Her eyes turned up toward the ceiling and when she spoke, it was a near-whisper, almost as if she was speaking to herself and not me. "God, I fell for you so hard and so fast I thought my head would spin clean off my shoulders."

My wide smile appeared all on its own. I had nothing to do with it.

"And my son...he fell for you, too. He adores you, Avery."

"I adore him," I said simply.

"I started to worry that it was all too good to be true and we went to dinner and Lauren showed up and said what she said..." Her voice trailed off.

"And suddenly it *was* too good to be true," I finished for her.

"Sure seemed like it." She dug her fingers into the arch of my foot and my eyes drifted closed for a moment, relishing her hands on my skin.

"Exes," I said finally, shaking my head. "Even when they're gone, they can mess with you."

"Or freak you out just a little." At my questioning look, Elena said sheepishly, "It was actually Cindy who made me see that I'd screwed up and needed to fix things with you."

"*Cindy* did?"

Elena shrugged. "She likes you. And she's right: I was a jerk. I left no room for defense or explanation or anything from you. I just wanted to protect my son. And I'm not sorry about that, but I am sorry that I hit you with both barrels the way I did."

"Okay. Now. Do I get a chance to clarify a few things?"

"Yes."

"You sure?" I teased.

She ran a fingernail up the sole of my foot, tickling me. "Yes."

"Okay then. This is going to sound really stupid— probably because my brain has gone to mush at this point —but when I was with Lauren, I was a different person. I know it wasn't that long ago, but I was at a different point in my life. I wasn't sure of anything except that I wasn't in love with her. Yeah, that's pretty cold. I know it, believe me. I loved her. She was wonderful, there's no reason not to love her. But there was no spark, no passion. Have you ever tried to tell somebody that? You don't want to be with them because you're not all that physically attracted to them after all?"

Elena shook her head.

"Exactly. She didn't deserve to be hurt like that and I probably stayed longer than I should have. But when she started talking about having kids...I just panicked. And I used that as an out. Which was wrong, I know."

"So, you wanted kids, just not with her?"

"Well..." I hedged. "That's not necessarily the truth either. I mean, look at my childhood." A bitter laugh bubbled up out of me. "I'm not exactly the poster child for normal family dynamics and I've always sort of fallen back on that, used it as a reason to not delve any deeper into my own psyche." I sat up and took one of her hands in mine, tracing her palm with my finger, feeling the delicate bone structure beneath the smooth skin. I cleared my throat and forced myself to continue. "But when I fell in love with you and spent time with you and Max, it made me really, seriously think about everything I've believed to be true about myself, about being afraid of so many things that stem from my own situation and you know something? I'm not afraid any more. I look ahead and I try to see the future, whether you and Max are there and guess what. You are. Front and center. And I don't want it to be any other way."

"Really?" She looked so like Max at that moment, her dark eyes uncertain, her voice small, and I couldn't help but smile at her.

"Yes, really. And, you know, it's probably a good thing that I've now had a taste of what an argument with you is like, that I should have my strategy planned ahead of time, since you won't let me get a word in edgewise."

Elena gave a snort of a laugh. "I'm bad like that, aren't I?"

"Yes, you are."

"My mom does the same thing. I'm sorry."

"Apology accepted." We were quiet for a moment. Then I asked, "So, what do you think? Are you willing to give this another try with me?"

When she stroked the side of my face, her touch was so gentle, her eyes wet and so, so loving, that mine welled up in response.

"Oh, *man*," I whined. "I don't want to cry any more today."

"It's okay," Elena whispered, her face close to mine. "They're happy tears. Happy tears are okay."

Then she kissed me.

Softly.

Tenderly.

Forever.

epilogue

As I sit here on a Sunday afternoon and watch the snow whip around outside the window, it's hard for me to believe it's been nearly four years. It's true what they say. Time does fly. And even faster when your life is wonderful.

I tuck the sunset-colored afghan my grandmother knit more tightly around my legs. Straining my eyes, I try to make out the bare branches of the trees in the backyard. I can't tell if it's actually snowing or if the wind is just blowing around the stuff already on the ground. Either way, it's looking awfully cold. A log in the fireplace pops loudly and Steve groans and shifts his body more tightly against my legs, annoyed to have his Sunday afternoon nap interrupted by anyone or anything other than Max.

Max. He'll be ten this spring. He's growing up so fast and both Elena and I are finding it bittersweet. I'll never forget the broken-hearted expression on Elena's face last year when he told her he didn't want her to kiss and hug him in front of his friends anymore. She took it like a champ, nodding, telling him, "Sure, no problem." Then she came home and cried for nearly an hour while I tried to reassure her that it was all part of the process, that it didn't mean he had stopped loving her.

He's such a great kid. Smart, with a wicked sense of humor. He loves to read, but hates writing. A math whiz, he shocks me with how easily he zips through his homework. I finally had to turn that over to his banker mother because I was embarrassed that it took me longer to check his assignments than it did for him to complete them. Numbers hate me. They love Max.

He still helps me bake. He'll even make a batch of chocolate chip cookies himself if he's feeling the urge. I think he's happy with the way things turned out; I think he's happy with me in his life. I know I can't imagine mine without him. He's with Cindy this weekend. She's another one who's amazed me over the past few years. I don't know exactly what happened, but once Elena and I began talking about moving in together three years ago, she really stepped up and began taking her role as Max's mother seriously. Now she goes to all his games, comes to parent-teacher conferences with Elena and me, and takes him all over the place. He spends at least two weekends a month with her, sometimes more. She's turned out to be an impressive parent, something I never thought I'd see.

Something else I never thought I'd see is me having a conversation with *my* mother. It took me nearly five months after Grandma's funeral before I worked myself up to contacting Samantha Carter again. Just an e-mail, just a few rather terse words to test the waters and see how it felt. Weird, was how it felt.

I had—have—so many emotions wrapped up and around my image of this woman…the first and foremost, of course, still being anger. To her credit, she's never offered excuses. She's tried to explain exactly what state she was in as a twenty year old with a kid. It's been a long, emotional haul trying to decide if it's even worth it to me to stay in contact with her. But circumstances change and lately I've been thinking so much of my grandmother and what she meant to me, and I think it's softened me a little. I'll probably call Samantha tomorrow.

I glance at the TV and an ad with dates for a museum exhibition downtown. My goddaughter Jaclyn, Josh and Nina's girl, will be three years old on one of the dates. Again, I'm astounded at how time flies. Seems like yesterday when I was in Nina's hospital room, holding Jaclyn for the first time, awed into tearful silence by her tiny fingers and itty, bitty pink lips. We spend a lot of time with Josh and Nina now, which is wonderful.

"Honey, I'm home," Elena calls out from the kitchen, a smile in her voice. She started using that corny line when we first bought this house. I love it.

She comes into the living room. I've never gotten used to her beauty; I don't think I ever will. There are days when I have to pinch myself to understand that this isn't a dream, that she is really mine. Her hair is still shimmering from remnants of snowflakes as she hands me a bag of salt and vinegar potato chips with a flourish.

"I come bearing gifts."

I snatch them from her like a starving woman. "Oh, my God, you are the most wonderful, amazing wife ever, ever, ever."

One eyebrow arches as she puts her hands on her hips. "You haven't moved at all since I left, have you?"

"Hey," I say with mock indignation and point to my swollen belly. "I'm making a baby from scratch here. I'm a little busy."

291

She grins at my standard line and turns to tend to the fire. "You've only got three more weeks to use that excuse, you know. After that, you're actually going to have to get up off your gorgeous ass."

"Wah, wah, wah," I say, munching more chips and running a hand over my tummy.

"I ran into Maddie in the grocery store," she says. "I invited them to dinner next week."

"That's great," I tell her.

Maddie has drifted from me a bit over the past year or two. I've noticed that it happens when children are involved. There seems to be a rather distinct line in the gay community between those with children or who want to have children and those without children who don't want to have them. Most of our friends now are people with kids, like Josh and Nina. We have more in common with them and we understand the needs of another family with children. And once this baby is born, it'll be even more pronounced.

I wonder if Maddie knows how much I miss her and I'm suddenly thankful to Elena for making the effort. I tell her, "I'll bake something special for Maddie."

Elena perches on the edge of the couch next to me and pulls the afghan down. Then she lifts my sweatshirt and kisses the bare skin, under which grows our baby. "Hi, Binky," she whispers. We don't know if it's a boy or a girl, so she's taken to calling it Binky, just to have a name. Her hand is surprisingly warm as she rubs my tummy.

My heart warms a bit and then my eyes well with tears —an unfortunate downside to all the hormones running roughshod through my system. I cry at the drop of a hat now. It's a little ridiculous. I sift Elena's hair through my fingers, enjoying the closeness. We chose a donor with Elena's characteristics, so I'm thinking (and hoping) her dominant traits of dark hair and those onyx eyes will win out over my copper hair and green eyes, but I guess we'll see in less than a month.

Less than a month.

God, I can hardly believe it. I feel like I've been pregnant for a hundred years and at the same time, it seems like it's been five minutes. I'll never forget the first time I felt the baby move inside me. I can't even begin to describe it, but that's the point that I knew, I *knew*, I wanted nothing more desperately than to be a mother.

That's also when the paralyzing fear set in.

Because once you feel that baby kick, your whole world changes and it all becomes real.

I think I'm ready. Well, as ready as somebody can be for parenthood, which is to say not at all. But it feels right and I'm ready to have my body back. And I'm ready to let Elena have my body back, too. All that stuff about pregnancy making you uncontrollably horny? Yeah, not so much, at least not in my case. My boobs were so sore, I didn't even want her to *look* at them, let alone touch. Believe me, she'll be just as happy to have this baby be born and out of my womb as I will.

The snow is letting up. I continue to play with Elena's hair as she hums softly to our child, a warmth fills me from the inside, and with all my heart I wish my grandmother were here. Missing her eased up a little bit after some time passed, but every now and then, I'm filled with such longing to see her, to talk to her, to ask her if she's proud of my choices and the home I've made with Elena, that I can hardly breathe. I want to ask her questions about motherhood and I wish from the depths of my soul that she could hold my baby. A small lump forms in my throat, as it always does when I'm missing my grandma.

As I've said before, I'm not a religious person at all and I've never thought of Grandma in a "better place." I've just thought of her as gone. But now, as I lie on my couch, with my baby growing inside me and the love of my life humming to it quietly, the snow begins to fall in earnest. It's not wind-whipped like earlier. Instead, big, fluffy flakes float to the ground silently and despite my disdain for all things below thirty degrees, it's a beautiful, tranquil sight to behold.

I smile and breathe deeply, completely content, utterly at peace. And deep down, I wonder if my grandmother isn't still looking out for me after all.

the end

Books By Georgia Beers

Novels
Starting From Scratch
Finding Home
Mine
Fresh Tracks
Too Close to Touch
Thy Neighbor's Wife
Turning the Page

Anthologies
Outsiders
Stolen Moments
The Milk of Human Kindness

To find out where to buy these books visit Georgia's website
www.georgiabeers.com